The Baby River Angel

Prairiescape Books

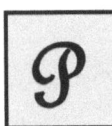

The Baby River Angel

a novel

by Robert Hays

Prairiescape Books
an imprint of
Herndon-Sugarman Press
Savoy, Illinois U.S.A.

ISBN-13: 978-0-9899926-2-6
ISBN-10: 0-9899926-2-4

To Mary, as always

❧ Be not forgetful to entertain strangers: for
thereby some have entertained angels unawares.
—BOOK OF HEBREWS

❧ 1 ❧

The makeshift raft, hardly more than a clump of brush, bobbed along in the ripples of the swift current close to the near bank of the river. When it was almost alongside the boat, Birdie raked it in with his fishing pole and the shallow reed basket lashed to two of the larger branches with a length of wild grape vine suddenly came alive. The two boys stared in fascination as he lifted a baby, arms flailing, and gingerly pulled back a corner of the cocoon-like blanket to reveal the tiny face.

"Lordy, child," Birdie said softly, "where'd you come from?"

"What is it, Daddy?" Birdie's oldest boy asked.

"Why it's a baby. Cain't you see that?"

The boy looked momentarily chastened, then pushed closer. "Let me see it," he said.

"Get the basket first. Set it down right there, in the bottom of the boat."

The boy did his father's bidding and Birdie carefully lowered the delicate bundle back into the basket. The boy stooped over the baby with an expression of awe while his brother, who had stayed back, crowded up close beside him. Once within reach, the younger boy gently lifted the frayed edge of the blanket so that he could get a better look.

"Whose baby you think it is, Daddy?" the younger boy whispered.

"Now how would I know that? You seen it floating down the river same as I did."

"I just wondered, is all."

"Yeah, well . . . I just wouldn't have any way of knowing. It sure

1

seems like somebody was awful careless to let the little thing go floating off on such a flimsy little raft as that."

The boys agreed. It sure did look like somebody wasn't taking very good care of the baby. How far upriver did he figure it had come from? Did he think maybe there was a nametag on it, like people looked for when they found a stray dog? What kind of baby did he guess it to be, a boy baby or girl baby? It looked tiny, did he know how old it was? Did he suppose whoever lost it was on a picnic and forgot and left the baby in the picnic basket?

"Now jest hold off with all your questions," Birdie demanded. "I already told you, I don't know any more about this baby than you do. All I know is it's a good thing we seen it when we did."

"How come you say that?" The older boy, again.

"Because it wouldn't have lasted long on the river, that's how come."

Now the younger: "You mean it would have drownded?"

"Most likely, yes. If that little bit of a raft got tore apart on a stob or something. This basket might have floated for a bit, but sure not for long."

Both boys were wide-eyed. Their daddy had just saved a baby from drowning and they had helped. Sobered by the weight of this dramatic reality, they sat quietly as their father turned the boat around and headed back toward the Cambria dock.

Back at the landing, Birdie gripped the basket firmly as he climbed out of the boat while the boys held fast to the pilings. He rushed to Sam Gowdy's bait shop.

"Sam," he called, breathless and red-faced from exertion, "you gotta see this!"

Sam Gowdy was not a man to hurry. He took his time coming from the back of the shop. When he saw the child Birdie Wilson held in the basket his jaw dropped in disbelief. "Where 'n hell did you get a baby?" he demanded.

"She was floatin' on the river," Birdie said. "I swear to you she was, Sam, on a flimsy little raft of a thing that would have sunk and drowned her the first rock or stob it hit in the water."

"The basket just setting on it?"

"It was tied on by a vine."

"Anything unusual about the basket?"

"It looks real old."

"What'd you do with the raft?"

Birdie looked surprised. "We didn't do nothing with it," he said. "I guess it just floated off. It wasn't nothing but a bunch of sticks. You think it might have been important?"

"I don't really know, Birdie," Sam Gowdy said. "It might have had some clues to where she came from."

"I never thought about that," Birdie said, almost apologetically. "Besides, we was busy just getting the baby and I was scared I'd drop her back in the water. What you think we oughta do, Sam?"

"We got to call the sheriff's office. I suppose they'll send somebody out for a case like this, even though most of the time they don't even know we're here."

Birdie agreed. Cambria would have been little more than a wide spot in the road, had it straddled a road instead of clinging to the river bank, and it barely registered with the rest of the county. The sheriff had never set foot there and sometimes it took a week to get a deputy. But Sam was right; a baby found floating on the Ohio River ought to get their attention.

Sam suggested that in the meantime they call Molly Hearst or one of the other Cambrian mothers who would know how to handle the baby until the authorities arrived and took her off their hands. Birdie did not disagree.

"Molly's had two of her own," Sam said. "A baby wouldn't be anything new to her."

Sam called the Fish and Fries Café where Molly Hearst waitressed. When he told her about the baby, she promised to come right away. The café wasn't far from Sam's shop and Molly arrived in minutes. She cooed over the baby, who stopped crying and smiled.

"Look at her little high-topped shoes," Molly said. "I've never seen any like them before. She's older than you'd think, being so tiny. I'd say probably nine or ten months." She promised that she would get the baby warm and dry and well-fed, took the basket and rushed out the door.

Birdie Wilson stared after Molly and the baby, almost with a sense of wonder. "What do you think the county's going to do with her?" he asked.

Sam Gowdy, who had not yet called the sheriff's office, offered a quick opinion: "I'd think they would have people just to take care of things like that."

"I expect they'd label her Baby Jane Doe and put her in the child welfare system."

"I don't think so, Birdie. They'd find out who she is and send her back."

"Back where? Looks to me like somebody didn't want her. Do you think they'd have floated her off down the river like that if they wanted her?"

Sam Gowdy, for one the few times Birdie ever had witnessed, seemed unsure of himself. "I guess you could be right about that," he said. "I just figured it was an accident that she got loose from somebody and floated away. You really believe anybody could do that on purpose?"

"All I know is, if it was an accident they'd a been lookin' all up and down the river. You seen or heard any kind of search goin' on lately?"

"No . . . not lately."

"You want that pretty little baby stuck away in child welfare?"

"But I don't see that we got any choice, Birdie. We got to call the law. Besides, we can't take care of a baby."

"Molly Hearst can, and some of the other women," Birdie declared. "There ain't any babies in Cambria anymore, which is one reason why folks get so disagreeable. But there's still mothers who ought to know what to do."

Sam took a minute before answering. Birdie could see that he was giving ground. "Well, maybe we don't have to call the law right away," Sam finally said. "Somebody'll come around looking for that baby anyway. We probably ought to let a few other people in on it, though, and that'll cause a ruckus. No two people in this town can agree on anything."

"You're sure right about that, Sam."

4

"I'll call the mayor. He may be able to pull everybody together on it. If there's anybody who can do it, it'd be Johnny."

Sam called Town Hall. Mayor Johnny White suggested that the two of them drop by and discuss whatever it was they had on their minds, given that Sam had made it sound particularly urgent.

Johnny White was not easily convinced. But he began to soften after he heard Birdie insist for the third time that the child welfare people would name the little one Baby Jane Doe. Birdie often was not too sure of himself, but on this issue he apparently held no doubt whatsoever.

"I do hate to think about her getting moved around in foster homes," the mayor said. "Father Jacob has told me often enough how hopeless that system is. If it's as bad as he says, she could get lost in it. No doubt about that."

"That's what I've been telling Sam," Birdie said, with a pleased expression on his face. "They'd call her Baby Jane Doe."

Sam Gowdy said, "You already mentioned that, Birdie—several times. Let's let the mayor handle this his way."

Johnny White rubbed his chin, hoping to look thoughtful. He liked to think of himself as a rational man who considered all the angles carefully before making a decision. He was confident that this was one of the main reasons he was well into his third term as mayor. Other Cambrians knew that nobody else would take the job.

"But the whole town would have to be in on it," the mayor said. "Can either one of you recall a single thing everybody in Cambria has ever agreed on?"

Birdie allowed that he couldn't.

Sam Gowdy took a different tack: "You have a lot of influence on the people of Cambria, Johnny. Given how they're all going to look on this little baby and see how precious she is and considering how Father Jacob has pretty much made the child welfare department seem like it was run by the devil hisself, you might be able to pull this off."

"But what about those who don't go to Father Jacob's church?" the mayor asked.

5

"I doubt that that matters much, Johnny. Everybody's probably heard him or one of his parishioners talk about it one time or another. I sure have."

Birdie nodded agreement. "Nobody wants her called Baby Jane Doe," he said.

The mayor still was not convinced. "I can just hear the folks down in the Canepatch claiming this is some kind of silliness their neighbors up on the hill dreamed up, which is reason enough for them to be against it," he said. "Or the other way around. We've got too many divisions in this town. The Methodists don't trust the Catholics, the Democrats don't trust the Republicans, the poor folks don't like the rich people—such few as there are—the fishermen don't like the guys with the big boats . . . If people start taking sides we'll never pull it off."

Sam Gowdy: "Like I said, Johnny. You have a lot of influence."

Johnny White sighed, signaling that he was about to give in on a point he still was unsure of. He looked squarely at Sam and then at Birdie and said, "Okay, if the two of you will back me up I'll see if I can get the town behind us. Once I start something, I don't like to fail."

On Friday night, Mayor Johnny White announced, there would be a citizens' meeting at Town Hall. All Cambrians were expected to be there. Word spread fast.

When the meeting time arrived, Town Hall was filled almost to overflowing.

Molly Hearst was there early, with Jay and Justine and the newest Cambrian, now snugly dressed and well fed and apparently satisfied. Birdie and Edna Wilson and their boys came right behind Molly and her kids, followed closely by Sam Gowdy and his wife, Alma. It was the best turnout for a town meeting anyone could remember. As usual, people clumped together in small cliques, those in one group eying the others warily.

Sam Gowdy whispered to Johnny White that the big crowd was ample proof of how much influence the mayor had over the citizens of Cambria. The mayor was clearly pleased. Sam actually was thinking to himself that the crowd proved that Cambrians had little else to do, but that was a thought he'd wisely keep to himself. Johnny White rapped on a table with his knuckles to gain attention. The room grew quiet and he got straight to the point. "You all know by now about that baby Birdie Wilson and his boys found floating on the river," he announced loudly from the front of the room. "That's what we're here to talk about. Molly's taking care of the child for now, so it's in good hands."

There was a stirring among those assembled as people turned to see Molly Hearst and the baby. Molly looked as proud as she might have had she just given birth to the little girl herself.

"Now there are a few things we all have to consider," Johnny White said. "First of all, is there anybody who feels strongly that we ought to bring the law in on this right away?"

"You think we might get in trouble if we don't?" someone called from the back of the room, a group on the right. There was more stirring.

Johnny White held up both hands to quiet the crowd. "Now I'm not an attorney, but I don't see how we'd be breaking any law," he said. "Is anybody here a lawyer?"

From the back of the room, in a group on the left: "There must be some law that says you have to report it when somebody abandons a baby."

"Well now, we don't know that she was abandoned. Who was that? Marylee? Okay, now, Marylee, since we don't know that she was abandoned, somebody might be looking for her right now. Wouldn't it be better for us to keep the little tyke safe and sound and have it here for its mama if she should show up?"

Marylee Tipsworth raised her hand. "I don't have any problem with that, Johnny," she said. "I was just saying that if she *was* abandoned we probably had ought to report it to the law. That's all."

Johnny White smiled at Marylee. "Point well taken," he said.

Jake Garner, among those in a small gathering closer to the front, had been shuffling his feet. "I got something to say, Johnny," he said loudly.

"You have the floor, Jake."

"I don't want this to be taken wrong, you know, but what I've been thinking is that it wouldn't be the worst thing in the world if we kept that little baby and let her grow up right here in Cambria. It's a good place for kids, and a lot of us are getting along in age. There aren't going to be many more children born in Cambria the way things are going. We'd be doing this little girl a favor and ourselves as well if we kept her. That's what I think."

"You stated your case very well, Jake," the mayor said. "Is there any more discussion?"

"I think we ought to call the sheriff."

Johnny White looked straight at Max Barnes, standing directly in front of him and not associating himself clearly with any particular group. "Are you set in your position, Max, or would you grant a little wiggle room?"

Max brought himself up to his full five feet, three inches in height and glared at Johnny White. "You sound like you're taking a position, Mayor," Max said. "I thought you were supposed to be neutral. I'm a reasonable man, you know that. But I can't see how we can justify not calling the law in on this. If the baby had been hurt or, God forbid, drowned, we sure would have."

"I can't quarrel with that, Max," Johnny White said. "Does anybody else want to state an opinion?"

"They'd call her Baby Jane Doe," Birdie Wilson called from the back of the room, the faction on the left. "That wouldn't be right."

Max Barnes slumped, and appeared to shrink an inch or so in height. He did a full about-face so he could see Birdie, but his view was blocked by a tall girl standing behind him. "You sure about that, Birdie?" he said, trying to look around the girl. "I'd think they would find out who she is, you know, and then call her by her real name. Don't you think?"

"How are they gonna do that, Max? She sure ain't carryin' no driver's license."

Max turned back toward Johnny White. "Do you think he may be right, Mayor? They might call her Baby Jane Doe?"

"Well, this is the child welfare people we're talking about. They seem to go by the book. If their rules say she should be called Baby Jane Doe, I'm pretty sure they would call her that."

8

"I don't like that," Max said. "I just wish we could be sure . . ."

Mayor Johnny White: "That sounds a bit like wiggle room to me, Max. Anybody else have anything to say?"

Margie Zielinski, in the group at the front, raised her hand and was acknowledged by the mayor. "I'd like to hear what Father Jacob thinks about all this," she said.

"Very good idea, Margie. Father Jacob?"

Father Jacob stood. Like Max, he appeared not to be a part of any particular clique. He looked about the room slowly and waited for quiet, as if to give his words more impact. "I doubt that there are many Cambrians who don't know what I think of the child welfare department," he said. "In my opinion, saving a child from that vile system is the Christian thing to do."

The priest sat down and Johnny White nodded approval. "Is Pastor Mike here?" he inquired. "Ah, yes, there you are. Would you like to say anything?"

Pastor Mike, also separating himself from any of the groups, remained seated. "Well, I don't want to make a habit of agreeing with Father Jacob," he said loudly, "but I don't think God would condemn us for doing what's best for one of the least of His children."

Johnny White: "Anyone else?"

No response.

"Okay then. We can inquire in good time about missing children and all that, because we want to do the right thing. But I've talked to a good many of you already and I know that while you have different views on how we ought to handle this, you all seem to agree that we don't want to see this innocent baby stuck away in child welfare somewhere."

Sam Gowdy, who rarely said a word at a town meeting, cleared his throat loudly and raised a hand. Johnny White nodded recognition.

"I've been thinking about this all afternoon," Sam Gowdy said. "It could be a good while before we know this little baby's real name. It seems to me we ought to give her a name ourselves, so's we can talk about her with one another and call her something besides baby."

9

Johnny White: "Anybody object to that?"

Murmuring in the crowd, but no response.

Sam Gowdy held up his hand again. Again, Johnny White nodded recognition.

"What I was thinking," Sam Gowdy said, "is she came to us like a little baby river angel. I move we name her Angel."

The murmur among people in the audience grew louder. Those in the group at the back of the room, on the right, began to whisper among themselves. Johnny White acted quickly. "If there's no objection, Sam's motion is approved," he proclaimed. "The little baby that Birdie pulled out of the Ohio River and saved, as long as we have her here in Cambria, will be known as Angel."

"Is Molly gonna keep her?"

"I didn't see who asked that question," the mayor said. "But the answer is yes, for now. Molly's agreed to take care of her here in the beginning. But over the long haul, depending on whether we keep her for just a little while or have her for a long time, everybody's going to need to pitch in. Anybody have a problem with that?"

The room was quiet.

"Okay, then. We'll start by taking up a collection right here tonight. Pitch in what you can to help Molly pay for the baby's food and get her the clothes and other things she needs. We'll develop an organized plan in a day or so—assuming nobody comes along looking for little Angel."

With that pronouncement, the mayor adjourned the meeting. A faction at a time, everybody gathered around Molly to see the baby. Johnny White set a wastebasket on a chair and made a show of dropping in a five-dollar bill. Sam Gowdy put in some carefully folded bills and Birdie's two boys came forward and emptied their pockets of change. The nascent Baby River Angel Fund was off to a good start.

Many of the Cambrians stayed around late into the night. Baby Angel was the most exciting thing to happen in town since most of them could remember, and those within every clique had ideas they felt obligated to share. Molly, at last, said she needed to get the child home to bed, leaving some of her fellow townspeople disappointed that they had not yet had their chance to hold the newest Cambrian. Johnny White stayed to the very end, accepting congratulations from many of his constituents and patiently hearing the concerns of others who were more cautious.

To his great relief, the mayor sensed no unified division among the people. Hill folks and Canepatch citizens went both ways, enthusiastic and cautious. The varied attitudes notwithstanding, the mayor recognized that this night marked the beginning of a new chapter in Cambria's history.

❧2❧

Early Sunday morning, Birdie showed up at Sam Gowdy's bait shop, his two boys in tow. Although there was a "Closed" sign on the door, the door was not locked. Birdie and the boys went in. Sam was puttering in the back. He heard the three coming and looked up with an expression of surprise.

"I'm closed, Birdie," he said. "Don't you know it's Sunday?"

"Oh, hell, Sam. You ain't never really closed. Everybody knows that."

"Well, I don't sell bait on Sunday. I probably ought to, 'cause I miss a lot of sales. But, heck, a man's got to have a day off once in a while."

"I didn't come to buy bait."

"Well, then, what can I do for you?" Sam put down the tackle box he'd been working on and walked closer.

"I wanted to talk to you about that little baby," Birdie said, his tone unusually serious. "I just cain't get over thinking that somebody might be looking for her. I'm wondering if you and me ought not to drive up to Wheeling and nose around and see what we can find out."

"That'd take two or three days, Birdie. I couldn't close my shop for two or three days this time of the year. I'd lose way too much money."

"Couldn't Alma run things for a couple of days? She's better at the business end than you are, anyway."

"Maybe so," Sam responded. "But do you think that old Dodge of yours would get us to Wheeling and back? That truck must be damned near as old as I am, Birdie. How many miles on it?"

13

"It don't show the miles anymore. That part's been busted for a while now."

"You ever think of getting a new truck?"

"Well now, if I had even half of old Miss Quattlebaum's money, maybe I would. But I ain't got old Miss Quattlebaum's money, and I don't expect she's going to split her money with me."

"Can't argue with you on that. Miss Quattlebaum didn't get to be the richest woman in town by giving her money away. I was just worried about your truck making it all the way up to Wheeling, is all."

"Oh, that old Dodge's nowhere near used up. I wouldn't worry about settin' off for California, or Alaska, even, in that truck. It's just about broke in good."

"Are you sure you're not just looking for an excuse to get away from Edna for a bit, maybe looking for some new stuff up in the city?"

"Don't talk like that in front of the boys," Birdie demanded, his eyes flashing rare anger.

"Yeah, I'm sorry for that," Sam said quickly. "But they're over there by the trophy case, too far to hear. Your boys are growing up pretty fast, Birdie. I can't hardly keep track of which one is which. The tow-headed one, the oldest, that's Ross?"

"That's Ross. His brother's Kyle."

"Well, you're lucky, Birdie. Those boys are going to make you proud someday."

Birdie grinned with pleasure. "They're good boys," he said "But how about Wheeling? You wanna go or not? I sup'ose I could do it by myself if I had to. It just seems to me like we ought to be making some effort to find the little girl's family if she has one. Just about anything that goes on up or down the river, they'd know about in Wheeling. Don't you think?"

"I expect they would, Birdie. I expect they would."

"Then you think we ought to go?"

Sam said, "Yes, I think maybe that would be the right thing to do. When you figurin' to leave?"

The two men talked about their schedules, pretending to have a

14

number of pressing matters to attend to. They would just have to put some of them aside for a while to make time for the trip to Wheeling. Hunting up Baby Angel's mama should be their first priority, though, and they were willing to let a few other things slide. They arranged to leave first thing Monday morning.

Birdie called the boys. They loaded into the old truck and drove the four blocks home, after which Birdie summoned the courage to tell Edna what he and Sam Gowdy were about to do. To his astonishment, his wife had nothing negative to say. She thought it was a good idea, in fact, and she would start packing for him right away.

"How long do you plan to be gone?" Edna asked. "I don't know how much to pack."

This was the first time Birdie had had reason to consider that question. His visit to Sam had been a spur of the moment thing, something he did on a mere whim. He hadn't calculated how long it would take to drive to Wheeling or thought about what they were going to do when they got there.

"Sam said two or three days," he told Edna. "I'd say three to be on the safe side."

Back at the bait shop, though, Sam Gowdy had found his wife much less receptive.

"What in this world do you think you're going to find out in Wheeling?" Alma exclaimed. "And even if it was a good idea, it's about the dumbest thing I can think of to set off on a trip like that with Birdie Wilson. I'd be surprised if Birdie even knows the way to Wheeling!"

Sam protested that Birdie actually was a pretty reliable fellow. Said, "He's been around more than you'd think, Alma. I believe he lived in Wheeling for a time. That would have been way back, but he probably still knows his way around."

"Well, if you're set on going there's nothing I can do about it. Still seems to me like a big waste of time, though."

And on that note, Alma set about getting things ready for her husband to pack. After twenty years of marriage, she knew Sam well enough to be confident that he'd never take what he needed if she didn't sort it out for him and put it all in one place.

15

❧

WHILE SAM AND BIRDIE were occupied with their serious plan-making, Molly Hearst was re-learning what it was like to have a baby in the house. Given that her youngest was now a strapping teenager, she'd found Baby Angel full of surprises—which in itself was a surprise. She had been sure that taking care of a little one, once you'd been through it a couple of times, was something you never forgot how to do.

She was wrong.

Baby Angel, of course, was a special case. Molly was afraid to leave the baby unattended for more than a few minutes at a time. She had been handed an important responsibility by Mayor Johnny White. Everyone in Cambria was counting on her to take good care of this unfortunate little one and she was determined not to let them down.

Molly would have expected to be the last person in Cambria chosen as Baby Angel's caretaker. Not that she doubted her own competence, but she'd felt strongly for some time now that nothing good was going to happen in her life ever again. Whether or not having a strange new baby in the house was a good thing—she still hadn't decided on that—being selected by Johnny White and her fellow Cambrians for the role they'd cast her in was a good thing. Yes it was.

Although Molly rarely missed church on Sunday, she wouldn't go today. Baby Angel had kept her awake most of the night and she was tired. She also didn't care to face all the curious church-goers. They would be full of questions about the baby and want to see her and hold her and they'd pass hints among themselves that maybe Molly wasn't the best one to have been given charge of the newest Cambrian. Not the Molly of recent years, always glum and unsmiling.

Justine and Jay went. When they got home they told her Pastor Mike was understanding, and sent his blessing to their mother and Baby Angel. Pastor Mike was never one to condemn.

Alma Gowdy called in the early afternoon. Was Molly manag-ing okay? she inquired, and was there anything she might need?

"I'm doing well enough, Alma," Molly said. "I will be needing some things, but so far I've not had time to think much about that. I'd forgot how much time a baby takes. "

"You need to make a list, that's for sure."

"I know. But what am I supposed to do with it? Do you know?"

"I can't say I do. Maybe give it to Johnny White?"

"I guess so," Molly said. "And sooner or later I'm going to need some help."

Alma suddenly became defensive. "Goodness knows I wouldn't know what to do," she said. "Besides, I'll be tied down with running the shop for a while."

"Oh? Something going on with Sam?"

"You won't believe this, Molly, but Sam and Birdie Wilson are leaving in the morning for Wheeling to see if they can find out something about the baby's family. I might be worried that Sam was looking for a fling, but if he was I can't imagine he'd be making the trip with Birdie. Do you think?"

Molly laughed. "That seems like a safe assumption to me," she said. "But I've got to go now, Alma. Angel's crying."

Molly hurried to the baby. She lifted the child from the makeshift bassinet—an old wicker laundry basket lined with towels and blankets—and comforted her until the crying stopped. She stood in the middle of the room for a time, swaying back and forth with the baby cradled in her arms, looking down on her little face. The baby smiled. Such a beautiful child! How could anyone have abandoned her?

She wished Roger were here beside her. Roger loved babies. And Molly missed him terribly.

Sometimes she had considered it a chore to wait up for Roger, always late getting home at the end of his long-haul road trip. She would wonder how she ever ended up married to an over-the-road truck driver, and feel sorry for herself. And then came that awful night when she got word of a massive pileup on an icy stretch of the Pennsylvania Turnpike. They said Roger heroically gave his life to save others, but the crash took him from her forever.

Raising Jay and Justine as a single mother had been hard. There

17

was little money left from Roger's insurance after a few years, and Molly had worked anywhere she could find a local job and tried to be home when the children needed her. Thanks to the generosity of Tom Johnson, she was able to work at his Fish and Fries Café on a schedule that fit her needs. Not much money, but enough to keep her going and take care of her family.

Molly thought about Birdie Wilson's lament: "They'd call her Baby Jane Doe." That would be in the child welfare system, where little Angel wouldn't have a real name, much less a real family. Jay and Justine had lost their father, but they had always had her and they'd always had each other. No child should be left with less. For the first time, Molly felt a true tug at her heart when it came to this baby girl.

"Don't worry, little river angel," she whispered. "If you don't have a mama out there somewhere looking for you, you have one here. I swear to God I will care for you and protect you like you were my own flesh and blood."

Her communion with the child was interrupted as Jay banged in from the side-porch, where he'd been making her a plant stand. He volunteered to do it. It pleased her when he knew she wanted something and set out to provide it if he could. Jay was a good son.

"Don't that baby cry a lot?" he said.

"*Doesn't*. And that's what babies do. But little Angel doesn't cry as much as you did—so far, at least."

"How do you know she's not sick or something?"

"She's not acting like there's something wrong, Jay. Babies cry when they wake up and want attention. It's normal."

"If you say so, Mom. I finished your plant stand. Want to see it?" Yes, she did. He brought the stand inside and she praised his work. Jay was handy with tools. He had been great help around the house in the last couple of years.

Molly was proud of her children. Jay, who looked more like his father every day, and Justine, always the more sensitive of the two, both of them growing up faster than Molly was ready for. They'd be finished with school too soon and go off to the city where they could find jobs and be independent.

She would worry plenty about Jay, of course, but even more about Justine. The thought of her daughter, a pretty young woman, alone in the city was almost more than Molly could handle.

"Don't forget," Jay said, "you've got to come and see my teacher tomorrow."

"Oh, no. I had forgot it, Jay. It's a good thing you reminded me. I just wish I didn't have to drive halfway across the county for it."

"But we have to ride halfway across the county on the bus twice a day, every day, Mom," Jay reminded her pointedly. "It's not that bad."

"I'm sorry, honey. It's not bad at all. I'm always happy to talk to your teacher. You know that."

As soon as Jay left the house, Molly was on the phone again. She called Kelley Peterson and asked if Kelley could keep the baby during the afternoon Monday. Kelley said she would love to do it, but she also had to be out of town. And please do call the next time Molly needed a hand.

Molly tried Janet Rider and Marlene Johnson. No answer at either house.

Marylee Tipsworth answered on the second ring. Molly skipped the usual small talk and went straight to the point: "Marylee, I really need somebody to take Baby Angel tomorrow afternoon while I go meet with Jay's teacher. Do you think you could do it?"

Marylee cleared her throat a couple of times. "Well, I'd love to help," she said, "but I have my hands full right now, Molly. There's been so much going on lately. And now Duncan's sick."

"Duncan? I'm sorry, Maryann, who's Duncan?"

"Oh, of course you wouldn't know—Duncan's my cat."

"I'm sorry to hear that," Molly said. "I hope he gets well soon." Then she hung up the phone.

There was hardly anyone left to call. Edna Wilson most likely would keep Baby Angel, but she had no home phone and didn't drive. With Birdie and his cell phone off on some wild goose chase with Sam Gowdy, Molly would hate to leave the baby there. What would Edna do in case of an emergency?

No choice, really. She would just have to take Baby Angel with her. The trip wouldn't be necessary if we had enough children in Cambria to support our own school, Molly reasoned to herself. But she couldn't change circumstances she had no control over. She started looking for a warm blanket to wrap the baby in just in case tomorrow turned out to be a cool day.

That night, Jay deftly cut slots in the sides of the wicker basket so that it could be strapped in the back seat of the car with a seat belt. Baby Angel would ride safely.

❧

MOLLY WAS NINE MILES out of Cambria when she saw the flashing red lights in her rear-view mirror. She eased her old Buick to the narrow shoulder of the road and stopped. A police cruiser pulled up close behind her, and in the side mirror she could see an officer checking her license plate. Then he was at her window.

"Good morning, ma'am," he said politely, tipping his hat ever so slightly. "I'm deputy Lynn Swafford, ma'am, and Sheriff Higgins sent me out to patrol this area this morning because we've had so many complaints about speeders on these county roads. I don't know if you saw me back there at that intersection, but I was on the north side of the road with my radar gun and—"

"No, I didn't see you," Molly said. "I hope I wasn't speeding."

"Ma'am, you were going twenty-two miles an hour over the speed limit. That's—"

"You can't be serious! I never drive fast. Are you sure that radar gun is working right?"

"Yes, ma'am, they're checked regularly. Not much doubt—"

This time it wasn't Molly who interrupted the deputy, but a loud wail from the back seat. Baby Angel had been awakened by the commotion and expressed her displeasure in terms too prominent to be missed by the adults up front.

"Ma'am, are you carrying a baby back there in that basket?" the deputy asked.

"Yes."

Deputy Swafford's astonishment was evident: "But didn't you know that's not legal? I mean, you have to have it in a safe child's seat. There are serious restrictions on that."

"The baby is safe," Molly insisted. "She's buckled in just like she would be in a child's seat. I wouldn't be driving around with her back there otherwise."

"Ma'am, I'm afraid this complicates things. I might have been able to let you off with only a warning on the speeding issue, but a child-seat violation is another matter. Sheriff Higgins gets his back up real fast over child-seat violations. If he found out I caught you in one and didn't write it up, I'd be in trouble up to my ears."

Molly could see that no amount of excuse-making or pleading for sympathy was going to bail her out. Deputy Swafford had impressed her as pretty nice man, and she might have talked her way out of the speeding ticket. But she had no choice now but to produce her driver's license and sit by idly while he wrote a ticket.

"Now, ma'am—Molly—I'm going to ignore the speeding," the deputy explained politely. "I have to give you a ticket on the child-seat violation, though, and the worst part is you have to make an appearance immediately."

"What does that mean, exactly? I have to go to court or something?"

"Well yes, in a way. I'm sorry, ma'am—Molly—but you will have to follow me over to Judge Winkler's house. Winkler is a semi-retired county judge who can set bond for you and let you be on your way. He lives right over yonder, just about a mile. I truly am sorry to have to put you through this, ma'am—Molly—but the judge will go easy on you. You'll be on your way pretty quick."

Molly was extremely irritated at herself. This was going to cost her money at best, and maybe even jeopardize her driver's license. And she'd be lucky if she made it to Jay's school on time. But she had no choice now except to follow the deputy as he led her to see the judge. As she drove, she considered Lynn Swafford. He was very nice, and also not bad looking. What she did not think about was the potential effect the visit to Judge Winkler might have if the topic of the baby's identity came up.

❧3❧

Birdie and Sam Gowdy arrived in Wheeling at mid-afternoon. They had tried hard, during the long drive from Cambria, to come up with a strategy. How was the best way to go about their mission? Or, at least, where should they begin? In spite of the lengthy discussion of several promising ideas, however, they had as yet come to no firm conclusions.

When Sam saw a sign that offered cheap rooms at the Highway Motel just ahead, he urged Birdie to stop. They also hadn't agreed on how long they might expect to be in the city, but they would need a place to stay even if for only one night. A cheap place.

"This one looks about as good as we're likely to find, don't you think?" Sam said. "Otherwise we keep on driving and don't see any place else we'd want to stop. It's not like we was looking for a fancy hotel."

Birdie agreed. He turned into the motel entrance and headed the old pickup truck toward the front door. There was an overhead canopy to protect visitors from the weather and a prominent sign warning that parking was only for registration. Violators would be towed. At the owner's expense, of course.

Once inside, they were relieved to find that the room rate first quoted would be pared significantly if they stayed for two or more nights. They assured the pretty young woman behind the check-in counter that they would be guests of the establishment for a minimum of two nights, and maybe even three.

Birdie explained: "We're on an important mission here, and we don't rightly know how long it may take us."

If the young woman was curious, her curiosity did not show.

She worked mechanically and soon had room keys in their hands.

Once they found a door with their assigned number on it, the two men entered and began to unpack. Toothbrushes and razors went on a bathroom shelf and each man had an extra pair of trousers and a shirt that went on hangers in the cramped little closet just inside the door. Sam had brought more clothes than Birdie had, and promptly filled a drawer of a shoddy dresser with underwear and socks. Birdie took another drawer and carefully placed in it a pair of colorful flannel pajamas.

"My mother always told me to be sure and wear clean underwear in case I got in an accident and had to be hauled off to the emergency room," Sam laughed. Birdie found no humor in that. He thought it was a good idea.

Their room had two standard double beds, although Sam commented that these looked to him to be a might narrow. But there would be only one man in each bed so he figured this didn't matter. Did Birdie have a choice as to which bed was his?

"A bed's pretty much a bed," Birdie said.

"All right then. I'll take the one nearest the window. This one here will be yours."

"I reckon one's about as good as the other, don't you think?"

"Yes, they should to be the same."

"Ought not to make any difference, then."

"That's what I just said, Birdie."

"So you're sure you want that one?"

"Doggone it, Birdie. It don't make no difference which bed is which. Do you have a problem with this one? If you do, just say so. I don't care which one I sleep in."

"No need to get riled up, Sam. I was just saying . . ."

"Okay, then. We're settled on the beds. What do you think we ought to do about supper?"

Birdie said he wasn't particularly hungry. He might not mind a beer, though, and didn't Sam see a bar next to the motel restaurant? "You su'pose it'd be open yet?"

Sam agreed that a cold beer would be an ideal way to launch their mission in Wheeling. They went downstairs just as the bar opened for dinner patrons and chose seats at a table in a dark corner. An overly perfumed waitress with a purple streak in her brown hair brought a bottled beer they never had heard of before, but it was the house special and the price was good. The beer turned out to be pretty good, as well, and soon they were on their third bottles.

When the waitress came around again, she inquired about their stay in Wheeling.

"We're on a mission," Birdie said. "We don't know how long it may take."

"My, that sounds mysterious," the waitress declared. "You must be spies or something!"

"Oh, no ma'am," Sam said quickly. "Birdie and me are ordinary civilians."

"Well, when he said you were on a mission, I just thought that maybe—"

Birdie was eager to get back in the conversation: "Our mission is a little girl. You ain't heard nothing about other folks looking for a little girl, have you?"

The waitress immediately began to back away from the table. She picked up their empty bottles and hurried toward the bar. Fortunately, she'd already brought their fourth bottles of beer and Sam and Birdie took long draughts and complimented each other on finding this new brand they never had seen or heard of before, and they wondered why because this was damned good beer. Sam excused himself to go to the men's room, and after he got back Birdie did the same.

Birdie had barely made it back to the table when two uniformed police officers pushed through the front door and walked straight to the bar. After only a few words with the waitress with the purple streak in her hair, the policemen approached Sam and Birdie.

"You fellows got some identification on you?" the first officer demanded. His attitude did not seem at all friendly.

"What the hell?" Sam exploded. "You think we ain't old enough to drink beer or something?"

The second officer stepped up closer to their table. In a calm but firm voice he said, "Now don't turn belligerent and make trouble for yourself. Officer Johnson just asked you if you had identification. Simple question. You got ID or not?"

"Sure he's got identification," Birdie roared. "Show him your fishin' license, Sam."

The first officer looked hard at Birdie. "Sir," he said, "are you trying to be funny? Because if you are, we've got a place for funny guys. Now how about you? You got any identification?"

Birdie deliberately let his face show his displeasure. But he dug into a back pocket of his jeans and pulled out a well-used wallet. He took out his driver's license and stuck it toward the policeman. "This here ought to do it, I guess," he said loudly.

The officer looked at the license briefly. "This license expired six months ago," he said.

Birdie's face reddened.

Sam stared at Birdie with an expression that bordered on total amazement. "Damn, Birdie," he said. "Have you been driving on an expired license?"

The first officer turned his attention back to Sam. "He's still ahead of you," he said. "You haven't produced any kind of ID at all. Now do you have some or not?"

Like Birdie, Sam pulled a wallet from his back pocket. He fumbled through the contents until he found what he was looking for. It was a boat owner's identification and registration card. He held it out to the policeman.

"Is this all you got? No driver's license?"

"I don't drive," Sam said. "Nothing but a boat, anyway."

The two officers looked at one another and the first one shook his head. Then he turned back to Sam and Birdie. "So you boys come up here from Cambria to have a few drinks and find yourself a little girl? You are an absolutely disgusting pair. Me and Officer Cross here are going to haul your sorry asses downtown and see that you get locked up for the night. You won't be picking up any little girls in Wheeling, not if I can do anything about it."

Sam started to protest. Officer Cross quickly shut him up. In the blink of an eye they were in the back seat of a squad car on their way to the Wheeling police department headquarters.

Once at the station, Office Johnson rushed them before a desk sergeant—his name, it turned out, was Wilson, which gave Birdie a brief bit of hope—who slowly and meticulously took down their identifying information. They emptied their pockets and Sam surrendered his watch, then they had to remove their belts.

"You'll get this stuff back when you get out of here—if you ever do," the desk sergeant explained.

Officer Cross, meanwhile, had sat down at a desk and begun typing something into a computer. "I haven't found anything on them yet," he called across the room to Sergeant Wilson. "But you damn well bet I will before I'm done. Get 'em locked up, and don't worry too much about keeping track of the key!"

Sergeant Wilson escorted them down a long hallway, through double steel doors to a row of barred jail cells. Only three of the cells were occupied, the prisoners apparently asleep. There was an overwhelming stench of unwashed bodies and alcohol mixed with a few even less pleasant odors.

"The drunk tank is a fitting place for you two filthy scumbags," Sergeant Wilson proclaimed as he unlocked the door to one of the vacant cells. "Get in here, Gowdy." Then he opened the door to an adjacent cell and shoved Birdie in. "We don't have to do anything to hold you over night, given the fact that you've been drinking and turned belligerent on us," he said. "And I'm betting that by morning we find out enough about you miserable perverts to keep you here for a long time."

After the door to Birdie's cell slammed shut, they could hear the policeman's footsteps echo a long way down the hall. Neither man spoke for a full five minutes after that.

Then, Birdie: "You think we're in trouble, Sam?"

"No shit, Birdie. We're in trouble deep."

"Ain't they su'posed to give us a phone call? I ought to call Edna and let her know we got here all right. I expect Alma's worried, too."

"Alma don't worry about me," Sam said. "Least not much. She won't expect me to call."

"You think they'll feed us in here? We didn't get any supper, not past them four bottles of beer. That was pretty good beer, wasn't it." This last bit was a statement of opinion, not a question. "So you really think we're in deep trouble?" This was a question, and it had a hint of urgency.

"They seem to think we're child molesters. That's a lot of trouble to be in."

"How could they think that? Hell, we come all the way up here to try and help out that little baby girl. Neither one of us would ever hurt a child."

"You know that, Birdie, and I know it. Problem is, how're we going to convince them? It sounded to me like those police officers had made up their minds."

Birdie didn't respond. It was beginning to sink in on him that Sam was correct—they were in deep trouble. What if the policemen thought they were somebody else? They didn't know anybody in Wheeling who could vouch for them. Maybe if they could get the policemen to call Johnny White . . .

"Birdie?"

"What, Sam?"

"Don't worry, Birdie. They'll get this straightened out. We'll be out of here tomorrow. Think you can sleep on that little cot over there?"

"I'd sleep better if I had some supper."

But the four bottles of that good new brand of beer had made sleep easier to come by. They never knew whether they were locked up too late for the evening meal or what, but nobody came with supper. Sam soon heard Birdie snoring loudly. A few minutes after that he was fast asleep, himself.

≈

"TAKE YOUR STUFF and get out of here." A different desk sergeant was on duty. He was no more polite than Sergeant Wilson. "We couldn't find anything to hold you boys on, but be damn sure you'll be watched as long as you're in Wheeling. Want my advice: Get back to Cambria and stay there. We don't want you in Wheeling, not now, not ever!"

28

They were dismayed to find that they had to get a taxi to take them back to the Highway Motel. The price of a taxi hadn't been figured into what they expected to spend. But at least they had had a free breakfast in jail. Although it wasn't much.

The first thing Birdie checked on when they got out of the taxi was his truck. It was just where he'd parked it the day before, right after they registered. He walked around it and looked it over carefully. "It looks okay," he told Sam. "You never know, in the city. Somebody could have took it while we was in jail down there."

"Birdie, who in hell would take that old truck?"

"Like I said, in the city you never know."

A motel housekeeping cart was outside their door and a maid was cleaning their room. She bustled about, looking embarrassed. Sam sat gingerly on the edge of a bed while she worked and Birdie stood and looked out the window. The maid quickly finished her work and asked if there was anything else they needed.

"I don't believe we need anything, thank you." Birdie replied. "But I was wondering if you'd heard anything about a little girl missing. That's what Sam and me are here in Wheeling for, looking for a little girl that somebody might be trying to find."

"Mercy, I don't think so," the maid said. "How long's she been missing?"

"She just got found last week."

"But if she got found—"

Sam interrupted. "Ma'am, we don't need to hold you up from your work. We appreciate what you did, cleaning up after us and all."

"It didn't take much. I couldn't even tell that anybody had slept in those beds."

When the maid was safely out of hearing distance, Sam challenged Birdie: "I don't think we better be asking anymore about little girls. That's what got us in trouble yesterday. We're going to have to figure out a better plan if we expect to find out anything in Wheeling."

"Maybe so. You got some ideas?"

"Well, we sure can't go to the cops," Sam said. "How about the

29

newspaper office? If there was a girl missing, wouldn't you think they'd know about it?"

"I reckon they would," Birdie agreed. "You got any idea where the newspaper office is at?"

"No, but I bet somebody at the desk could tell us."

They decided to clean up before starting anything else, feeling pretty scruffy after their night in jail. They took turns in the shower and in front of the mirror shaving and, after Birdie put on the only extra shirt he'd brought along and Sam put on both fresh shirt and pants, they went to the front desk to inquire.

"The Newspaper office? Do you mean the *News-Register*?" The smiling young man behind the counter, who spoke with an east-Asian accent they found somewhat difficult to understand, seemed unsure. "I think it's down on Main Street."

"You think, or you know?" Sam asked.

"I'll find out for sure." The young man turned and went some-where in the back, and was gone for several minutes. He returned with a broad grin. "I'm for sure," he announced. "The newspaper office is down on Main Street."

They chose not to press their luck by trying for more specific information. The newspaper office ought not to be too hard to find. They climbed into Birdie's old truck and set out for downtown. Even though it had been years since he lived in Wheeling, Birdie soon was getting a sense of direction and remembering his way around. Finding the newspaper office was surprisingly easy.

Once inside they made their way to a receptionist's desk, where a middle-aged woman with premature white hair put down her steaming cup of coffee and offered a friendly smile. "May I help you?" she asked.

"We'd like to inquire about a missing little girl," Sam told her. "We wondered if there had been any stories on her in the paper?"

"Would that have been recently?"

"She was just found last week," Birdie said.

"I'm a little bit confused," the woman said. "I thought you said she was missing. But she's been found, you say?"

Birdie responded to her friendly demeanor, with a broad smile

30

of his own. "Yes, ma'am, that's right," he told her. "She was found last week. Me and my boys found her, floating on the river."

"Do you have a name?"

"Oh, excuse us, ma'am," Sam said. "I'm Sam Gowdy and this is Birdie Wilson. We're from Cambria."

The receptionist smiled again, this time in actual amusement. "I'm pleased to meet you," she said. "But I meant do you have a name for the missing girl?"

"Yes, ma'am, we give her the name Angel," Birdie said. "Sam here is the one that suggested it, and Johnny White took right up on it."

The woman looked a bit uneasy. She picked up a telephone on her desk and said, "Excuse me just a minute, please," and pressed a button on the base of the phone. "I have two gentlemen here you might want to talk to," she said. And, turning back to Birdie and Sam, "Would you two mind waiting right over there for a moment? Somebody will be with you right away."

Birdie and Sam stepped back, to an area near the door that she seemed to have indicated. There were no seats and no clearly defined waiting space so they just stood awkwardly and waited for an editor or reporter or whoever was going to come out and give them information on any missing little girl. The first person to approach them was a uniformed security guard.

"Do you gentlemen have a problem of some kind?" the guard asked, showing little real interest.

"Well, no," Sam responded. "We was just interested in finding out any information about a missing little girl. Looks like it would have been in the newspaper."

"I don't believe we've had any little girl missing," the guard said, still without expression. "If we had I'd remember it. So why don't you fellows just move on along now, and don't take up any more of Miss Jensen's time?"

The two Cambrians, quite unimpressed by the overall reception they had received at the newspaper, left through the same heavy doors they'd entered by and stepped out onto the sidewalk. It was beginning to rain. They were soaking wet by the time they got back to Birdie's truck. It had a parking ticket on the windshield.

"I thought I remembered Wheeling being a more friendly kind of place," Birdie said, once they were out of the rain and seated in the pickup. "Seems to me like some city people just ain't as nice as Cambrians."

Sam was wiping his wet face with a handkerchief. He kept on wiping as if he hadn't heard a word Birdie said. Birdie observed Sam for a time, then shook his head sadly and started up the truck and headed back out of town, toward the Highway Motel. Neither man spoke on the way.

The drive took less time than the trip into town had, in spite of the rain and the poor performance of the truck's wipers, and they were at the motel in what seemed no time at all. When they got back to their room, Sam took his battered suitcase down from a shelf and pulled out the dresser drawer and began to pack his extra socks and underwear. Birdie sat on the bed and watched.

Finally, Sam spoke. "Birdie, we're not going to find out anything in Wheeling. We may as well go home."

"We got to stay tonight, though. We signed up for that."

"We'll stay tonight, then get up early in the morning and head back to Cambria."

Birdie offered no dissent.

❧4❧

Judge Harold Winkler was an elegant man, simple in speech and dapper in appearance. He welcomed Deputy Lynn Swafford and Molly Hearst as if asking friends or relatives into his home. "And look at this precious little bundle," he crooned, gazing adoringly at the baby cradled in Molly's arms. "I've not seen you in a while, Lynn. Been hard at work, I guess?"

"Yes, sir, I have."

"Tell Sheriff Higgins we could use a bit more presence out in this part of the county. Would you do that?"

"Yes, sir, I will."

"Getting in any fishing now that the weather's turned more to spring?"

"No, sir, I'm not."

"Would you care for some coffee?" Judge Winkler said, turning to Molly but clearly directing his query to both. "I've just made a room and invited fresh pot." He motioned them into the living them to sit.

Deputy Swafford declined the coffee, and Molly followed his lead. She had never before appeared before a judge or any other person of judicial authority. She had no idea how to act. But she supposed the judge would tell her what to do in good time, and meanwhile she simply would watch Deputy Swafford.

The judge suddenly stopped short. "Excuse my terrible manners. Ma'am, I'm Judge Harold Winkler. I don't believe I have had the pleasure of making your acquaintance."

Lynn Swafford put a hand on Molly's shoulder. "This is Molly Hearst," he said. "We just met a little while ago over on one of the county roads. I'm sorry to have to intrude, but the reason—"

Judge Winkler interrupted. "I'm very pleased to meet you, Miss Hearst—or is it Mrs.?"

"It's Mrs. I'm a widow."

"Well I'm very sorry to hear that."

Lynn Swafford shuffled his feet awkwardly. Then he cleared his throat. "Judge," he said, "the reason I brought Mrs. Hearst in front of you this morning is that I had to write her a ticket for carrying a baby in the back seat of her car without having a proper car seat. Now I will say that she had it strapped in securely, in a basket that served as a nice little bed. But as you know the law is very strict on this matter."

"Is this the baby?"

"Yes, sir, it is."

"She's a very beautiful baby, Mrs. Hearst. What's her name?"

"Her name is Angel, your honor."

"Oh, please. Dispense with the formality. Call me Harold. And how old is little Angel?"

Molly was hesitant. "We think she's about eight or ten months, but we're not really sure."

"Oh, I see—she's not your child, then. But of course you said you're a widow. Is she related? I hope you're not a paid caretaker. That would complicate the situation—the legal circumstances, you know."

Molly Hearst felt as if her mouth was full of cotton. "Yes, she's somewhat related," Molly stammered. "I mean I am taking care of her but not like I'm being paid or anything like that and I had to bring her along because I'm supposed to be visiting my son's school for a conference with his teacher but I'm going to be late and I wouldn't have brought Angel but I couldn't find anybody else to take her on short notice and I didn't have a proper car seat so Jay, he's my son, made the basket so it could be fastened with the seat belt. I wouldn't do anything in the world to hurt Baby Angel, your honor."

Deputy Swafford laid a gentle hand on Molly's arm and Judge Winkler looked as if he felt guilty for having asked her a troubling question. "Please, Mrs. Hearst, sit here on the couch and relax," the judge said. "You can put baby Angel down beside you there. She must be getting heavy by now. Let me get you some coffee. You too, Lynn. How do you both take it?"

Deputy Swafford said black and Molly once again followed his lead. The judge left the room and the deputy sat down across from Molly, in an antique upholstered chair with hand-made doilies protecting the arms and headrest. He looked at Molly with an expression of near-pain. He started to speak, seemed to think better of it, then started to speak again. But neither he nor Molly said a word before Judge Winkler returned with two cups of steaming coffee on a tray along with silver cream and sugar dispensers, spoons, white linen napkins, and a plate of cookies.

"Mrs. Winkler made these this morning," the judge said. "I regret that you missed her. She's off to town today and she'll be sorry she wasn't here for your visit."

Deputy Swafford stood. He took the tray from Judge Winkler and placed in on a coffee table in front of the couch. Then he took one of the cups of coffee and went back to his chair, while Molly took the other cup and nervously poured cream and added sugar. The deputy took two sips of the hot coffee before addressing Judge Winkler directly: "We sure appreciate your hospitality, judge, but the truth is I need to get on with my patrol. Sheriff Higgins wants us out there where the traffic is. I don't mean to be impolite, but it really would be good if we could get on with business. As I said before, Molly—Mrs. Hearst—was driving—"

"Oh, hush, Lynn. I know why you're here. I'm supposed to act on your ticket and decide what to do with this very nice lady and her beautiful little baby. But you're the one who wrote the ticket. What do you recommend?"

Deputy Swafford flushed red with embarrassment. "I don't know if it's for me to say, judge," he said. "We, that is the sheriff's department, will respect your ruling, whatever it is. And I expect Mrs. Hearst needs to get on her way to her boy's school."

"Well then, Lynn, I have two options. Either I can dismiss your ticket or I can set bond for Mrs. Hearst—"

Baby Angel chose this instant to wake, and as usual did so with a loud wail. Molly quickly set her coffee cup on the table and picked up the baby, rocking her in her arms. But this time, what had worked well before had no effect whatsoever. Angel not only continued to cry, but her cries became louder and more demanding. She was hungry and she was determined to make everyone in the room aware of it.

Lynn Swafford stepped to Molly's side. "It's been a long time, but I used to have a way with babies. If you'll let me . . ."

Molly quickly handed Angel over. The deputy held her upright, against his shoulder, and began to hum, all the while swaying in time with his own music. Baby Angel stopped crying.

"Looks like you're still good at it, Lynn," Judge Winkler chuckled. "You raised a couple of your own, if I recall correctly."

"Yes, I did. After we lost Jane, I had to bring up the boys all by myself."

"I've not had the pleasure of seeing your two sons for some time now, but it sure was clear you did a good job."

"Thank you, Judge Winkler. Now—"

"Yes, I know," Judge Harold Winkler said. "I suppose you're right. We need to get on with business. You ought to be back out on the road pointing your radar gun at unsuspecting motorists, I imagine. And Mrs. Hearst needs to get on to her boy's school."

"Yes, sir, I think that about covers it."

"Lynn, I appreciate the fact that your job is to enforce the law. And I understand how Sheriff Higgins gets bent all out of shape over baby-seat violations. And he's right about that. Our children are all precious and we have to make sure they are protected. But you tell me that Mrs. Hearst had this beautiful baby—Angel, didn't you say?—she had Angel securely strapped in and she looked pretty safe to you. So here's what I'm going to do. I'm going to void your ticket. Mrs. Hearst, I must say it's been a pleasure to meet you and your little Angel. Now you are free to go on, and get to that boy's school."

Molly's relief gushed out, first to Judge Winkler: "Your Honor, I don't know what to say except thank you. And you can be sure I'll take care of little Angel." And to Deputy Swafford, who waited until this instant to return Angel to her: "You were very polite to me and I'm really very grateful for the way you took Angel and stopped her crying. She seems to like you."

Lynn Swafford reddened again. "I'll see you to your car, Mrs. Hearst," he said. "And thank you, Judge Winkler. I think you were more than fair to Mrs. Hearst."

"Get back some day when you have time to go fishing," the judge replied. "And Mrs. Hearst, any time you happen to be back this way please stop in to say hello and let me see how that little baby's doing. Will you do that?"

Molly was backing toward the door, which the deputy held open for her. "Yes, sir," she said, "I will."

Once outside, Molly and the deputy walked to her car. He held the back door open while she strapped the baby into the basket that now had judicial blessing as a certified car seat. Molly backed away and bumped into the deputy, who was fumbling with his book of traffic tickets. He dropped the tickets and quickly stooped to pick them up. His policeman's cap fell from his head. He reddened even more.

Molly felt the heat of a deep blush creeping up her neck. She wanted to help this man, and make him more comfortable. But he was so clumsy, what could she do?

After several more awkward minutes, she was at last on her way again. Baby Angel slept peacefully in her basket in the back seat.

Molly knew that she would be late for her appointment with Jay's teacher. She considered her options, and decided it would be best simply to tell the truth—she had been delayed by a speeding ticket. At the very least this would substantiate the fact that she'd been hurrying in an effort to be on time.

She was almost an hour late, but Jay's teacher, a dowdy woman named Mrs. Kobel, was understanding. She was sorry for Molly's inconvenience at the hand of the law and appreciated her visit. Jay, she said, was an excellent student and she could tell that he had his mother's support at home.

"I try my best," Molly said. "It's not easy being a single mother, but of course I'm sure you hear that all the time."

"Yes," Mrs. Kobel replied, "and I know it's true. But I do believe it's unfortunate that Jay doesn't have a man's influence in his life. These formative years are critical, Mrs. Hearst. Does he have anyone who might serve as a male role model?"

"Well, no . . ."

"I'm sure you do your best, Mrs. Hearst. As I said, Jay is a good student and a fine boy. But I do believe he misses having a strong male figure he can lean on. Did he and his father get on well?"

"Yes," Molly said, "but he was still little when he lost his father. He missed him a lot then but he hardly remembers him now."

"And there hasn't been a man's influence since?"

"Well, no, not directly. But there's Pastor Mike and other men and boys he has plenty of contact with—"

"Yes, of course. As you say. I didn't know he had a baby sister at home."

"Oh, no. Angel isn't his sister. I'm just keeping her for someone, and I had no choice but to bring her along."

In what Molly found to be a very condescending tone of voice, Mrs. Kobel said it was commendable to help another mother even though time spent caring for other children was time away from her own. But she trusted that Molly was able to keep things in proper balance and even if she devoted all her time to Jay he still would be missing the male influence he needed, anyway.

Molly was tempted to answer in similar tone, but was saved by a loud wail from the wicker laundry basked she had deposited on the floor at her feet. Baby Angel apparently felt that it was time for this particular teacher's conference to be over. Mrs. Kobel did, too, and brusquely signaled that Molly's time was up.

Molly left the classroom and picked up Jay, who waited for her outside the school office. His face lit up with a big smile when he saw her approaching.

"How'd it go, Mom?"

"It went very well, Jay. Mrs. Kobel said you are a good student and a fine young man. But I already knew that, of course."

"Did you like her?"

Molly hated to lie to her son, but she did: "Yes, she seems nice."

"Did she want to talk to you about anything in particular—like any problems I have or stuff like that?"

"No, it didn't seem like it to me. Didn't she schedule meetings with all the students' parents?"

"I don't think so, Mom."

Molly stopped walking and, when Jay stopped too and turned back to face her, demanded of her son: "Jay, have you been having problems at school that I don't know about? Why would your teacher make an appointment with me and not the other parents?"

Jay obviously was embarrassed. "I think I know, Mom," he said. "But I'd rather wait and talk about it in the car if you don't mind."

By the time they reached the car and had Baby Angel's basket secured in the back seat, Molly's tension had escalated until she could feel her heart pounding in her chest. What in the world was going on with Jay in school?

For once, Jay got right to the point. They were barely out of the parking lot when he started his explanation. "Mom, I'm straight, okay? But Mrs. Kobel somehow seems to have got the idea that I'm gay."

Molly was speechless.

Jay watched her for a minute and, getting no reaction, went on. "She's never said it, but I can tell. She's always saying things about how boys act, and lots of times what she says doesn't fit me at all. Is that what she wanted to talk to you about—me being gay?"

"No, she never said—wait, she did seem concerned that you have no male influence in your life. Good lord, Jay, you're right. She does think you're gay."

Jay smiled as if quite pleased with himself.

"See, I had her figured out," he said. "So what did you tell her, Mom?"

"Well, nothing. I didn't know what she was getting at, Jay. I just told her your father's been gone for some time now and you don't really have a good male role model. That's what she asked."

"What do you think we ought to do?"

"Jay, I have no idea."

And she didn't. The last thing in the world Molly wanted to do was let down her son. If he was in physical danger she'd lay down her life for him in the blink of an eye. If he had emotional needs, she would spend every waking minute trying to help him. But what was she supposed to do with a stupid (*don't say that out loud, Molly*) old school teacher who thought her son was gay and what difference would it make anyway?

In the end, she chose to emphasize that last point—what difference would it make if he were homosexual?—and talk with Jay about all people being unique and how she'd always taught him and Justine not to discriminate against anyone they thought was different. Jay seemed content with her suggestion that they let the matter ride for now and talk about it more over the weekend. He probably knew that this was her way of putting off dealing with something she had no clue how to handle. Whatever.

To their mutual relief, they found other things to talk about the rest of the way back to Cambria. Molly felt much better by the time they got home. But her comfort turned to anxiety when she saw a clearly marked sheriff's department automobile parked in front of the house.

❧5❧

Sam Gowdy and Birdie might have made it back to Cambria without incident had it not been for Sam's over-active bladder. When the stretch of highway between stops got too long, Sam finally had to insist that Birdie pull off the road so that he could get out and relieve himself in the bushes. Everything went okay until they were ready to get back on the road, but at that point their troubles began.

Birdie started the engine and put the pickup in gear, then looked in the side mirror to make sure nothing was coming up behind. The highway was clear. He released the clutch. The truck didn't move. Instead, one rear wheel spun impotently in the mud of the highway shoulder.

"Give it more gas," Sam Gowdy directed.

Birdie did.

The result was even more futile wheel spinning. "Rock it back and forth a little," Sam said.

Birdie shifted into reverse and once again released the clutch and gunned the engine. More spinning. Not only was the truck not moving, but the spinning wheel was digging deeper into the soft ground. The truck had begun to tilt toward the roadside ditch. Birdie shifted gears again and tried to urge the old Dodge forward. The truck didn't move.

"We're stuck, Sam," Birdie announced matter-of-factly.

"Let me get out and push. Rock it a couple of times, then really give it the gas."

Sam stood behind the truck, a little to the side, while Birdie shifted back and forth from forward to reverse a couple of times, trying to gain some movement. Then he stepped squarely in back when Birdie shifted to low gear and revved up the engine. Sam pushed as hard as he could. Birdie pressed hard on the gas pedal and cursed. The truck didn't move, but Sam was splattered with mud thrown back by the spinning wheel.

"It's no use, Birdie," Sam called. "We're not going anywhere." Birdie cut off the engine and stepped out to survey the situation. He shook his head sorrowfully. The pickup's right rear wheel was buried deep in the soggy ground. Water had started to seep into the hole around the wheel.

"Gonna have to find us some help," Birdie said. "It'll take some pretty good power to pull us out now."

"I'm sorry, Birdie. If I could have waited a little bit longer we wouldn't be in this fix."

"Don't worry about that, Sam. A man's gotta go when a man's gotta go."

"What do you figure to do?"

"I guess somebody'll come along and give us a ride, else we'll have to walk. Probably a gas station down the road a piece. How far do you guess we are from the river?"

Sam looked off toward the west. "See that row of trees way over yonder?" he said. "I believe that might be the river. I'd make it, what, about a quarter of a mile? Why?"

"Well, if we could find some river rats like us we know they'd help us quick as a possum up a gum tree, that's all."

Sam nodded in agreement. "You're right about that," he said. "Right now, though, I'd settle for an old dirt farmer with a mule."

As Sam spoke, a man in a new-looking black Mercury pulled up beside the mud-stuck pickup and stopped. He lowered the window on the passenger side of the car and called to Sam and Birdie: "Looks like you boys could use a hand. Get in and I'll drop you off down the road at Scudder's place. There's likely somebody there that can help."

Sam got in beside the driver and Birdie crawled into the back seat. The Mercury was spotless inside and still had a distinct new-car smell. Birdie looked down and saw that he'd left a big muddy footprint on the light-gray carpet. He pulled a handkerchief from his pocket and tried to lean down without being obvious and see if he could wipe it up. Sam and the driver were talking and Birdie's motion went undetected. But when he wiped at the mud, all he managed to do was spread it even more widely. He tried to stuff the muddy handkerchief back in his pocket and in the process left an ugly smear on the seat.

"Where you fellows from?" the driver was asking.

Sam told him they were from Cambria and on their way home from Wheeling. On the way, that is, until they got mired down back there.

"I do at lot of business in Wheeling," the driver responded. "You fellows up there on business or pleasure?"

Sam swallowed hard. "We were there on a little business."

"What kind of business are you in?"

"I run a bait shop and Birdie there is a fisherman, I guess you'd say."

"So you were checking out new fishing gear or the like?"

Sam had his left arm over the back of the seat, his hand dangling downward. He began to wave his hand vigorously, hoping Birdie would pick up the cue and jump into the conversation. Sam needed help.

Birdie, who'd been busy trying to erase his muddy footprint from the floor, had not been paying attention to the conversation in the front seat. He had no idea what Sam wanted. But Sam's hand-wagging looked to portend something serious, and Birdie naturally was concerned.

He leaned forward and said, "You hurt your hand pushing back there, Sam?"

"You say you hurt yourself?" the driver asked. "Do you need a doctor? If you do, I ought to turn around and head back the other direction."

Sam hoped the relief didn't show in his voice. He was extremely happy to have the subject changed from their business in Wheeling. "No," he said, "I'm okay. I didn't hurt myself. Good thing, too, since my pushing didn't help any."

"That's good," the driver said. But he would not be deterred so easily. "Like I was saying, you boys looking for new gear or something up in Wheeling?"

Birdie said loudly from the back seat, "No sir, we were looking for somebody who could give us information on a little girl."

"Oh, so you're interested in little girls?" The driver suddenly appeared to be more attentive. "You like pictures?"

"No, we don't have a picture—Sam, we ought to have got us a picture—"

"How about video tapes? I've got a real nice selection in the trunk that you boys might like to see. I can make you a good price on 'em, too."

Sam Gowdy stiffened. "Hell no, we're not interested in pictures or video tapes of little girls. We were trying to find out about the family of one little girl. Stop and let us out, you dirty pervert."

"Hold on, now," the driver whined. "Maybe I misunderstood something. And maybe I misled you fellows. I'm not into that kind of thing. No siree."

"Then what were you going to sell us?"

"I think this was all just a misunderstanding. Why, I love kids myself. Have two little granddaughters. But look, here's Scudder's place. There will be somebody here who can give you a hand." He pulled into the driveway of a combination gasoline station and country general store. "I'm just glad I could help you fellows out. Sorry about the misunderstanding. Just forget it, okay?"

Sam and Birdie got out and their benefactor sped back onto the highway.

"You really think he was a pervert, Sam?" Birdie asked.

"Hell yes. Driving around with a trunk full of pictures and video tapes of little girls. Wish we'd got his license number. I'd sure call the law if they got a phone in here."

"How'd you catch on to him?"

Sam Gowdy looked at Birdie with an expression somewhere between pity and astonishment. "I smelled him, Birdie," Sam said. "You can smell a pervert from a mile off. And you couldn't see 'em from the back I guess, but he had on green shoes. Brightest

44

green I ever saw. That was the dead giveaway, green shoes."

Birdie's confusion was apparent. Then he broke into a wide grin and said, "You're pulling my foot, ain't you, Sam."

"Yeah, Birdie, I'm pulling your foot."

But once inside Scudder's, they had more pressing things to worry about. Could they get a tow, back up the road a piece? Yes, their pickup was stuck in the mud on the shoulder, headed south. No, it most likely would not take much to get them out. Sure, Scudder's Jeep Cherokee probably would do the job.

Scudder wanted fifty dollars. In advance.

Birdie and Sam got together and counted their money. Between them, they had fifty-eight dollars left. Scudder got the job.

It took no more than twenty minutes for Scudder to have the old Dodge unstuck and back on the highway. Birdie calculated that they had plenty of gas to make it to Cambria. They would be home before dark. He thought their trip to Wheeling had been worthwhile, didn't Sam agree?

"We didn't find out anything, Birdie," Sam protested. "How is that worthwhile?"

"Don't you see, Sam, if anybody had been looking for our little Angel we surely would have heard about it. Since we didn't hear anything, that means nobody ain't looking for her. If nobody ain't looking for her she's been abandoned. If she's been abandoned, Cambrians can take care of her and raise her up just like family."

"If we can keep her out of child welfare."

Birdie made a sound that was halfway between a snort and a grunt. "I'd sure hate for them child welfare people to get hold of her," he said. "They'd name her—"

"I know, Birdie. They'd name her Baby Jane Doe."

Birdie Wilson drove in silence for the next twenty minutes, something very rare for him. But he had sensed that Sam was not always taking him seriously. He wanted to think things through before he started another topic. The problem was, he couldn't come up with another topic. Baby Angel had so stuck in his mind for the last couple of days that she was all he could find to talk about. Then he remembered that it was Sam who had suggested in the town meeting that the baby be called Angel. This was an opening he could take advantage of.

"You really believe in angels, Sam?"

"I don't know, Birdie. Do you?"

"I'm not too sure about it, myself. Seems like lots of people do."

"All I know is that I've never seen one."

"Maybe they're invisible."

"I expect they might be—if they exist."

Birdie hesitated, then charged ahead. "The reason I was asking, Sam, is that you was the one who said we ought to call that little baby Angel. You said she come to us like a little river angel. Ain't that what you said?"

"That didn't necessarily mean I believe there are real angels, though. I was just saying—"

"But you said she come to us like a little river angel. I remember exactly what you said."

"Birdie, it doesn't matter what I said. I was just saying we ought to give her a name, and it seemed like under the circumstances Angel was a proper name to give her."

Sam said this in a voice loud enough that Birdie could tell he was irritated. He decided to give up talking entirely for a while. Whatever was stuck in Sam's craw would probably go away in good time, and maybe he'd just wait and let Sam Gowdy speak first next time. They drove all the way back to Cambria without talking. When they arrived in town they saw a sheriff's department patrol car parked in front of Molly Hearst's house. Mayor Johnny White stood beside it, talking with an officer.

6

Johnny White had few options. He must get things organized in a hurry. Three clangs of the bell atop Town Hal was the signal that summoned the town's volunteer fire department, and the mayor gave the bell rope three vigorous yanks. The toll of the bell rolled over Cambria like God striking a celestial anvil with a sledge hammer. Within minutes, eight volunteer firemen—the entire department save two—were assembled.

"We've got a problem, men," the mayor announced earnestly to those gathered before him. "Maybe some of you saw the sheriff's car over in front of Molly's house. I tried to call Molly and nobody answered. My guess is, she saw the car in time to duck out the back door with the baby and right now is on the run. If the sheriff gets ahold of that little baby, she's headed for the child welfare system for sure."

"Birdie says they'd name her Baby Jane Doe," Kirk Mendenhall called from the back of the group.

Johnny White held up his hands for silence.

"We ought to listen to Birdie. He's the one that found her." This from Gordon Blessing, standing square in the middle of the group of assembled firemen.

Morris Layman, at the front of the group: "That's right, mayor. Birdie says they'll name her Baby Jane Doe and we ought to listen to Birdie since he's the one that found her."

The mayor again signaled for quiet. "That's why I called you all together," he said. "If the sheriff decides to look around town, we need to keep that baby moving. I want all of you to go home and be ready to take little Angel in at the drop of a hat."

Morris Layman raised his hand. Johnny White nodded his way. "That doesn't make a lot of sense, Johnny. How are we going to know where she is and when to get her?"

"I'm coming to that, Morris. I'll be on my cell phone, following close behind the sheriff. I'll know where the baby is and which way the sheriff is headed, and I'll call one of you as appropriate to pick up the baby and take her back to your house. Use the back door, and keep low."

Kirk Mendenhall: "So the plan is just to stay a step ahead of the sheriff. And you'll be in command, right?"

Johnny White nodded affirmatively. "That's exactly right, Kirk," he said. "I have all your phone numbers. I need for you to get on home and stay by your phone. Now I won't be calling everybody. Who I call and when depends entirely on the sheriff's movements. Any questions?"

There was plenty of mumbling and even a bit of grumbling among themselves, but no questions from the volunteers. They scattered quickly. Johnny White set out for Molly Hearst's house to begin his observation of the sheriff. He walked fast.

Even as he rounded the corner of Molly's block, he could see that the lone occupant seated in the patrol car did not look like Sheriff Higgins. This was good, because the sheriff was a dogged man who, once he smelled prey, wouldn't give up the trail until they got snow in the summertime. Although the sheriff had never set foot in Cambria, Johnny White had met him twice in the county seat. He'd admired his work through the years. If there was a criminal on the loose, nobody you'd rather have chasing him than Sheriff Clarence Higgins.

But now the shoe was on the other foot, so to speak. Little Baby Angel was the prey—or, rather, the people who had Baby Angel. If Sheriff Higgins had heard that Cambrians were hiding an abandoned child from the child welfare agency, he would never give up till her found her.

The mayor had a hunch how the sheriff had come to know about Baby Angel. Max Barnes. In the assemblage in Town Hall where Cambrians had made the decision to keep little Angel out of the child welfare system, Max had stated flatly that they ought to call the sheriff. So Max had gone against the decision of the people and called the sheriff on his own! Johnny White seethed with anger.

Keep your cool, Johnny, he exhorted himself. If Max already had reported the presence of Baby Angel, it was even more important that they keep the child hidden. The law couldn't take her if they couldn't find her.

The mayor made a snap decision. Instead of trying to conceal the fact of Angel's existence, since the sheriff apparently already knew, his duty now was to create as much of a distraction as possible and give Molly more time. Yes, he'd have to find an opening to call one of the volunteer firemen when the time came, but he'd play that card when it was dealt. Right now, he simply needed to face the sheriff's man head-on.

Johnny White strode manfully up beside the police cruiser and rapped hard on the window. The man inside, who might have been sleeping, looked up, startled, and lowered his window. He was a deputy the mayor had not met before.

"I'm Mayor White," he said. "Is there a problem here, deputy?"

The deputy pulled himself up straighter in the seat, then looked to think better of that and opened the door and got out. He stooped to pick up his hat, which he'd knocked off in the process.

"No, sir," the deputy said. "I'm just here to follow up on something. No problem at all."

"I don't believe we've met."

"Excuse me. I'm Lynn Swafford, sheriff's deputy. Sheriff Higgins doesn't send us over this way very often."

"I'm very much aware of that, Deputy Swafford. You might tell the sheriff we pay our taxes the same as everybody else in the county. Seems like we have a right to the same protection."

"Oh yes, Mr. Mayor. The sheriff would be the first to say so."

Johnny White felt that he'd beat around the bush long enough. Time to get straight to the point: "I expect you're here to check on that baby, right?"

"Sir?"

"The baby. I assume you are here in response to a call about the abandoned baby Birdie Wilson found floating on the river."

Before Lynn Swafford had a chance to answer—fortunately, because he was quite confused by Johnny White's question—Molly drove up from behind. The deputy turned toward her car with a smile that was partly a sign of relief and partly a sign that he was happy to see Molly again.

Johnny White was virtually panic stricken.

Molly got out of her car and approached the two men, while Jay opened a back door and began to undo Baby Angel, sound asleep in her secure laundry basket. He hoisted the basket and followed his mother.

"Molly—Mrs. Hearst—I'm happy to see you got home safely," Deputy Lynn Swafford greeted her. "And the little one is still riding safely, I see."

Molly feared that her pleasure in seeing Lynn Swafford again was obvious, though she tried valiantly to hide it. She was curious, though, and asked in a manner a bit more harsh than she intended, "What are you doing here? Is something wrong?"

Jay stood awkwardly beside his mother, holding the laundry basket and sleeping baby. Mayor Johnny White took a step toward Jay, then turned to Molly. "I thought you were away, Molly," he said politely. "I see you're still keeping your cousin's baby. Is she going to pick it up some time soon?" There was an expression of pleading in the mayor's eyes, as in "please, Molly, please go along with this."

Now it was Molly who was confused.

This time, Lynn Swafford came to *her* rescue. "I don't think Judge Winkler understood that she was your cousin's baby," he said. "That might have simplified things. Or maybe you said so and the judge and I just missed it."

"Judge . . . Winkler?" Johnny White stammered.

"It's a long story," Molly said. "But if you men will excuse us, we need to get this tired and hungry baby inside. It was nice to see you again, Deputy Swafford."

Molly started toward the house. Jay followed with Baby Angel.

Deputy Swafford raised a hand as if to signal the two to stop, but stood silently as they disappeared through the front door. Then he turned to Johnny White.

"I'm sorry, Mr. Mayor," he said, "what were you saying about an abandoned child? If there's an emergency, I'll get on the horn and get more help out here right away."

"Please. Call me Johnny."

"Yes sir, Johnny. But like I was saying, maybe I better call in and let Sheriff Higgins know about that abandoned baby. They ought to get it to the child welfare people, for starters. Who found it, did you say?"

"I didn't say. I assumed Max Barnes told you folks all that when he reported the situation."

"I'm sorry, Mr. Mayor—Johnny—but I haven't seen a report on an abandoned child. I'm going to have to call the sheriff's office and see if there's something—"

Johnny White suddenly brightened. Birdie Wilson's old Dodge pickup was coming up behind Molly's car, and he could see that Sam Gowdy was riding with Birdie. Any interruption that would cause the deputy not to call in to his home base looked to him like a good interruption, as welcome as an unexpected thunderstorm on a hot August day.

Birdie and Sam crawled out and stretched arms and legs after their long ride. The mayor rushed to them, impatient for a report on the success of their mission. When Sam told him they hadn't learned anything, Johnny White's relief was apparent. But now he whispered a quick explanation of the newest threat to Baby Angel's wellbeing: the arrival of the sheriff's department.

"Max Barnes must have called the sheriff's office after all," the mayor said quietly. "This deputy seems a bit confused about it all. He said he hadn't seen the report yet, but he drove right up to Molly's house so he must know more than he's letting on."

"He'll take her to the welfare department," Birdie declared.

"Thing is," Johnny White whispered, "he doesn't know that Molly has the abandoned child. He thinks Baby Angel is her cousin's baby. What we have to do is keep him confused about that."

Sam Gowdy shook his head. "It's a dangerous game, holding out on law enforcement," he said. "If the sheriff's office knows about the baby, maybe we better just give her up."

"They'd name her Baby Jane Doe." This from Birdie, of course.

"Cambrians made up their minds from the beginning to keep this little girl out of the child welfare system," Johnny White declared. "I just can't see that little angel of a thing put in some foster home where they didn't care anything about her. It looks pretty clear that whoever abandoned her is not going to take her back, so she'd be passed around forever. I just can't let that happen."

"Well, you're the mayor," Sam Gowdy said. "You took your oath of office to see to the interests of us Cambrians, and we'll stick by you."

Deputy Swafford, meanwhile, had been on the radio with the sheriff's department dispatcher. Sheriff Higgins was gone for the day and the dispatcher didn't know anything about an abandoned child report. Deputy Swafford hurried over to the mayor and his two constituents.

"Mr. Mayor—Johnny—I can't get anything further on that abandoned child report, so I probably should just look around some and talk to a few people and see what I can find out. Sheriff Higgins most likely will send me back tomorrow anyway, so I may as well try and get a head start. You mentioned a Max somebody?"

Johnny White felt compelled to lean over and re-tie a shoe before he responded. While he was thus occupied he developed a sudden interest in the deputy's patrol car.

"You don't need those tall antennas anymore, looks like," he observed, straightening to a standing position. "This little bitty one adequate to keep you in touch with your base?"

Sam Gowdy picked up on the mayor's cue.

"Radio systems have come a long ways," Sam said. "I expect the dispatcher in the sheriff's office can keep in touch with you deputies, and the sheriff hisself, of course, without much trouble these days. You probably don't use a phone very often."

Birdie was not as swift as Sam. But he was interested in radio communications because he was hoping to get a radio on his boat.

He asked Deputy Swafford, "What kind of radio does it take to be part of a system like that? Is there one that would work with just two radios? Like if I had one on my boat and Edna—that's my wife, Edna—if Edna had one at home, could we keep in touch that way? Of course you never know, I might want to get three some day if we get another boat when the boys get a little bigger."

Johnny White became the perfect host. "Now Birdie, we can't expect the deputy to take too much time answering technical questions. He probably has a long drive home. Do you have a family, Deputy Swafford? Birdie here has two fine boys at home."

Lynn Swafford responded exactly the way the mayor hoped he would. He said he was a single father with two grown sons, regretted that he didn't have at least one girl, and could tell that Birdie was proud of his children. And yes, he did have a pretty good drive. Maybe since he hadn't been able to find out anything more on the abandoned child report he might as well call it a day and get on home. He was happy to have made the acquaintance of Mayor Johnnie White and Sam and Birdie.

As he crawled into the sheriff's department sedan, Deputy Swafford added a sinister note to his leave-taking. He was sure he would be back in Cambria tomorrow to pick up where he left off, he announced. An abandoned child report was a serious affair and the sheriff's department would treat it accordingly.

As the patrol car moved away, Sam Gowdy looked at the mayor expectantly. "What do you think we ought to do now?" he asked.

"That deputy will be back tomorrow with some kind of warrant, mark my word on it," Johnny White answered. "We've got to get the baby out of Molly's house, for starters. He bought the story that she was keeping her cousin's baby, but if Max told them she's got the abandoned child they'll want to get in there and check. He said an abandoned child should be in the hands of the child welfare department, but if they can't find her they can't get hold of her and turn her in."

"They'd name her Baby Jane Doe," Birdie said.

Johnny White rubbed his chin. The strain of responsibility was beginning to show. He clearly was giving serious thought to what he was going to say next. After a long pause he finally said, "I have the volunteer fire department on alert and ready to act. Seems like the best thing to do now is call one of the men and have them pick up the baby from Molly."

"Not Max Barnes, though," Sam said.

"No. Max was one of two firemen that didn't show up. I'll call Larry Zielinski first. Him and Margie raised five of their own so I expect they'll know how to take care of a baby for a while. But we've got to keep her moving. Baby Angel, I mean."

Sam Gowdy looked skeptical. "How long do you figure we can keep this up, Johnny? If the law gets to looking seriously for an abandoned baby, they won't give up easy."

"I know, Sam. This could turn into a long fight. But we Cambrians are pretty good at sticking with something once we set to it. None of us wants to see Baby Angel in the child welfare system."

Birdie shook his head. "They'd name her Baby Jane Doe," he said. "They sure would. Baby Jane Doe."

❧7❧

M olly had become irrevocably attached to Baby Angel. So had Justine and Jay. It was as if this beautiful baby girl had been sent from heaven just for them. She was the center of attention, the three of them vying for the privilege of holding her and feeding her when she was hungry and changing her when the need arose and taking care of any other wants she might have.

Molly understood the danger. Sooner or later, the authorities might step in and take the baby. The mere thought of Angel being placed in a foster home made her ill. Still, when Johnny White called, Molly resisted.

"They're going to be looking for an abandoned child," the mayor said. "That deputy may have been fooled by the claim she's your cousin's baby, but they're going to check on that, Molly. Do you even have a cousin with a baby?"

Molly admitted that she didn't. At least none that she knew of.

"Then you can see what we have to do. If they can't find her they can't get her."

"Johnny, I know you're right," Molly said. "But it's like she belongs here. I just can't tell you how much I hate giving her up. Even when I know it's temporary."

Johnny White assured her that Baby Angel would be returned as soon as it was safe. And meanwhile she would be well cared for. In spite of the way they usually squabbled over every issue, he promised, Cambrians all were committed to saving the child from the welfare people. Molly was proving herself a good mother. Nobody would object to the baby ending up with her in the end.

Reluctantly, Molly's accepted the mayor's dictum. She got together Angel's things, such as she had. Then she sat on the couch, holding her baby in her arms, and waited.

Larry and Margie Zielinski showed up on Molly's doorstep within the hour and took Baby Angel away. Molly lay awake most of the night, wishing she could get up and tend to the needs of the baby that was not hers but had stolen her heart. It was nearly dawn before she finally went to sleep. When she woke, the sun was shining brightly through a bedroom window and somebody was knocking on her front door.

It was Deputy Lynn Swafford.

Molly pulled her robe tighter and opened the door. "I didn't expect to see you back here again," she said. "Is something wrong?"

Lynn Swafford blushed. "No, no. Nothing wrong. It's just that, well, I didn't have a chance to talk to you yesterday, with the mayor there and all that. So what I did was, I came back to finish my business with you. You know, the business I didn't get done yesterday."

"You have business with me?"

"I didn't really mean business literally, Molly—Mrs. Hearst. I only meant that what I came to check on, you know, I didn't get to check on."

"Okay. So what did you come to check on? Yesterday, I mean."

Lynn Swafford took off his cap. He shifted his feet. He cleared his throat—twice.

"Molly," he said, "I was going to say I came back to check on your license plate or something like that. Something official, you know. But that was just an excuse. What I really came for—yesterday, I mean—what I really came for was to see if you'd like to have dinner or something."

Molly felt a sense of giddiness she hadn't experienced for years. This modest, polite man had actually come to ask her for a date! She would not be coy. In fact, she would make clear to Lynn Swafford that she was happy he had come and she would be perfectly delighted to have dinner with him. And she did.

Deputy Swafford was quick to accept her invitation to come in

56

for coffee. There was a brief period of awkward conversation, after which they became comfortable and allowed themselves to enjoy each other's company. Neither would have guessed that it had been years since the other had taken this much pleasure from the mere proximity of one of the opposite sex. It was a full hour before Deputy Swafford admitted reluctantly that he was on duty and needed to get back to work.

"If I don't check in pretty soon Sheriff Higgins himself will be out looking for me," he joked. "I didn't tell the dispatcher exactly where I was."

"But you wouldn't be in trouble just for stopping by?"

"Not as long as I could give them a reason—like checking on your baby. And by the way, where is she? I hadn't even noticed that it's been quiet all this time."

Molly felt her heart skip a beat. Why would he even mention checking on Baby Angel? Maybe Johnny White was right. Maybe the sheriff's department had received a report of an abandoned baby. Maybe Lynn Swafford was lying. Maybe he was here to take Baby Angel and turn her over to the child welfare people. Then she looked Lynn Swafford straight in the eyes. This was a good and decent man. This was a man she could trust. But, unfortunately, this was a man she had to lie to.

"Oh, the baby," she said innocently. "They picked her up. I don't have her anymore."

Lynn Swafford smiled. "That may be a good thing," he said. "I won't have to write you any more tickets for hauling around a baby in a—what, a laundry basket?"

Then he was gone. But he would be back Wednesday at six o'clock to take her to dinner.

Molly called the Zielinskis. She could pick up Baby Angel at any time, and they needn't worry, the authorities weren't looking for an abandoned child. How did she know? She knew because a sheriff's deputy had just left her house. And he knew nothing about an abandoned child. Therefore, the sheriff's department had not received a report of an abandoned child and Johnny White and the rest of them had been worried for nothing.

Margie Zielinski seemed unsure.

No, she said, Larry had ordered that no one could see Baby Angel until Johnny White said so. She had been expecting to hear from the Mendenhalls, not Molly, because the Mendenhalls were supposed to take the baby next.

"But Margie, there's no need for the Mendenhalls to take her. Nobody's looking for her. She can come home," Molly said.

"But Molly, couldn't I keep her for just a bit? She's so precious."

Molly gave in. She was being selfish. Baby Angel belonged to Cambria, not her. And Johnny White had promised that the child would be returned to her in due time. She would have to be patient. But she already missed the little one terribly much.

She found consolation, though, in looking ahead to Wednesday night. She had not seen another man since losing Roger. It was beginning to sink in that she actually had a date, and further that she had no notion how to act. Going out with Lynn Swafford would not be like her first date with Roger. They'd been teenagers. She and Lynn Swafford were adults—previously married adults with children, yet. She had ample reason to be nervous.

Molly made it a point to occupy herself with routine house-keeping chores for the rest of the day. In recent months, she often had been too depressed to care about the house and there was a lot to catch up on. The day passed swiftly and before she knew it the school bus was stopping at the front door and first Jay and then Justine came spilling out.

As soon as they got inside, both of Molly's children began look- ing for Baby Angel. It wasn't at all clear to them why the Zielinskis had taken her. Molly tried to make it simple. Baby Angel belonged to the community, she explained, and other Cambrians also had a right to her. Wasn't that only fair?

"But how can it be good for her to be passed around like that?" Justine asked.

"I don't think this will last long, honey. Johnny White said—"

Justine snorted. "Johnny White doesn't know pigeon crap about anything."

"Ignore her, Mom," Jay chided. "She's got boy troubles."

Justine stuck out her tongue at her brother. Molly called for peace before the sparring got out of hand. Jay and Justine got along well, but either could get impatient with the other in an instant. Jay, though, had given her an opening.

"Since you mentioned boy problems," Molly said, hoping to make her revelation sound light-hearted, "I have news. Wednesday I have an actual date. With a man."

"Way to go, Mom!" Jay exclaimed. "What took you so long? I mean, you're still pretty and you've got nice—you know, what men like."

Justine turned and left the room.

"Don't pay any attention to her, Mom," Jay said. "She's probably jealous."

"Jay, I need to make something clear. I've not seen another man since we lost your father. I didn't want you or your sister to think I was trying to replace him. Or his memory. But it's been a long time and I still have a life to live. You two won't be living here forever."

"So you're in a hurry to get rid of us?"

"You know that's not what I mean," Molly said, giving way to her irritation.

"What about Baby Angel?"

"Yes, I want her to be my child. But things are very uncertain. We'll have to wait and see how they play out."

Once assured that Jay had no problem with her dating Lynn Swafford, Molly went to Justine's room and knocked gently. Justine invited her in.

"Honey," Molly said, "I want you to understand that I'm not trying to replace your father. He'll always be the love of my life. But you and Jay will be gone someday and I still have a life to live. Anyway, going out to dinner isn't making a commitment. He'll probably turn out to be a jerk!"

Justine laughed at this. She admitted that she was being childish and insisted that she actually wanted her mother to develop a social life. "Maybe you'll even get out of this dumb place," she said. "But what about Baby Angel, Mom?"

"Jay just asked the same question. And I'll tell you the same thing I told him. I want Angel to be my child, but things are very uncertain. We have to accept the fact that we may not get her, Justine."

"Anyway," Justine said, "I'll take care of her if we have her back by Wednesday night. You can go out and have fun and not worry about the baby."

❧

THE ZIELINSKIS kept Baby Angel overnight. Mary and Kirk Mendenhall picked her up the next day. After them came the Garners and then the Blessings. Mayor Johnny White stuck to his duty roster, notifying each Cambrian family as its turn came up. When Juanita Blessing questioned whether this still was necessary, the mayor defended his tactics on the grounds that he still expected the sheriff's department to show up at any time looking for an abandoned child. But this was good training even if turned out to be a month before that happened.

"Baby Angel belongs to Cambria," Johnny White said, "and all Cambrians should share in her safekeeping."

In any event, the baby had not been returned to Molly by Wednesday. Justine's disappointment at not getting to babysit Angel was offset by helping her mother get ready. She urged Molly to wear more makeup and put on her nicest dress. And if she really wanted to impress this guy, she must wear her highest heels!

Molly accepted her daughter's pushing as an excuse to do what she really wanted to do anyway. She was giddy as a schoolgirl. This might have been first date and prom night all rolled into one, except that she'd never had a prom night and her first date had been when Roger bought her ice cream at the Dairy Queen. No matter. It all seemed new and exciting.

Justine and Jay stood by like proud parents as she and Lynn Swafford left the house. In what Molly suspected was a pre-planned move, they simultaneously demanded that she not stay out too late.

Lynn Swafford had dressed up, too, in his best suit. Well, actually his only suit, saved for very special occasions.

He had made a reservation at the sole quality restaurant within driving distance of Cambria. When they got there, it was closed. A sign on the door said a power outage had caused a loss of refrigeration and the place would reopen once the spoiled food had been disposed of and refrigerators and freezers cleaned. It gave no date.

"I'm sorry," Lynn said. "I didn't plan for anything like this."

"It's not your fault. And it doesn't matter, we'll just go somewhere else."

"But they say this place is nice—"

"Lynn, do you know where I'd like to go? Would you take me to a Dairy Queen?"

"Molly, I'll take you anywhere you like. Dairy Queen? There's one right down the road. We'll be there in five minutes."

And they were.

Maybe it was Lynn Swafford's pleasant company, or the beautiful evening, or simply the Dairy Queen, but for whatever reason Molly felt fifteen again. She could not remember being happier, ever. They sat at an outdoor table and ate ice cream and talked and watched the teenagers and all the parents with children who came for treats. Some took tables, as they had, and stayed a while, as if reluctant to give up time under the stars on such an evening as this.

Lynn talked about his two boys and Molly talked about Jay and Justine. They exchanged stories about all the challenges of being single parents with children.

"You said you're a widow," Lynn said. "I don't mean to pry, but what happened to your husband. I mean, okay, I know he died, but—"

"He was a long-haul truck driver. He was killed in an accident on the Pennsylvania Turnpike."

There it was. A simple statement of fact, like she was discussing a stranger. For the first time since Roger's death Molly found herself able to talk about it without the deep hurt. It was a release that had been far too long in coming.

"I'm sorry," Lynn Swafford said. "That kind of thing, suddenly and without warning, that can be pretty hard to take."

"And you lost your wife some time ago?"

"My wife didn't die. She left with another woman."

"I don't know what to say, Lynn. I didn't expect that."

"Of course not. No reason you should have. I've been over it a long time. I guess she was a lesbian all along, but I didn't know."

Molly, to her own dismay, burst out laughing. "I'm sorry," she said. "I laughed because what you just told me reminded me of something really, really stupid. I've tried to take it seriously, but I can't. Jay's teacher thinks he's gay. He wants me to tell him what to do about it, but I haven't a clue."

"Is he? Gay, I mean."

"I'm sure he isn't, and he says he isn't. But if Mrs. What's Her Name sees him that way, I don't know how he's supposed to prove otherwise."

After Molly's explanation, Lynn was smiling again. "I have an idea," he said. "See if Jay has a girlfriend. There's bound to be one girl in his class that he has warm thoughts about. When it's as simplistic as Mrs. What's Her Name sees it, he only needs to show in front of her that he likes girls."

"Lynn Swafford, you're a genius," Molly said. "No, actually it's pretty obvious. I should have thought of it myself."

"Just don't offer any daughter problems. I have sons. I don't know about daughters."

"I feel lucky to have one of each."

"My biggest regret after Jane left us was the fact that we didn't have one more chance to have a baby girl. I'd always wanted a daughter. The baby girl you had, little Angel—what a darling. To tell you the truth, I was disappointed to find out she was your cousin's."

"Lynn . . ."

"What?"

"Never mind."

❧8❧

When it came to religion, Cambria was pretty much like any other small town. About a third of the people belonged to Father Jacob's flock and rarely failed to attend mass at the old Catholic church on the high side of town, where it could be seen from almost everywhere. Another third were members of Pastor Mike's congregation in the Methodist church, which was located on the low side of town, nearer the river, in the area commonly called the Canepatch. The Methodists' edifice was quite modern compared to the Catholics' and had a basement recreation area that was a popular gathering place for such as there were left of the younger generation.

As to the other third of the Cambrian populace—well, suffice it to say that had any of them entered a place of worship the shock might have been so great that the walls crumbled around them. Good people, yes, but not of a religious bent.

Father Jacob and Pastor Mike were beloved figures among all Cambrians. They were gentle men, and wise. Their opinions counted. But they were far too competitive. Each was forever seeking an edge over the other. Much of their competition centered on Ida Quattlebaum, sole heir to the Quattlebaum Steamboat Company fortune, who very well may have had more money than all the other Cambrians combined. To their discredit, this concern had more to do with their interest in beating one another in fund-raising than it did with Miss Quattlebaum's soul. But they played fair and if they were open to criticism it was only because their competition was not related to the service of God. No, it was personal.

Pastor Mike was years younger than the venerable priest and

used this to advantage whenever he could. Especially on occasions such as Spring Carnival, when there were contests of physical performance: baseball throwing, horseshoe pitching, sack racing and so on. Father Jacob was a gracious loser.

Competition flatly ceased in times of community need, however. During wet springs when the river got out of banks and the Canepatch was flooded, or when winter storms or house fires or other disasters affected Cambrians, Father Jacob and Pastor Mike always stood shoulder to shoulder doing what they could to help.

Father Jacob had a long-standing feud with the child welfare department and rarely missed an opportunity to speak his mind on the subject. Most Cambrians assumed—though no one knew for sure—that his views were based on personal experience. He accused the agency of placing children in homes where the foster parents were more interested in the money they were paid than the wellbeing of the children, and then ignoring them. Pastor Mike agreed with this view, but was less vocal.

When Jake and Carrie Garner showed up at Father Jacob's Sunday service with Baby Angel, the good father got so emotional he almost had to cancel mass.

"This beautiful little child of God must never be allowed to fall into the hands of the child welfare department," he declared. "She needs the love and care of Cambrians—all of us. I include her in my prayers every day."

The following week, in the care of Marlene and Tom Johnson, the baby arrived at the Methodist church and promptly got the full attention of Pastor Mike. He changed his sermon to preach about little children, drawing his text from the Gospel According to St. Mark.

Birdie Wilson also was in attendance, with Edna and the two boys. As Pastor Mike got into full voice Birdie supported him with irregular shouts of "Amen" and when the preacher mentioned the child welfare department Birdie called out from his seat near the back of the sanctuary, "They'd call her Baby Jane Doe." Pastor Mike was momentarily flustered, but regained his rhythm quickly.

"Birdie's probably right," the minister proclaimed, "Baby Angel might very well become anonymous in their heartless system."

In the days that followed, both the Catholics and the Methodists talked about the religious leaders' commitment to the protection of Baby Angel and the non-faithful Cambrians were impressed by what they heard. Outside of Johnny White, Father Jacob and Pastor Mike were the closest thing Cambria had to civic leaders. With their voices added to that of the mayor, there was hardly a soul in town who didn't accept the idea that saving Baby Angel from the child welfare department was a critical undertaking that they all needed to be part of. Just telling friends and neighbors that they supported the effort made folks feel good.

Sam Gowdy, as proprietor of the town's main bait shop, was in a position to have a steady finger on the pulse of Cambrian public opinion. He told Birdie, "What you and I started with that little baby has become a cause for everybody now."

"Nobody wants her in the child welfare system," Birdie said. "They'd call her—"

"Birdie, don't say it. I've heard it too many times already."

Birdie was subdued. But he would stick to his guns. "Well," he said, "they would."

Johnny White, meanwhile, had been racking his brain for ideas about raising money for the Baby River Angel Fund. Cambrians were generous to a point but that point probably had come and gone. To wring any more out of people, the mayor had to come up with something different. The only thing he could think of was a raffle. And with Spring Carnival right around the corner, now was the time to do it.

Spring Carnival was a Cambrian tradition that went back as far as any of the locals could remember. It was a weekend set aside for fun and games. Some said it was the only time all year long that Cambrians all agreed on something. Just what it was they all agreed on wasn't really clear.

Johnny White decided to buy a fancy crib for Baby Angel, pay for it from the raffle proceeds, and award the winner the opportunity to present it as a gift from the whole town. He expected enough five-dollar raffle tickets to be sold to raise a nice profit, and every cent of that would go into the Baby River Angel Fund.

First, the mayor approached Father Jacob and Pastor Mike and solicited their support. Both thought a raffle was an excellent idea. They had to, of course, having themselves used raffles as fund-raisers a great many times over the years.

He asked Sam Gowdy to set up a display at the bait shop to promote raffle ticket sales. Sam agreed, and said he'd be more than happy to sell tickets at the shop. And further, he'd help Johnny White contact other businesses in town—such few as there were—and get them involved. No Cambrian would be immune from the pressure to buy one or more lottery tickets for the benefit of Baby Angel.

Johnny White got everything in order. He set up a Town Hall display, where an expensive baby crib in beautiful pecan finish was the main attraction. He had an ample supply of numbered yellow lottery tickets printed. Ticket sales were brisk.

As Cambria got ready for Spring Carnival, the Baby River Angel Fund grew by leaps and bounds. Johnny White was immensely proud of his effort, and Father Jacob and Pastor Mike praised members of their respective flocks for their generosity. Each was determined that his church sell more tickets than the other. The carnival spirit pervaded the little river town. And, in the churches, the spirit of stout competition.

Molly Hearst had regained temporary custody of Baby Angel. With Lynn Swafford now a regular caller, she was growing more and more nervous. How long could she carry on the deception that Angel was her cousin's baby? Moreover, she felt terribly guilty for lying to this man who had come to mean a great deal to her.

"Mom, you can't lie to him like this," Justine scolded. "Lying is not the way to start a relationship. How are going to explain it if he finds out?"

"I know, Justine. I know. But if I tell the truth and they come and take her . . ."

Justine and Jay worried about that possibility as much as she did. Their attachment to Baby Angel was a joy to behold. Still, Molly knew that there soon would come a time when she had to confess her deceitfulness to Lynn and take her chances. She understood, also, that she faced certain heartbreak if her confession led to the loss of either the baby or Lynn Swafford.

Justine had decided that she was too old to participate in frivolous things like Spring Carnival. She volunteered to stay home and keep the baby so that Molly and Jay could be free to enjoy the carnival weekend.

Lynn came for Molly shortly before noon on Saturday. It was a beautiful morning. When they arrived at the carnival area downtown, it seemed that most Cambrians were there ahead of them. Surveying the crowd, Lynn stopped short. Coming toward them was Sheriff Clarence Higgins, dressed in full uniform, complete with a shiny badge on his chest and a conspicuous handgun holstered on his hip.

The sheriff, a wide smile on his face, approached with extended hand. "This is a surprise, Deputy Swafford," he said jovially. "I didn't expect to see you here." And to Molly: "Good morning, ma'am. I'm Sheriff Clarence Higgins."

Molly introduced herself. The sheriff engaged in brief pleasantries and excused himself, hurrying off as if on a vital mission.

"You'd never guess there was an election coming up," Lynn Swafford said sarcastically. "That's the only thing that would bring him out for something in Cambria."

"I don't think he's been here much."

"Never. And in uniform so's everybody will know who he is. He never wears a uniform on the job. Did he win your vote?"

"I think it might take more than showing up for Spring Carnival to do that."

❧

SHERIFF HIGGINS walked fast, hoping to see and be seen by as many of Cambria's citizens as possible. He made it a point to stop in places of business and chat with whoever he found inside. This eventually led him to Sam Gowdy's bait shop, and the first thing he saw there was a large, hand-lettered poster promoting lottery tickets for the Baby River Angel Fund. The establishment appeared to be empty except for two boys handling fishing lures.

"You boys serious fishermen?" the sheriff inquired.

"Yes, sir," the taller boy replied.

Sheriff Higgins: "Well, I like fishing myself. I don't get time to do much of it, though. I'm Sheriff Higgins." He thrust a friendly hand toward the taller boy. "What's your name?"

"Ross Wilson."

"I'm glad to make your acquaintance, Ross. Who's your friend here?"

"My brother Kyle."

"Glad to meet you too, Kyle. I was wondering about that sign at the door. Can you tell me about the Baby River Angel Fund?"

"It's money for Baby Angel," Kyle said.

"Baby Angel?"

"Yes, sir. She's the abandoned baby Ross and me and our dad rescued from the river. If we wouldn't have saved her she would have drownded."

"You don't say!" The sheriff's surprise was genuine. "You say she was abandoned?"

"Yes, sir," Kyle told him.

Sheriff Clarence Higgins, having made the trip to Cambria expecting nothing more than a good day of campaigning, went into lawman mode. At full throttle. "Who abandoned her?" he demanded of Birdie Wilson's boys.

"We don't know," Ross said.

"Well who has her now?"

"She belongs to all of Cambria," Ross said. "She's probably over at Molly Hearst's, though. Molly keeps her most of the time."

When Ross Wilson said Molly's name, Sheriff Higgins remembered at once where he'd heard it before. He set out immediately to track down Molly and Deputy Lynn Swafford. He grew more angry as he walked. What the Wilson boys had told him didn't make much sense, but if all this involved an abandoned baby he needed to know about it. And he was certain there hadn't been an abandoned baby report in the county during the last two years. He found Lynn and Molly in Town Hall, examining a baby crib.

Coming up behind them, Sheriff Higgins said brusquely, "Miss

Molly, I understand you keep an abandoned baby at your house."

Molly turned. She was stunned by the sudden charge. Taken off guard, she was at a complete loss for a response. Lynn Swafford rushed to her rescue.

"You may have been misinformed," he told the sheriff. "Molly keeps her cousin's baby."

"Then that's not the so-called river angel this crib's intended for?"

"No, sir. It wouldn't be."

"Deputy Swafford, do you know anything about an abandoned baby being kept here in Cambria?"

"No, sir," Lynn Swafford said. "I haven't heard about anything like that. And Molly certainly would know."

The sheriff looked Molly intently in the eyes. "What is this Baby River Angel Fund for, that I've seen advertised all over town?" he demanded.

Molly's resolve melted under Sheriff Higgins's withering stare. "It's for a baby girl Birdie Wilson and his boys found floating on the Ohio," she admitted. "The whole town sort of adopted her."

"The whole town was in on it?"

"Yes, sir."

"Including the mayor?"

"Yes."

"Can you explain why an abandoned baby was not reported to the authorities?"

"No, I can't."

Lynn Swafford's face was a mask of confusion and disbelief.

The sheriff, his face beginning to redden, turned to his deputy. "And you're telling me you knew nothing about this, Swafford?"

"He had no way to know, sheriff," Molly said flatly. "I guess nobody thought to report it. Everyone was too busy taking care of the baby."

"Well it's going to be reported now!" Sheriff Higgins exploded. "I'll have the full story within the hour or somebody's in crap up to their ears. Swafford, call the child welfare people. Have them pick the baby up immediately."

Deputy Lynn Swafford had a hand on Molly's arm. She could feel the tenseness in his fingers. His uncertainty was reflected in his tone. "But we don't know where it is," he told the sheriff. "How can they pick it up if we don't know where it is?"

"I believe Miss Molly here knows where it is. Isn't that right, Miss Molly?"

"Yes. She's at my house."

"Deputy Swafford, call the child welfare department right now. Then get over to Miss Molly's house and wait. I'm going to find that mayor and get some answers."

When Molly finally had the courage to look at Lynn, she could see the hurt. "I'm so sorry about this," she said. "I didn't want to deceive you, Lynn. It's just that—I don't know how to explain it. It got too complicated. We were all afraid of losing Baby Angel. And I don't think I can stand to give her up now. Can you understand that?"

"Molly, I wish you had trusted me with the truth."

"But you would have had to report an abandoned child."

"I guess you're right. But maybe I could have helped work things out. Now, I don't have any way to go except to follow the sheriff's orders. I'm sorry, but we have to go now, Molly. I'll call the child welfare people from your place."

Molly's house was less than three blocks away. The two walked in painful silence. When they reached their destination, the house was empty. No Justine, no Baby Angel.

ᢒ9᠖

ather Jacob was having more fun at Spring Carnival than he ever had had before. At first he thought this was because the winter had been long and cold and he had been looking forward to spring even more than usual. But on further reflection, he decided it was because of the general gaiety of the occasion. No, not the occasion, the people. He could not recall a time when Cambrians had come together in such jovial spirit.

He watched the children scamper about, making up games as they went. The adults all stood around in small groups, talking and laughing. Johnny White had been up and down the street several times meeting and greeting his constituents. And Father Jacob had even seen Sheriff Clarence Higgins making a show of his presence.

It was almost time for the organized games and contests to commence. Father Jacob had mixed emotions. He loved to compete, but he was tired of losing to Pastor Mike.

As he strolled among the happy throng, Father Jacob heard none of the usual complaints. Those from the Canepatch had no harsh words for those who lived on the hill. Those from the hill spoke no criticisms of the Canepatch residents. The Catholics apparently admired the Methodists and the Methodists seemed to believe that the Catholics were the salt of the earth. Cambria's Spring Carnival was awash in goodwill.

The climactic event of the day would be when Mayor Johnny White drew the winning lottery ticket. Father Jacob hoped fervently that if he could not be the winner himself, it would at least be one of his faithful parishioners. He had worked hard to sell tickets. The mayor had yet to make an announcement on ticket sales, but he felt sure that the Catholics had bought more than the Methodists. This would be one competition, at least, in which he bested Pastor Mike.

The loudspeakers suddenly came alive with the voice of Charlie Tipsworth, chairman of this year's carnival committee. Charlie thanked the mayor and other members of the committee and wished every Cambrian a safe and happy carnival. Then he announced the first competition. The baseball throw.

Father Jacob had thought about not participating in the carnival games this year. Given his advanced years, people surely would understand. But he had too much pride to pass up an opportunity to compete with Pastor Mike. Maybe just this once . . .

Charlie Tipsworth sang out "last call" for the baseball throw. Eager participants already had lined up at the site. Each one signed his or her name on a slip of paper and the slips were put into a hat—one of Larry Zielinski's old summer straws—and then they drew for order of competition. Each participant would get three throws.

Kirk Mendenhall would throw first. Kirk was a large man with a strong right arm. Everyone expected him to be a top contender. For some reason, Kirk decided to forego a running start and throw from a still position. He lofted the baseball high in the air and instead of traveling in the proper flat arc for distance the ball dropped at an embarrassing two-hundred feet. Those who had heard Kirk's swearing over minor incidents were surprised at his good-natured acceptance.

Next in line was Larry Zielinski. He made a show of demanding his hat back, then warmed up his throwing arm with a few windmills. He threw from a running start. The crowd applauded as the ball struck ground beyond the three-hundred-foot mark.

Pastor Mike was the third man to throw. His effort was well short of Larry's, as was that of Jake Garner. Ross Wilson threw an impressive distance for his age, after which Tom Johnson and Juanita Blessing took their turns. Sam Gowdy and Morris Layman performed poorly. Marylee Tipsworth became the second woman competitor, and beat three of the men.

Then it was Father Jacob's turn. His best hope was to not make a fool of himself. A lefty, he flexed his arm a few times, backed away from the line to give himself a running start, and heaved the ball with all his might. He saw that his throw went somewhere just beyond the 250-foot mark. Poor performance, even for him.

The last to throw was Max Barnes. It was well known that Max had made it to the minor leagues, playing for a Pittsburgh Pirates' farm team. Max always won the Spring Carnival baseball throw. Max took the ball six feet behind the line, shuffled forward in quick side steps, and launched a high line drive that landed a good thirty feet beyond Larry Zielinski's ball.

One of the volunteer markers brought results to the launch area and called out his report. Max Barnes's 350-foot throw led the competition, followed by Larry Zielinski's throw of 310. Father Jacob's throw of 260 feet was ten feet short of Pastor Mike's effort.

Competitors made their second throws without much change in the results. As expected, after two rounds Max Barnes was still the one to beat. And now it was an even greater challenge, as Max added ten feet to his first mark.

Four people decided to pass on round three.

Kirk Mendenhall, having performed pitifully twice in a row, was determined to salvage his reputation on his last effort. From a running start, he threw the ball at least 325 feet. If the markers recorded it correctly, that should put him in second place. The onlookers cheered and Kirk took a modest bow.

Pastor Mike's last throw was his worst of the day. Jake Garner's was remarkably consistent with his first two. Tom Johnson threw well. Juanita Blessing and Marylee Tipsworth made all the Cambrian women proud with efforts that assured they would finish well up in the listings.

Now it was Father Jacob's turn. One more time. The overall competition was meaningless. He would, finally, beat Pastor Mike. He took the baseball, stood as still as a statue for a full minute, breathing deeply. Old joints and old muscles ached their discouragement. *One can only do one's best.* That was what he believed. And he would.

The wiry old priest took two shuffling steps like he'd seen Max Barnes do and flung his whole body into his throw. The baseball went high and long, as if aided by a divine gust of wind, and sailed far beyond the last distance marker. Gordon Blessing would contend later that Father Jacob's ball cleared the tall cottonwood trees and splashed down in the Ohio River, more than 500 feet away.

The crowd was silent. Father Jacob turned slowly. He looked into the faces of his Cambrian friends and neighbors and saw stunned disbelief. Then the applause began. The gathering was not large, but their roar of approval was remarkably loud.

Max Barnes, standing by for his final throw, dropped the baseball he held and rushed to Father Jacob's side. He took the old priest's left arm and held it high in the air, like he was signaling the winner of a championship boxing match.

Shortly afterward, Charlie Tipsworth's voice boomed over the speakers: "Ladies and gentlemen, it looks like we have a new champion in the baseball throw. They won't be able to mark the distance, but we hear that Father Jacob threw the longest ball ever seen in Cambria. Folks, let's give the good father a well-deserved round of cheers."

Once more, the cheering began.

❧

IT TOOK SHERIFF HIGGINS longer to find Johnny White than he expected and with every minute it took, his anger grew. Who did these Cambrians think they were? How did they think they could get away with such blatant disregard for the law? It was about time they learned some respect for the system.

The mayor had joined the celebration of Father Jacob's astonishing baseball throw. Like other Spring Carnival goers who had not actually seen it, he had heard the uproar and hurried to see what it was all about. He made it just to the outer fringe of the cheering crowd before Sheriff Higgins caught up with him.

The sheriff wasted no time on pleasantries. "Mayor, I need a word with you—now!" he demanded.

A wave of dread swept over Johnny White. From the moment he discovered that the sheriff was in Cambria, he had expected the worst. This probably was it. "Why, Sheriff Higgins," the mayor said, trying to feign surprise. "Of course. It's always good to visit with our lawmen. What can I do for you?"

"You can damn well explain to me why it is that everybody in your town seems to disrespect the law, that's what."

"I'm sorry, sheriff. I don't believe I know what you're talking about. But let's go up to Town Hall and find some coffee and you can explain your concern."

Sheriff Clarence Higgins was a large man, over six feet tall and overweight. He tended to be somewhat red-faced and breathless even under ordinary circumstances. Just now, his face was livid. Whether or not he intended for other Cambrians to hear, when he spoke he was loud enough that all those within several feet in all directions stopped talking and listened.

"You know damned well what I'm talking about," the sheriff bellowed. "How come nobody reported that abandoned child to the authorities?"

Johnny White was the model of innocent ignorance. "Why, I don't believe there's been any child abandonment here," he said softly. "Have you had a report on something I'm not up on?"

"You know what I'm talking about! You got signs up all over promoting lottery tickets for that Baby River Angel Fund. Now I know where that so-called river baby come from, and I know she was abandoned. What I don't know is why in hell somebody didn't report it."

Johnny White was pensive.

"You know, sheriff, it never occurred to any of us that the child might be abandoned," he declared. "We expected to find out that she was just lost. You know, somebody's likely to be around any minute now looking for her. Abandoned would imply that it was deliberate, wouldn't it? How in the world could anyone deliberately abandon a child?"

Sheriff Higgins was not to be so easily placated. "Somebody is going to answer for this, mayor," he said sternly. "And I'll tell you something else. My deputy is on the way over to Molly what's her name's house right now to get that little baby and call the child welfare people. We'll have that baby in their hands before dark. I guarantee it."

With that threat, Sheriff Higgins stormed away.

Sam Gowdy, who had been standing near enough to hear the entire exchange, edged closer and said, "What are we going to do now, Johnny? I don't see any way we can save Baby Angel. I expect the deputy is already over at Molly's, or he will be before we can do anything to warn her."

Johnny White smiled. "Sam," he said, "you underestimate me. I got to work on things the minute I saw Sheriff Higgins this morning. If they can't find the baby, they can't take the baby. Right?"

"You're right about that, Johnny. But the sheriff won't stop until he gets his hands on Baby Angel. He'll get a court order, don't you think?"

"Yes. But like I said, if they can't find her they can't get her. Here's Birdie. Maybe he can tell us something."

Birdie Wilson, who had just walked up, showed a big grin. He looked somewhat sheepish, like the cat that had just swallowed the goldfish.

"I did exactly what you said, Johnny," Birdie proclaimed.

"Anybody see you, Birdie?"

"No, sir. Justine packed up the baby real quick and we slipped out the back door. I know nobody didn't see us. You got a plan from here on, mayor?"

"I guess you'd say it's the same plan, revised," Johnny White said. "One way or another, we have got to be able to keep Baby Angel moving."

Sam Gowdy: "Stay one step ahead of the law, so to speak."

"In simple terms, yes, stay a step ahead of the law. The longer we can keep Sheriff Higgins from getting his hands on that baby, the better chance we have to figure out a way to keep her out of the child welfare system."

"They'd name her Baby Jane Doe," Birdie said, shaking his head sadly.

❧10❧

"I can't imagine where they could be," Molly said. "Justine promised to stay and take care of the baby. She wouldn't have gone out. Lynn, I'm scared. Something must have happened to them."

In spite of his earlier irritation, it was painful for Lynn Swafford to see Molly in distress. He wanted very much to comfort and reassure her. "There's no sign of a break-in or anything like that," he said. "Something probably came up that Justine had to see to, and of course she took the baby with her."

Molly burst into tears. "I don't know what to do, Lynn," she said between sobs. "I'm scared. Whatever happens now I know we're going to lose Baby Angel. And I love her so much . . ."

Lynn Swafford took her in his arms. "Don't cry, Molly," he whispered. "Don't cry. This will all work out. I'll do anything in my power to help you save that baby."

"But what can you do now? The sheriff ordered you to call the child welfare department."

"I can't call the child welfare department if we don't have the child."

Molly pulled back, so that she could see his face. She looked into his eyes. Yes, she trusted this man. And she loved him. Her despair was replaced with modest hopefulness. She recalled Mayor Johnny White's plan.

"Lynn," she said, "would Cambrians be guilty of a crime if they deliberately hid little Baby Angel to keep her out of the hands of the child welfare department? I mean, if there was an organized effort that everybody was in on?"

"Are you telling me that's what's going on here?"

"All I can say is, that's possible."

"Don't tell me any more right now, Molly," Lynn Swafford said. "I'm going to be in a tough predicament, between a rock and a hard place any way you look at it. So right now the less I know, the better."

"I'm so sorry I got you into this situation. The last thing I wanted was for something to come between us."

"Nothing has come between us, Molly. And nothing will. I'm not going to be that easy to get rid of."

"Promise?"

"Promise."

They stood in a long embrace. Then Lynn Swafford led Molly to the couch and urged her to sit and rest. He went to the kitchen and made tea. He returned with two cups and set one on the coffee table in front of her.

"Do you know where Jay is?" he asked.

"He's taking in the carnival, no doubt. He was looking forward to it."

"And Justine didn't want to go, you said?"

"Yes. She thinks she's too old for such childish things."

Lynn Swafford laughed. "Every adult in Cambria probably is out there," he said. "It's funny that she thinks of it as childish."

"Oh, that's just Justine," Molly answered. "She's trying to act grown up."

"Remember, I don't know much about girls. But I guess all kids reach that stage at some point. A stage where they want to look mature."

"Yes, I think they do. But we're just making small talk, Lynn, to avoid the discussion we didn't finish. What are you going to tell Sheriff Higgins?"

Deputy Lynn Swafford stood and walked across the room to a window. He looked out for a time before responding. When he turned back to face her, his countenance was grim. "I have to tell him what I know," he said. "He'll get a warrant that allows him— us—to search for the missing baby. I'll have to do my duty, Molly, because I took an oath. But I hope to God we don't find her."

"How long will it go on, do you think?"

"I wish I could say it will be over soon, but I don't believe that. He'll get a judge to issue the warrant, then the judge will know about it, too. The news will be all over the county by nighttime. The genie is out of the bottle, Molly, and I don't see any way to get it back in."

"That sounds pretty hopeless, then."

Lynn sat beside her on the couch again. He put an arm around her shoulders and drew her close. Molly lay her head against him and slipped her hand into his. At this instant she might have wished there never had been a Baby Angel, that she and this man she loved might sit this way forever without a worry in the world. And yet—had it not been for Baby Angel, she never would have come to know Lynn Swafford. And she did love and want the baby so very much.

"It's never hopeless, Molly," Lynn Swafford said. "I'll fight beside you as long as there's any way to go on this. For starters, as soon as I leave call Johnny White and find out what's going on right now. Tell him what I told you—about the sheriff's warrant and all—and make sure he understands there must be a plan to keep the baby on the move. If Sheriff Higgins finds her, it will be very difficult to head off the child welfare people. Now I have to go and face the wrath of Sheriff Higgins."

Molly escorted him to his car. Once he was seated behind the wheel, she leaned in through the open window and kissed him sweetly.

"I trust you, Lynn," she said. "I know you'll do what you can."

"Yes," he said, and drove away.

Molly went back inside and called Johnny White, but there was no answer. Her helpless feeling returned, stronger than ever. It was a familiar mood, one she still fell into much too easily. And it was a mood that often had led her to question whether life was worth living.

Deep inside, she had known that it was not. Only the existence of Jay and Justine had kept her from giving in to her depression and doing something desperate. Just when she'd decide that the children would be better off without her, here they'd come, dirty and hungry, tired but excited, full of stories about their day in school or on the playground, and need her to fix their dinner or wash their clothes or do some other caring thing. And she would know there was no one else to look after them, these innocent children she loved. And so they would have saved her for another day.

Baby Angel had brought her such joy. Jay and Justine would be grown up and gone all too soon, but if she had Baby Angel and— dare she dream it?—if Lynn were still in her life, she could be happy again. Like she had been in the days before that terrible accident on the icy stretch of the Pennsylvania Turnpike.

Molly's mood swung again, in full circle, from helplessness and hopelessness to determination and confidence—determination to do whatever she could to help save Baby Angel and confidence that, especially with Lynn on their side, the good people of Cambria would win this battle. She called Mayor White again. This time he answered.

"Molly," the mayor said, "Justine and the baby are okay. We know where they are. You stay there, just in case the sheriff has somebody watching your house."

"Do you really think he would do that?" Molly asked, somewhat incredulous.

Johnny White, firmly: "I've no doubt of it. Sheriff Higgins is offended, and when Sheriff Higgins gets offended he's like a rabid bull terrier. No way he's going to let go of this until he finds the baby. This may be tricky, Molly, but if we all stick together I think we can win. But it may go on for a long time. Are you up to that?"

"Johnny, whatever it takes."

"I'll get back to you, Molly," the mayor said. "We've got the upper hand just now, and we'll have a plan. Cambrians don't give up easy. But you know that."

❧

LYNN SWAFFORD tried to prepare himself for what he was about to face. Sheriff Higgins would be angry when the deputy reported that the abandoned baby was not at Molly Hearst's house. Very angry. The only thing he could think of was a verse he'd learned in Sunday school: "A soft answer turneth away wrath."

The sheriff met his expectations, and then some. Not just angry, furious.

"Deputy Swafford, if you plan to stay on my force you damned well better find that baby," the sheriff admonished. "And I mean fast!"

Lynn was careful to show respect. "I always follow your orders, sheriff. You know that. By the way, how long's it been since you've been fishing? The locals tell me the river is yielding some pretty good catches these days. Since we're here I thought we might rent a boat and get a couple of hours on the water."

Sheriff Higgins was livid. He all but sputtered when he spoke: "You're thinking about fishing at a time like this? There's an abandoned child here somewhere, deputy!"

"Well, I'm concerned about that child, of course," Lynn said, keeping his voice low. "But from what I hear that baby is being well cared for. I doubt that it matters much whether we find her now or next week some time. You think?"

"Swafford, I don't know why I ever hired you. Well, yes I do, I hired you because your daddy hired me when he was sheriff. But that sure don't guarantee you a badge forever. Do you get my drift?"

"Yes, sir, I do. And I remember my father saying you were the best deputy he ever had."

"I learned everything I know about law enforcement from him," Sheriff Higgins said. He had cooled off perceptibly, was almost calm now. "We better get back to work, I guess."

"What do you want me to do?"

The sheriff laid out his plan, based on circumstances as he saw them at this point. He would head back to the county seat and get a warrant from Judge Chester Gilbert. Gilbert was a tough law-and-order man who no doubt would give them whatever they needed. He expected to be back before dark with a general, broadly drawn warrant that would get them into any house in Cambria.

Lynn Swafford would stay and ask around. "Find out anything you can," Sheriff Higgins said. "Somebody here knows where that baby's at."

"Yes, sir. I'll dig up what I can."

"And Lynn, save a day before too long for that fishing, okay?" "I sure will sheriff, I sure will."

As the sheriff turned and walked back toward his car, Lynn Swafford sucked in a long, slow breath and blew it out forcefully. He had managed a calm veneer while inside he'd been jumpy as a cat. Sheriff Higgins was not a man easily talked down. He understood, though, that this was the calm before the storm. The sheriff undoubtedly would get whatever he wanted from Judge Gilbert. He would be back with a sweeping warrant, as promised.

Lynn saw no choice now but to play both sides as best he could. He must convince his boss that he was fulfilling his duty, making every effort to find the abandoned child. At the same time, he recognized the bottom line: He was in love with Molly Hearst, he would do anything he could to help save her baby. This was going to be pretty tricky.

How would he handle Johnny White? It was unlikely that he could gain the mayor's confidence at the same time he gave appearances of working closely with the sheriff. But Johnny White was in command of the Cambrians, it was Johnny White whose plan they would be carrying out, and without Johnny White's trust he'd have a very hard time gaining enough inside information to help protect the baby from discovery.

The obvious answer was that he must depend on Molly. And she on him.

Much as he wanted to run straight back to Molly, Lynn Swafford decided that it would be best to get a sense of things from other Cambrians first. Were they all in on the mayor's tactics? Was there someone who might be a weak link, someone who might tell more than he should? Or *she* should. He presumed that the town's women were in on all this at least as deeply as the men. Oh, yes. They were mothers.

Lynn Swafford knew where to begin.

Sam Gowdy's bait shop usually was the busiest place in town. The front door stood ajar. There was an "open" sign in the window. But when he got inside, the shop appeared to be deserted. Lynn looked about the place much like a customer, handling lures and tackles and other fishing paraphernalia. He was examining a small tackle box when Alma Gowdy came out from somewhere in the back.

"You're the sheriff's man," Alma said. No approval, no condemnation. Merely a statement of fact.

"Yes, I am."

"You can hurt Molly a lot, you know."

"Ma'am?"

"You may not know it, but that girl's been through some rough times. Losing her man and all. Now she's all wrapped up in that baby, and that's the best thing that's happened to her in a long, long time."

"I know she loves that baby."

"And I love Molly," Alma told him. "I'd hate to see her heartbroken over that child."

"Are you Sam's wife?"

"Yes."

"I met Sam the other day, over in front of Molly's house. He struck me as a pretty solid guy."

"He is. But you're changing the subject."

Lynn Swafford had not intended to lead their conversation in a new direction, but he realized she was right. The truth was, he wanted very much to talk about Molly. And the baby. "Sorry," he said. "I didn't mean to."

"Well, I can tell you this. That little baby's brought this town together. Everybody's pulling in the same direction for the first time in as long as I can remember. All the petty little quarrels forgot about, too. All because of that baby."

"I've got two sons of my own, Mrs. Gowdy. I know what children can do."

Alma shook her head. "I'm not talking about a normal situation, you know, where a new baby is born into a family and all that,"

83

she said. "This little baby is special. She's got no right to be alive. If Birdie Wilson and his two boys hadn't found her floating on the river right when they did—well, I doubt she'd of lasted five minutes longer."

"I need to talk to Mr. Wilson. Can you tell me where he lives, give me some directions?"

"You're the lawman. Do some lawman work and find out for yourself. You'll get no help from me."

With that stinging rebuke, Alma Gowdy turned her back and walked swiftly toward the rear of the shop. Lynn Swafford was left standing alone, regretting that he'd ever taken the deputy's oath or even heard of Sheriff Clarence Higgins. Whatever he did next, he wanted more than ever to make it a step toward saving Baby Angel—Molly's Baby Angel—from the child welfare system.

As he walked back toward the two blocks of downtown where the Spring Carnival still was in full swing, he passed a small knot of children fixated on their sidewalk chalk drawings. He stepped off the curb to go around and the children hardly looked up. Up ahead, he could see that the crowd had thinned somewhat but still was large by Cambria standards. Continuous reports came over the loudspeakers as Charlie Tipsworth made announcements and read lists of winners from various competitions.

"Ladies and gentlemen," Charlie was saying, "in just five minutes I'm going to announce the name of the raffle winner. Which lucky Cambrian will have the honor of presenting that handsome new crib to the baby river angel? You all bought tickets, and you won't want to miss the announcement."

Lynn stopped right where he was. He stood directly in front of Town Hall. That's where the presentation would be made. Was it even conceivable that the abandoned child would be present? And if not, who would represent her? Who would be there to accept the crib? And where would the crib go, if not to Molly's house?

He sat on the curb and waited. Charlie Tipsworth's announcement would come at any minute now. Mayor Johnny White walked toward him.

"Having a good time, deputy?" the mayor asked.

Lynn Swafford stood as the mayor came close. "Not bad at all," he said. "Looks like the carnival is going real good."

"I assume you're mixing business and pleasure today."

"I guess you could say that."

"Your boss almost ruined my day, getting all stressed over that baby. You have any idea why he got so uptight about it?"

"Sheriff Higgins has devoted his life to law enforcement," Lynn said. "He's pretty strict when it comes to anybody he thinks is going against the law."

"How do you feel about this particular case, deputy?"

"Please, call me Lynn. I don't really have any choice. I have to follow the sheriff's orders. I swore an oath that I would always do my duty to the best of my ability and that's what I try to do."

Johnny White scratched his head. "A whole lot of Cambrians have stuck their necks way out to protect that baby," he said. "Nobody wants to see her end up in the hands of the child welfare people where she might be passed around among uncaring foster parents. You can understand that, can't you?"

"I understand, mayor. But I guess I have a better view of the child welfare folks than that. I believe they would have the baby's best interests at heart, just like you good people in Cambria."

Johnny White turned toward Town Hall, then looked back at Lynn Swafford. His smile disappeared. "Like I told the sheriff," he said frostily, "you'll have to find that little baby before you can take her. That may not be as easy as you think. Now I've got to go in here and make a presentation. Come along if you like."

At that instant Charlie Tipsworth's voice echoed through the streets of Cambria: "Ladies and gentlemen, it's time to announce the lottery winner. This is what you've all been waiting for. The mayor's ready to present the winner over in Town Hall, and the winner will accept the crib for Baby Angel. And the winner is . . . Molly Hearst."

❧11❧

Justine was beginning to enjoy the intrigue. She had doubted Birdie Wilson when he came running up to the back door, panting and red-faced, and told her she must get out of the house quickly and take the baby to Marlene Johnson. Now that she was here, and understood why, she found it exciting to have a role in the Cambrian deception.

Baby Angel showed no sign of distress after the dash across five backyards and a nearly dry creek bed to the secluded Johnson house, but Justine was determined to stay as long as she could and make sure. Marlene Johnson was an old woman, in her view, and probably hadn't taken care of a baby for years. The baby still was Justine's responsibility, and it was a responsibility she took very seriously. Her greatest concern now was that her mother would be terribly worried until she found out where they were.

"Do you think I could call my mom in a little bit and let her know we're here?" she asked Marlene Johnson.

"We probably shouldn't," Marlene advised. "She'll know to get in touch with Johnny White, and he knows where we are. Johnny has stressed several times that his plan won't work unless we all follow his instructions."

"Does Johnny White really have a right to run things like that?"

"I don't think this is the time to raise that question, Justine. He organized everything on the spur of the minute, and so far his plan has worked just fine. I think we need to stick to what he tells us until this is all over."

"Marlene, do you think we'll be able to save her?"

Marlene Johnson put a hand on the girl's arm, a calming gesture, and smiled. She said, "Child, when you've lived here as long as I have, you'll know that Cambria has some mighty hard-headed people. We don't always pull in the same direction the way we ought to, but we are all together on this. Yes, I do think we'll be able to save her."

The older woman's confidence was reassuring. Justine lifted Baby Angel from her basket and carried her across the room to an area where the sunlight poured in through a wide floor-to-ceiling window. The window offered a striking view of the woods behind the Johnson house on a steep slope that extended all the way to the river. The mere sight of the Ohio always was comforting to Justine, as she imagined it was to all Cambrians.

She heard the Johnson phone ring in the hallway, and saw Marlene rush to answer. Marlene listened intently for a few minutes. "Yes, we will," she said. "Thank you, Johnny. We'll stay in touch."

It was the mayor, Marlene reported. He had called Molly and let her know where Justine and the baby were. And he also had more disturbing news: Sheriff Higgins was back in town with a search warrant for Molly's house, looking for an abandoned child. Fortunately, the warrant covered no other property. When the sheriff failed to find the baby there he wouldn't be able to search anywhere else.

"Now you understand Johnny's reasoning," Marlene said.

"I already did," Justine told her. "But I guess I understand it better now."

"They know we have the baby somewhere here in Cambria. The sheriff found out about the lottery. I'm thinking that lottery wasn't Johnny's brightest idea."

"They're going to find stuff at our house, too. Baby things. And the big basket she sleeps in."

"That's not what you carried her over here in?"

"No. It was too big for me to carry. I put her in the old basket Mr. Wilson found her in, floating on the river."

Marlene Johnson assured Justine that she would keep the baby safely hidden. Johnny White would give them instructions about what to do next. Justine could stay as long as she wanted to, or feel free to go on home any time she felt like it. On second thought, though, it might be better for her to stay away until they could be sure the sheriff was gone. He'd no doubt press her hard if she showed up now.

Justine agreed. Not only did she want not to jeopardize Baby Angel in any way, but she also knew she would be scared to death if she had to face the sheriff.

She returned the baby to the basket she'd brought her in and put her down gently. The baby smiled and waved her arms. The lowering sun shone all the way across the room now, and a beam of bright sunlight fell on the basket. Justine saw something no one had noticed before: On the side of the basket were faint markings.

"Marlene, look at this," Justine called.

Marlene Johnson came across the room and stooped down to get a closer look. "I can't make it out," she said. "Can you?"

Justine studied the markings closely. "It says 'the' something, but I can't read the rest of it," she said. "Maybe if you hold the baby I can pick it up and get a better look."

Marlene gently lifted Baby Angel from the basket and cradled the child in her arms. Justine carried the old basket over to the window where the sunlight was brightest. She traced the markings with a finger, trying to make out letters.

"'It's 'Magnolia'. That's the other word. It says 'The Magnolia' on the side of the basket, Marlene."

"That sounds like a flower shop, don't you think? Years ago, they used to sell flowers in baskets like that."

"I guess that was before my time," Justine said. "Was there ever a flower shop in Cambria."

"Not that I know of."

Justine placed the basket back on the floor and Marlene put the baby back in it. Baby Angel had slept soundly through the whole transaction. She sighed when Justine pulled a blanket up to her chin, as if satisfied to be back where she belonged.

"We'll never know what it means," Marlene said.

"You're probably right. But I wish we could find out."

WHEN SHERIFF HIGGINS arrived at Molly's front door, he was accompanied by Deputy Harlan Gidcomb. Deputy Lynn Swafford was there to meet them. The sheriff waved a warrant, duly approved by Judge Chester Gilbert, that granted a thorough search of Molly Hearst's house for "an unnamed abandoned child."

Lynn Swafford pretended to be supportive. "What about the wider warrant, one to let us search all over town?" he inquired.

Sheriff Higgins was palpably irritated by the question. Deputy Gidcomb answered for him: "You know Judge Gilbert, Lynn. Goes strictly by the book. He said we didn't have enough evidence that this thing was—"

"Never mind that crap now," the sheriff commanded. "Let's do what we came to do. Knock on her door, Lynn."

Lynn Swafford had prepared Molly for this event. He knocked lightly and she opened the door and invited the three inside.

"We don't mean to cause any problem for you, Miss Molly, if you just turn the child over to us," the sheriff declared. "We've got a child welfare department woman on the way, and she'll take good care of that little one."

"I'm sorry," Molly said, "but my two children are still out enjoying Spring Carnival. There's no child here."

Deputy Gidcomb edged past the others and looked about the living room. He went into the kitchen, then moved systematically through the three bedrooms. He came out of the third bedroom carrying the wicker laundry basket Molly had used as a car seat for Baby Angel.

"This looks like a baby basket to me," the deputy told Sheriff Higgins. "It's got a blanket and stuff in it, too."

"That's just an old laundry basket," Molly said innocently.

Lynn Swafford took the basket from Deputy Gidcomb. "Sheriff," he said, "and Harlan, I can vouch for Mrs. Hearst's honesty. If she says there's no abandoned child here, then we're not going to find one." He placed the basked on the floor next to the couch.

"Let's go find that mayor," Sheriff Higgins snorted. "They're hiding that abandoned child somewhere and I'm going to find out where. Lynn, you come with me, and Harlan, stay out front and wait for the woman from child welfare."

"What am I going to tell her, sheriff?" Deputy Gidcomb asked.

"Hell, I don't know. Tell her she can wait around if she wants to, or we'll call her again when we need her. You take care of her as you see fit."

The sheriff turned to Molly and tipped his cap. "I beg pardon for the intrusion, Miss Molly," he said politely. He added, sarcastically, "You know things you're not telling, and I know you know. You may not have seen the last of us." He left the house, Lynn Swafford and Harlan Gidcomb close behind.

Molly dropped onto the couch and began to cry. The outward calm she had displayed, feigned with tremendous and determined effort, gave way to her true feelings. How could Cambria possibly maintain this sham? Sooner or later, the sheriff would find Baby Angel. The baby would be placed in the hands of the child welfare people. And then what? Would she, Mayor Johnny White, and other Cambrians be charged with some kind of crime? How much trouble would Lynn Swafford be in?

Moments later, she heard a car drive up in front. She pulled herself up from the couch and looked out and saw Deputy Gidcomb conferring with a woman who looked briefly toward the front door. The woman raised her hands in a gesture of utter frustration, appeared to say angry words to the deputy, and got back in her car and drove away. Deputy Gidcomb set out in the direction the sheriff and Lynn Swafford had gone, walking fast.

Molly missed Baby Angel. She wanted Justine to come home from the Johnson house, and Jay to come home from wherever he was. The house felt empty without the children.

If the child welfare department took Baby Angel away, this is what her future held. Justine and Jay would soon be gone and she would be alone. Unless . . . She'd tried to stop thinking about a future with Lynn. Maybe he wasn't looking for a serious commitment. And who could blame him? His last one hadn't worked out so well.

She heard another car and nearly panicked. Was it the sheriff coming back? But it turned out to be Birdie Wilson. Molly peeped out through the curtains and saw Birdie on the front step, with Kyle and Ross standing close behind. To her even greater surprise, Birdie was holding a baby crib, folded so that it was long and flat and stood upright.

Molly opened the door and Birdie beamed, as if eager to share good news. "I guess maybe you haven't heard, but you won the lottery," he proclaimed. "Since you wasn't there to take this crib for Baby Angel, I volunteered to bring it over. The prize is the honor of giving it to the baby and I guess the mayor figured you'd be as likely to find her as anybody." He winked.

"So Johnny White sent you with this?"

"He shore did. Why?"

"I'm just not sure it's best for me to have it right now, Birdie. Does Johnny know the sheriff was here, with a search warrant?"

"Johnny figured once the law had been here hunting for the baby and gone they wouldn't come back," Birdie declared. "You think he might be wrong about that?"

Molly stepped back. "I don't know what to think about anything, Birdie," she said. "Go ahead and bring it in."

Birdie Wilson lifted the crib over the doorsill and rolled it into the living room. The boys helped hold it upright. Once they had it unfolded and set up it looked much larger. Birdie sent Ross back to the truck to bring in the mattress. He placed it in the crib, stood back and studied his handiwork, then took the mattress out and turned it over.

"I believe I got that right," he said. "Do you need anything else, Molly?"

Molly said she didn't and thanked Birdie and the boys for what they'd done. After they were gone, she rolled the crib to one side of the room. It took up more space than she would have guessed, dominating the area. What a ridiculous claim it would be now to say she knew nothing about the abandoned child. She could only hope that Johnny White was right about the sheriff not coming back.

Justine got home a few minutes later and came in through the back door. "I looked to make sure the cops were gone," she said.

"Johnny White called Marlene and told her they were here. What'd they do when they didn't find Baby Angel, Mom?"

"I don't know, Justine. But they're going to find her sooner or later. I wonder if it wouldn't be better just to give her up—turn her over to the child welfare people. We're going to lose her, I know we are."

Although she tried hard not to, Molly began to cry again. Justine stood by helplessly.

"Don't cry, Mom," Justine said. "Please don't cry. Johnny White has a plan all worked out to save her. All we have to do is keep her hid until they give up looking. How long do you think they're going to keep trying if they can't find her?"

"They'll never stop looking, Justine. Sheriff Higgins will tear down every house in Cambria if he has to, to find that baby. He's got his back up on it and he's not going to give up."

"Mom, you always told Jay and me to have the courage of our convictions," Justine said firmly. "Now I want you to follow your own advice. Everybody in Cambria is in on this, and determined to save Baby Angel. Marlene says Johnny White has a good plan and if we just stick to our guns we can win. I believe that. Don't you?"

Molly tried hard, and managed a bit of a smile. "If you feel that strong about it, honey, I feel better about our chances. What are we supposed to do now?"

"Wait until we hear from Johnny White, I guess. He'll tell us what to do next."

"I guess there's nothing else to do. I wish Jay would get here."

"Don't worry about him, Mom. He loses track of time when he's having fun. That means he's enjoying Spring Carnival. Maybe I missed something, after all."

Jay arrived a full hour past the time Molly had set for him to be home. She was beginning to scold him when a soft tapping on the front door signaled the return of Lynn Swafford. Justine let him in and Molly and the two children all waited expectantly for him to tell the latest happenings.

His report was mixed, some good news and some bad.

Everything was calm for now, Lynn said. Once Sheriff Higgins exercised the search warrant at Molly's house and came up empty handed, he was left with no place else to turn. He tracked down Johnny White and demanded angrily that the town give up its efforts to keep the abandoned child hidden. The mayor pretended ignorance.

"He'll be back tomorrow or the next day with a new warrant," Lynn said. "Judge Gilbert will no doubt listen to his case and might very well issue a warrant that allows a wider search, lets them go from door to door."

Jay, who had shown great interest in what Lynn had to say: "But what is their case, Lynn? If nobody reported a baby abandoned . . ."

"Johnny White's lottery. And one of Birdie's boys told the sheriff an abandoned baby was found floating on the river. That will be enough for the judge."

"Lynn, I wish this had never started," Molly said. "How can it end any way except heartache for us all. We're going to lose Baby Angel, and maybe be charged with breaking the law. I wish Johnny had just called the sheriff at the beginning."

Justine's eyes flashed with anger toward her mother. "Mom," she said, "you promised! Courage of your convictions, remember? If we don't pull this off we'll probably never see Baby Angel again. Is that what you want?"

"You know it's not, Justine. It's—it's that I'm so afraid of losing her, and I couldn't stand to give her up now."

Molly was still fighting to hold back tears. Lynn stepped close and put an arm around her shoulders. Jay and Justine also drew near and awkwardly tried to show sympathy. Jay sought a distraction and pulled Justine across the room to the new baby crib. The two of them made a show of admiring it, talking too loud and speculating how Baby Angel would love it.

Lynn Swafford, meanwhile, guided Molly into the kitchen. She took a seat at the table and he made tea—the single example of domesticity Molly had seen from him as yet—and poured each of them a cup. Lynn put a hand on hers and looked into her face.

"Molly, Molly," he said, "I can't stand to see you unhappy. What can I do to bring a smile to your pretty face?"

Although she was touched by his sympathy, Molly also saw something comic in his exhibit of earnest helplessness. She did not want to laugh, but she did. Lynn was embarrassed, but happy to see her tears replaced by giggles. Molly, for her part, regretted making him uncomfortable. Both felt obligated to make amends. In an instant they were hugging playfully.

Which led to a tight embrace. Which led to a passionate kiss. Which led to more passionate kisses.

When Justine saw what was taking place in the kitchen, she quietly ushered Jay onto the side porch. She told him about rushing Baby Angel to the Johnson house and he told her about Father Jacob's miraculous baseball throw. They made their stories exciting, with only modest exaggeration.

Jay also had a revelation to share: "Guess what, Justine. I have a girlfriend!"

"You? What girl would be interested in a little twerp like you?"

Jay was used to her teasing, and in fact expected it. He went on with his report, unabashed.

"Nellie Rider," he said. "We took in most of the Spring Carnival together. The next time we're in school, me and her are going to parade by old Mrs. Kobel and carry on like lovebirds. Me gay? I don't think so!"

Justine could not hide her smirk, but she assured her brother that no one with any sense had ever thought he was gay. Then she echoed her mother's sentiment: "Anyway, what difference would it make?"

And Justine had another matter of intrigue to tell about. She described the marking on the basket Baby Angel had been found in. She made it sound mysterious, if not sinister. Somewhere, she predicted, was information that would identify The Magnolia and shed some light on the abandoned baby's background. Only she didn't used the word "abandoned."

❧12❧

The rains commenced the day after Spring Carnival and the river began to rise two days after that. All fishing stopped. Simply getting around town meant running from under one roof to the next as umbrellas offered little protection from the wind-driven downpour. Cambrian men who worked outdoors, including the fishermen, spent most of their days in Sam Gowdy's bait shop drinking coffee and telling stories. Baby Angel was very much a topic of discussion.

Sheriff Higgins, meanwhile, had been thoroughly frustrated in his plan to get a blanket warrant from Judge Chester Gilbert. The judge said there was no clear evidence that the whole town was involved in concealing an abandoned child. The sheriff could obtain warrants one house at a time, and only one warrant a day. If evidence that a baby might have been there turned up in several Cambrian homes, this would be enough for him to issue a blanket warrant. That was the best he could do.

Judge Gilbert went on to assure that he was a tough law-and-order jurist and wanted very much for the sheriff to succeed. An abandoned child should be in the custody of the child welfare people. Period.

Once outside the judge's chambers, Sheriff Higgins vented his anger freely. His deputies were subjected to the longest rant they had heard from their boss in years. With expletives deleted, the sheriff's complaint could be boiled down to a fear that Judge Gilbert was more interested in maintaining his image than he was in justice. Not the kind of judge those on the front lines of crime fighting could admire. The two most experienced deputies were recalling—silently, of course—the times they had heard the sheriff praise Gilbert as the "best damned judge in the state."

Whatever. Limited to a single warrant, the sheriff chose Birdie Wilson's house as his next target. His rationale was that Birdie and the boys found the abandoned child floating on the river and one of the boys told him about it. Surely Molly Hearst would be afraid to bring the child back to her house. The Wilsons might be the next most likely place.

Sheriff Higgins was no dummy. He understood full well the futility of going one house at a time in his search. That Cambrian mayor had the whole town organized. But by thunder, abandoned children belonged in the child welfare department's hands. That was the law. It was his job to enforce the law. This had become personal.

And sooner or later, criminals always screwed up.

The sheriff had assigned his four other deputies to take care of the rest of the county, and Deputy Lynn Swafford was working with him on the Cambria case. He liked Lynn. Liked him too much, maybe, because he had some doubts about Lynn's commitment to finding the abandoned child. Lynn had taken an oath to perform his duties loyally, though, and Lynn was not one to violate his oath.

The two of them rode together in the sheriff's old Ford Explorer. Lynn had left his department cruiser at the courthouse.

"This is about the last time you'll be riding in this old bus," the sheriff said. "I'm getting a brand new GMC Acadia next month. County auditor has already approved it."

"Probably about time. This one's seen better days."

"It went over a hundred thousand miles six months ago."

Lynn Swafford hoped the sheriff would continue to talk about mundane things like the old SUV all the way to Cambria. He had no desire to discuss today's mission or anything else related to Baby Angel. But he wouldn't be that lucky.

"What can you tell me about this fellow, Birdie Wilson?" the sheriff asked.

Lynn was hesitant. "Honestly," he said, "not much of anything.

He fishes in the Ohio River and he has two boys. His wife is said to be a salt-of-the-earth type woman. That's all I know."

"Well, I can tell you this: They're hiding that abandoned child somewhere and we're going to find it."

"Sheriff," Lynn Swafford said cautiously, "I don't mean to speak out of turn here—you know, overstep my place or whatever—but it seems to me like maybe you're taking this case too seriously. I worry that you're getting too uptight about it."

Sheriff Higgins took a moment before responding, and when he spoke it was with lowered voice. "Lynn, let me tell you something," he said. "You wouldn't have any reason to know this, but Margie and me—well, we had a baby and lost it. Way back when I was a deputy working for your daddy. We wanted it so bad. Margie just about died over it. But the point is, I still think of that little baby girl sometimes and, knowing that we never could have another, it makes a baby just about the most precious thing in the world to me. Nobody ought to be able to abandon one and get away with it. And if we can't find it we don't have much chance of finding out who left that baby floating on the Ohio River."

"I'm sorry." That's all Lynn Swafford could think to say.

After a period of quiet, the sheriff turned to the topic of fishing. Had Lynn been on the river any this spring? Did he suppose the water was getting too high for fishing now? Had he thought any more about the two of them taking a day off sometime to go fishing together? What kind of fishing gear did he have? Did he get to go fishing with his father much when he was a boy?

Lynn was glad for the change of subject. He was finding his own duplicity in the abandoned child case more taxing than he had ever imagined. He felt like a traitor when he was with Sheriff Higgins, yet he could never bring himself to let down Molly. Fishing talk lessened the tension. The rest of the short ride to Cambria was much more pleasant.

They stopped in front of the Wilson house, and both men started toward the door. Lynn sensed movement behind him and turned. The sheriff's Explorer was beginning to move. Lynn ran back and jumped into the driver's seat and hit the brakes.

When the SUV came to a stop he set the parking brake and got out. Sheriff Higgins stood facing him, hands on hips, glaring at the old Ford.

"I meant to tell you, the transmission's been slipping out of gear when it's parked," he called. "It's just about more than I can keep up with, having to set the brake every time I get out of that damned thing."

Lynn walked back to where he sheriff stood, on the path toward Birdie Wilson's door. "It didn't get far this time," he said. "Be patient. You'll get that new car soon."

"Well, thanks for catching it, Lynn. Now we better get back to business."

Birdie answered their knock.

"Mr. Wilson," the sheriff said, "I have a warrant duly approved by Judge Gilbert that gives us access to your house to search for an abandoned child. Please step aside and give us entry."

Birdie Wilson looked somewhat bewildered, but quickly backed away from the door and motioned them inside.

"Are you alone in the house?" Lynn Swafford asked, trying hard to sound friendly.

"Edna's in the back room, making up the bed and stuff."

Lynn asked about the boys. Birdie said they were already up and out, and who knew where they might be now that school was out and the river was too high for fishing. But he expected they'd be back sometime soon and could he have Edna get Lynn and the sheriff coffee or anything?

"We shouldn't be here too long, Birdie," Lynn said, again making his best effort to be a friendly public servant.

Sheriff Higgins, meanwhile, had stood in the middle of the living room and gazed about, visually examining the room's furnishings. He went to the sofa, stooped and lifted the cushions and looked underneath.

Without saying anything to Birdie, he made his way to the kitchen and repeated his deliberate eyeballing. Then the bathroom. Where he opened the medicine cabinet and took note of its contents. And the boys' room, opening drawers and closets.

It occurred to Lynn Swafford that the sheriff looked very efficient. Rude, perhaps, but efficient.

Edna emerged from the other bedroom. To Lynn Swafford, she looked somewhat tired and careworn. He felt sorry for her. He was embarrassed for her and embarrassed for himself. He hadn't been involved in many searches, and most of those he had taken part in were about drugs or stolen merchandise. If you thought you were searching the lair of a drug dealer or thief you didn't feel nearly as bad as this.

Edna smiled at them, though. She said she had just made fresh coffee and wouldn't they like a cup? She apologized for the state of disarray in the bedroom. She hadn't had time yet to get things straightened out.

Sheriff Higgins took only a few minutes to finish his superficial search of the Wilson house. There was nothing here to indicate the presence of a baby, now or any time in the recent past. He apologized to Birdie and Edna for any inconvenience even as he tried to maintain his tough demeanor.

Just as the sheriff was finishing his stern lecture on obstructing justice and other crimes horrible to law enforcement professionals, the Wilson boys banged in through the back door. They clearly were startled to find Sheriff Higgins and Deputy Lynn Swafford in their house.

The sheriff greeted them like long-lost comrades. Especially Kyle.

"I believe this is the young man who first reported the abandoned child," he said pleasantly. "You boys been doing any fishing lately?"

"No, sir," Ross answered. "River's too high."

"Well, I'm sorry to hear that. Deputy Swafford and me have been wanting to get out there one of these days and do a little fishing, ourselves. But if it's too rough for serious fishermen like you two, I guess we'd better wait till the water runs down before we take to a boat."

Kyle smiled proudly.

"By the way," the sheriff went on, "you don't happen to know where that abandoned child is right now, do you?"

Kyle said, with some show of excitement, "No, sir, but she usually stays over at Molly's house. That's where we took the new crib."

"Who took the new crib?"

"Me and Ross and our dad. Johnny White sent it over to Molly after the lottery."

Lynn Swafford could see the color creeping into the sheriff's face. An angry outburst was coming. A real volcanic eruption.

"Mr. Wilson," the sheriff exploded, "weren't we just now talking about obstructing justice? Do you understand what obstructing justice means?"

Birdie said meekly, "No, sir. I don't reckon I do."

"Well for starters it means lying to a duly authorized police officer. That would be Deputy Swafford and me. So if I ask you a question and you lie to me, that's prima facie obstruction of justice. People go to jail for obstructing justice. You understand what I'm saying?"

"Yes, sir, I think I do."

"All right, then. I'm asking you this: Have you ever had that abandoned child here in this house."

"No, sir. She's never been in this house."

"But you admit there is an abandoned child?"

"Oh, sure. I ain't never denied that, sheriff. Me and the boys found her floating on the river."

Kyle jumped in, excited again: "We saved her from drowning." Sheriff Higgins faltered, as if not quite sure where to take his interrogation next. "You did a good thing," he told Kyle. "But now we need to find that baby and get her into the hands of the child welfare folks so they can take care of her."

"They'd call her Baby Jane Doe," Birdie said quietly.

Kyle spoke again: "Yes, sir, they'd call her Baby Jane Doe."

The sheriff apparently had regained control of his temper. "The law is the law," he said, this time not shouting. "An abandoned child ought to be in the hands of the authorities. Now you folks know it's your duty to report that kind of thing."

Birdie Wilson brightened, as if he'd just discovered an opening. "Yes, sir," he said. "And that's exactly what we did. Me and Sam Gowdy went straight to the mayor after we found that baby. In Cambria, the mayor is the highest authority we got."

The sheriff turned to Deputy Swafford. "I think we may as well go now," he said. "I think we've done all we can do here."

They ran through the rain to the SUV. Both were soaking wet. Once settled inside the vehicle, Sheriff Higgins vented his frustration. "Lynn, did anybody ever notice that man might be a brick or two short of a load? I went from mad to just about to bust out laughing."

"I think he's a good man, sheriff. He tries to do the right thing, from what I hear."

"Maybe. But he's sure not the smartest man in town."

Now it was Lynn who recognized an opening. He recently had thought of a new ploy and had been waiting for a good time to try it out. Anything to tone down the sheriff's all-out assault on Cambria. Otherwise, like a hungry hound tracking a rabbit, the sheriff wouldn't let up until he found what he was looking for.

"I don't know about Birdie Wilson," Lynn said, "but I understand that Cambrians are pretty active voters. Maybe you could do a little campaigning while we're going around town."

Sheriff Higgins seemed uncertain. Lynn held his breath. "Yes, I suppose I might," the sheriff finally said. "I've been spending too much time around here not to get something out of it."

Lynn Swafford pressed his advantage. "Of course, it's hard to charge into somebody's home with a search warrant and then ask them to vote for you when you're done," he said. "I was just thinking, if we keep this up we're going to lose every vote in Cambria this fall. That might be just enough to tilt an election, don't you suppose?"

The sheriff's thoughtful demeanor gave Lynn an instant of optimism. It didn't last long.

"You know, Lynn," Sheriff Higgins said, "I don't care if it costs me an election. It's the right thing to do. I'm going to find that child. I guess we might as well head on back to the courthouse and hit up Judge Gilbert for another warrant. I want us to get back over here tomorrow."

"Yes, sir. Not much more we can do here today."

"But I believe I'll see if I can find that mayor, first."

The sheriff started the engine and released the brake. After turning around in the street, he headed toward Town Hall. Lynn hoped they wouldn't find Johnny White, though he was not sure why. Well, yes, he did know why. The more time Sheriff Higgins spent in Cambria talking to people, the more chances there were for somebody to say the wrong thing and lead him to Baby Angel. The Wilson boy certainly hadn't helped things any.

Once again, Lynn Swafford felt the pain of guilt. Deception was not in his nature. He wished he could see Molly. He hadn't considered how hard it would be for him actually to be in Cambria but not able to stop by her house. He consoled himself by vowing to call her as soon as he had a chance.

Sheriff Higgins drove slowly. They met Pastor Mike, walking in the rain. The young minister carried no umbrella and wore no rain gear. He was, from all appearances, simply enjoying his stroll. He waved merrily as they passed.

They found Johnny White in Town Hall.

"Sheriff Higgins!" the mayor exclaimed, extending his hand in greeting. "What a pleasant surprise. And it's good to see you too, Deputy Swafford."

The sheriff apparently was not impressed. "You knew I'd be back," he said flatly. "And you know I'll be back tomorrow and the day after that, for as long as it takes. You're hiding that abandoned child somewhere in Cambria and I mean to find her."

Johnny White held his ground: "Now sheriff, we have talked about this matter before, as you may recall. I don't deny there was a child found on the river, but we have no way to know how she got there. I've heard that some good Cambrians have pitched in to take care of her until her momma shows up. Birdie Wilson and Sam Gowdy even made a trip up to Wheeling to see if they could find out about her family, with no luck. But like I told you before, I don't concede that this is a matter for the law."

Sheriff Higgins stiffened. "And I'll bet you don't concede that you know where that abandoned child is hidden, either?"

"I concede neither that she is abandoned nor hidden."

Lynn Swafford stood back from the sheriff, a couple of steps behind. He could look Johnny White in the eye without his behavior being visible to Sheriff Higgins. He suddenly felt proud of the mayor. This man believed he knew what was right and it was apparent that he would stick to his guns. Lynn felt somewhat less guilty about his own double standard, and a great deal more determined to stand by all these Cambrians—but especially Molly—until they'd seen this battle through. His best hope still was to find a way to reach the sheriff and get him to call off the dogs.

❧13❧

Before Lynn Swafford called Molly that night, he wanted to think of a good excuse for needing to see her right away. The best he could come up with was to suggest that they ought to get together and compare notes on Cambria's war with Sheriff Higgins over Baby Angel. Sure. This was dear to her heart. It was reason enough.

But when Molly answered the phone all he said was, "I want to see you tonight."

"Then come as soon as you like," Molly replied.

On the way to Cambria for the second time that day, he was euphoric. This time he wasn't going to search somebody's house for signs of an abandoned child. No, this time it was to see the woman whose company had become his greatest joy.

If only they could get past the sheriff's campaign to find the baby, maybe he and Molly could settle into a normal man-woman relationship. Whatever that meant. He had believed that he had such a relationship once in his life, though it didn't turn out so well. But there had been a few good years, and he had two great sons to show for it. Morgan and Patrick would be home from college soon and he was eager to see them.

How would the boys like Molly? Given the time their mother had been gone—and considering the circumstances under which she left—he doubted they would resent her being replaced by another. Not much, anyway.

Lynn already had come to feel that he was on good terms with Justine and Jay. They had grown up without an adult male in the home and he'd recognized from the beginning that they took to him as the father figure they had missed. Given his feelings for Molly, he welcomed the prospect of that role. He was starting to imagine them all together as a family.

And how would Molly like Morgan and Patrick? Well, it probably didn't matter much. His boys were almost grown now and soon they would be on their own. But they were good kids. Molly was open-minded and accepting, so he expected her to like them just fine. As the kids today would put it, "What's not to like?"

Lynn smiled as he passed the intersection where he'd operated the radar gun that day and caught Molly speeding. The location was fortunate because of its nearness to Judge Harold Winkler. Otherwise, Molly most likely would have had to appear before Judge Gilbert—and most likely would have faced a much different outcome. He was sobered by the thought that that entire drama might never have taken place. It was just coincidental. Or was it?

The rain hammered on the windshield. At times he found it hard to see. Nothing else would bring him out on a night like this. But he was on his way to see Molly. The difficult driving conditions were only a minor inconvenience. If the drive to Cambria seemed long it wasn't because of the weather. It was because he was impatient to be there.

How long had it been since he'd known the real comfort a woman could provide? The mere idea of it struck him as remote and foreign. It might as well have been forever.

Just as he drove into Cambria, the rain let up slightly. Lights were ablaze at Father Jacob's church but beyond this there were scant signs of life. The little town was mostly dark, with few street lights, and Lynn watched carefully for the shadowy corner where he needed to turn. Then he was on Molly's street and almost at once he saw her old Buick. He parked behind it and ran up to the house.

Molly held open the door. At this moment, she was the prettiest sight Lynn Swafford ever had seen.

❧

HIS PREDICTION that news of the drama playing out in Cambria would spread came true even faster than Lynn Swafford himself had expected. Monday's *County Star* newspaper carried a banner headline, "Cambrians Hiding Child." The story was based entirely on an interview with Sheriff Higgins.

The sheriff charged that the whole town was in on the conspiracy and vowed to do "whatever it takes to find that abandoned child." He also made a pointed reference to the county elections coming up in the fall: "I want the voters to know that I enforce the law, and the law clearly says that child should be turned over to the authorities." He said his department would see to it that the child was properly cared for by the child welfare people.

The story was written by Nate Hynes, the *Star's* police reporter. Hynes happened to be a nephew of Sheriff Higgins. Few of the newspaper's readers were aware of this fact, however, and Hynes had a good reputation as a reliable newsman.

Two days later, a white Dodge van painted with the gaudy logo and slogan of a Pittsburgh television station pulled up in front of the Cambria Town Hall. Sheriff Higgins in his old Ford SUV was close behind.

Two hefty young men emerged from the van and set up an aluminum frame that they covered with a blue tarpaulin to create a shelter from the rain. They hauled out lighting and sound equipment and two video cameras. One man began taping background scenes, including Town Hall, and walked down the street until he could get a clear shot of the river.

The other man got Sheriff Higgins and brought him under the tarp.

After everything was set, the reporter—young and blonde and pretty—exited the van and hurried under the shelter. She introduced herself to the sheriff and carefully outlined the story she wanted to do.

Even though the rain had continued all day, Cambrians were out and about, catching up on things put off too long because of the weather. A small crowd of onlookers quickly gathered before the television station's portable production tent, with umbrellas overlapping until they formed an almost solid roof over their heads. They were curious, excited to see a television crew right here in

Cambria, and squeezed in close enough to see and hear what was going on,

"If we do this right, I think I have a good chance of getting on the national network with it," the pretty reporter was saying. "Hey, guys, hurry up and get a mike on the sheriff. I'm ready to get this show on the road."

One of the young men turned on the lights, on tall stands and aimed directly at the sheriff and the pretty reporter. The sheriff looked blinded momentarily but quickly recovered by turning sideways. The pretty reporter licked her lips and shook her head from side to side to fluff her hair. She pointed to the cameraman and began, "Okay, we're taping in three . . . two . . . one . . . This is Tippi Grant with an exclusive report on the strange conspiracy here in little Cambria to hide a child from the authorities. Sheriff Charlie Higgins, explain to our viewers what's going on."

She moved the microphone from her own face into the face of the sheriff. He looked uneasy, swallowed hard and, squinting in the bright lights, said rather nervously, "Excuse me, ma'am, it's Clarence. Clarence Higgins."

"Cut!" the pretty reporter called to the camera operator. She motioned with the fingers of a flattened hand as if slashing her own throat. "I'm sorry, guys. Let's start over. Okay, we're taping in three . . . two . . . one . . . This is Tippi Grant reporting from little Cambria on a strange conspiracy to hide a child from the authorities. Here for an exclusive interview is Sheriff Clarence Higgins. Sheriff, explain to our viewers what's going on."

She repositioned the microphone again. This time the sheriff began smoothly: "Well, it all started with an abandoned child that a man named Birdie Wilson found floating on the river—"

"Who is this Birdie Wilson? Does he have a criminal record?"

"No, ma'am."

"What can you tell us about him?"

"He seems okay."

"Would you say this Birdie Wilson is a hero?"

"I guess some would say so."

"What do you say?"

"Well, I give him credit for saving that child."

"And your concern now is that the child is missing?"

"I don't suppose I'd say she's missing. It's just that she's not in the hands of the authorities."

"You said she. So the child is a little girl?"

"Yes, ma'am."

"So this Birdie Wilson saved a little girl from the river. And then what? Did he notify the local police?"

"No, ma'am. Cambria doesn't have any police department, just volunteer firemen."

"If there are no police, who takes care of crime in Cambria?"

"That's my job. I'm county sheriff."

"I understand. Did Mr. Wilson notify you, then?"

"No, he didn't."

"Who did?"

"I wouldn't say I was notified, exactly. They had a lottery, just before Spring Carnival. That's how I found out."

"A lottery? That had something to do with . . . Cut! Turn it all off, guys. This has gotten just too damned screwy. I want a good clean tape. The network eats up this human interest crap. Take a couple of minutes and we'll start over."

A soft murmur rolled through the little knot of onlookers. The crowd had grown by a half-dozen more Cambrians, the last one to arrive being Juanita Blessing. Johnny White had stepped out of Town Hall to see what the commotion was and he, too, had joined the group. They all had stood in silence while the pretty reporter went about her work.

Now they were free to talk: "The sheriff looks kinda scared up there." "You'd be scared too, if you got put in front of a camera." "I hope this don't make Cambria look bad." "Are they from Pittsburgh, did you say?" "That young woman is right pretty." "Maybe we'll make the big time with all this hubbub."

The pretty reporter fluffed her hair and licked her lips again. "Okay," she said, "let's try this again. Guys, turn on the lights, please. Ready? We're rolling in three . . . two . . . one . . . This is Tippi Grant with an exclusive report on a bizarre conspiracy the people here in little Cambria are engaged in. So Sheriff Clarence Higgins, you say it's a criminal act. Can you explain why?"

"Well, somebody should notify the law when a child gets abandoned."

"And that's what happened here? Who abandoned the child?"

"We don't know."

"But you believe the whole town's in on it somehow?"

"Depends on what you mean. They weren't in on the abandonment. We don't know who did that."

"I understand. But sheriff, can you explain what it is the people of Cambria are doing that you say is illegal?"

"Yes, ma'am. They're hiding the child."

"The abandoned child."

"Yes, ma'am."

"And you feel they're endangering the child?"

"No, ma'am, I wouldn't say that. I expect they're taking good care of her."

"You said her. So you know it's a girl?"

"Yes, ma'am."

"If you're not concerned for the child's safety, sheriff, what is your main concern?"

"It's the law."

"What do you mean, exactly."

"The law says an abandoned child should be reported."

"Maybe I'm missing something here, Sheriff Higgins. If the abandoned child was not reported, how did you come to know about it—I mean, you're here investigating, right?"

"Yes, ma'am, I am."

"So how did you know?"

"They had a lottery. I saw the posters. Right before Spring Carnival."

"Just so our viewers understand, can you explain in a bit more detail exactly how the lottery tipped you off? On the abandoned child, I mean."

"Yes, ma'am. The lottery had to do with the baby river angel."

"Baby river angel? That's fascinating. What information . . .

what do you know about this baby river angel?"

"Nothing at all, ma'am. That's why we're looking for her. I should have said earlier, I've never seen her."

Color had begun to creep up the pretty reporter's neck. The dampness was starting to straighten her hair. She cast a sideways glance at the young man holding the camera. "Sheriff Clarence Higgins," she said, "I want you to look straight into this camera and tell our viewers what's going on in this town—here in little Cambria. Just start from the beginning, okay?"

The sheriff took the microphone from her and held it up close in front of his face. He looked directly into the camera. He said: "The beginning, as I understand it, was when Birdie Wilson and his two boys was out fishing. Birdie's youngest boy, I can't remember his name, is the one who explained to me about the lottery. He said the baby river angel was usually over at Molly Hearst's house and so that's where my deputy and I looked first. I'd like to give credit here to Deputy Lynn Swafford, by the way. Anyhow, we looked at Miss Molly's house and there was no sign of the baby river angel. I went back to Judge Gilbert to see if we could search all over town. All over Cambria. I thought Judge Gilbert would approve, because he's a strong law-and-order judge who says abandoned children should be in the care of the child welfare department . . ."

Someone in the small crowd of onlookers—most said it was Margie Zielinski—shouted, "Birdie says they'd call her Baby Jane Doe. Is that right, sheriff?"

Sheriff Higgins stopped with his mouth open and looked at the pretty reporter for direction. The pretty reporter yelled "Cut!" and once again gave the throat-slashing sign to the cameraman. At that instant, the aluminum frame holding the rainwater-laden tarpaulin over their heads gave way. The tarp dumped the water directly onto the pretty reporter and the sheriff.

From beneath the tarp, the onlookers could hear the pretty reporter cursing. Sheriff Clarence Higgins tried to console her. When she'd finally clawed her way free, she ran to the van and jumped in and slammed the door. The two young men gathered up equipment and hurried it into the back of the van. In almost no time at all the van and the television crew from the city were gone.

Sheriff Clarence Higgins took advantage of the opportunity to compliment the good people of Cambria for coming out in the rain to watch the big production and thank them for their attention. He handed out cards and asked for their votes in the fall.

Cambria's promise of network fame vanished as quickly as it had begun. There was no exclusive videotaped interview with Sheriff Clarence Higgins that night on the national news, nor even on the Pittsburgh television station's local evening report. Correspondent Tippi Grant's story was replaced by a superficial thirty-second item read with a dead-pan expression by a middle-aged male news anchor. He called their town Cambridge.

No matter. The Pittsburgh television station was not seen in Cambria, anyway.

❧14❧

Granny Vogler was the closest thing Cambria had to a town sorehead. His real name was Granville and he'd been dubbed Granny long before he gained his reputation for being cranky. In the last ten or fifteen years, though, the nickname had seemed to fit especially well. Some said his grouchy disposition came from the lack of a woman's influence since that bad winter when the influenza took his wife of more than forty years. Others contended he was just born that way.

Granny was pretty much a recluse. He would be seen trudging around town in his old slouch hat and heavy woolen shirt, even in hot weather, but he seldom stopped to talk. He almost never went to public events of any kind.

Even so, Molly Hearst was surprised to hear that Granny didn't know about Baby Angel. She'd assumed that, by now, everyone in town knew all about the little one. The baby had been the principal topic of discussion among Cambrians for a good many days.

Granny showed up at Molly's door early in the morning, the day after Cambria's near brush with fame. He had been among those standing in the cold rain watching and listening as the pretty reporter from the Pittsburgh television station interviewed Sheriff Clarence Higgins. To say that Granny was confused would be a gross understatement. But he had heard the sheriff say that Baby Angel usually was at Molly's house and he understood that this matter some way involved the whole town.

Molly invited Granny in and poured him a cup of hot coffee. She let him know that his appearance at her door had come as a surprise, although he was always welcome. Granny seemed uncertain how to respond. He'd nearly finished his coffee before he finally spoke of what was on his mind.

His inquiry was blunt: "Where's your baby?"

"Why, Granny, I don't have a baby," Molly answered.

"I mean the little river angel that TV lady came to find out about. The sheriff said it usually is at your house. I ain't seen a little baby in so long I just wanted to see it, is all. Sounded kinda like it was community property."

"Oh," Molly replied, "the little river angel. I don't keep her here all that much. Other people keep her, too, and Johnny White is pretty well in charge of where she is at any given time. Like you said, she is kind of community property."

Granny set his cup aside and stood. "Well, Molly," he said, "I thank you for the information. I suppose I'll go down and see Johnny and find out where she is. I thought if she belonged to the town maybe I could help provide for her. If you think that might be appropriate."

"Yes, of course," Molly said, trying to hide her surprise. "That'd be very generous of you, Granny. It costs a lot to raise a child these days."

"That's what I figured. I reckon Johnny would take a check?"

"Why, yes, I think so. He has a fund set up for the baby. The Baby River Angel Fund, it's called."

Granny edged toward the door. He said, "You know I'm not rich, Molly. But I'm getting by pretty good. It don't take a lot for an old man to live on, living by hisself."

Molly wondered if Granny Vogler had been judged too harshly by other Cambrians. And she felt guilty. How many times in recent years had she even greeted him on the street, much less offered friendly words of conversation? She couldn't think of a single one.

"I don't see you around as often as I used to, Granny," she said. "How've you been?"

Granny Vogler reacted as if he was surprised that she took the time to ask. "I'm tolerable well, thank you," he said. "I guess I just don't see much reason to get out anymore."

"I'll tell you what, Granny. Let me walk down to Town Hall with

116

you. We can talk more on the way. Is that okay with you?"

"Why, I'd be honored, Molly. Yes, I'd be honored."

Molly cleared the table. She put the cups and spoons in the sink and turned back to Granny Vogler. "I'm ready when you are," she said. "Is it still raining?"

Granny said it was, but not very hard. He had walked in the rain coming over to Molly's house and didn't feel the worse for wear. She might want to carry an umbrella, though, or maybe put on a raincoat if she had one.

Molly got an umbrella from the closet and led the way. They had barely left the house when the rain picked up again, coming down in sheets. Her umbrella and his slouch hat offered little protection and they were thoroughly soaked by the time they got to Town Hall.

Johnny White stood up from his desk and welcomed them. "You two look like a pair of drowned rats," he observed. "I assume it's still raining?"

"You assume right," Granny Vogler told him. "But we're here for something important, mayor. I want to give you a check for the baby fund."

"Yes, of course. We'd appreciate that," the mayor replied. "The good people of Cambria have been generous, but we can't ever get too much in the Baby River Angel Fund."

Granny pulled out his checkbook and sat down and began to write. "Miss Quattlebaum give you anything yet?" he asked.

"Well I don't know if anybody's approached Miss Quattlebaum about it," Johnny White said. "Folks don't see her much."

"I'll ask her. She's got more than I do, that's for sure."

Granny handed his check to Johnny White, then turned to Molly. "I expect you may want to wait here till it slacks up some," he said. "But if you don't mind I think I'll go on over to Sam Gowdy's bait shop and see what's going on."

Molly smiled. "Granny, I can't get much wetter," she said. "I believe I'll just tag along. Let's go!"

The rain soon slackened again, to little more than a shower. Molly furled her umbrella. This made it easier to walk closer to

Granny Vogler and talk. She'd sensed during their trek to Town Hall that he was beginning to feel more at ease. And express himself more freely. She hoped that would continue.

It did. By the time they got to Sam Gowdy's bait shop, Granny not only was speaking freely about things going on around town but also was laughing and making jokes.

The bait shop was crowded. Molly hadn't intended to stay, but she actually was beginning to enjoy Granny's company. She also was curious to see how the old man behaved in a roomful of other Cambrians—and how they treated him.

Once inside, Granny looked about as if searching for a familiar face. Molly was surprised. She would have thought that the old man knew everyone there. It turned out that he was looking for a place to hang his hat and, finding none, jammed it back down on his head and joined the gathering of his neighbors.

He walked over to Kirk Mendenhall and Gordon Blessing and slapped Kirk on the back and shook hands with Gordon. In no time at all, the three of them were carrying on a jovial discussion of the weather, the price of gasoline, and the flood level on the Ohio River. Jake Garner soon joined in and after him, Max Barnes.

Molly, meanwhile, had spied Margie Zielinski across the room. Margie was sitting in an old steel folding chair, backed against the wall with a cup of steaming coffee in her hand. She brightened when she saw Molly coming her way.

"Bless you, girl!" Margie sang out. "I didn't think there was going to be another woman here today. If I had to set and listen to the men's tall tales much longer I'd have been out of here pretty soon."

Molly found an empty chair and pulled it close.

"Did you come in with Granny Vogler?" Margie asked. "I've not seen him around here in months."

"I think he wanted company. Men's company, I guess. But I have to tell you something you may not believe."

"If you tell it, I'll believe it, Molly. What is it?"

Molly leaned close and kept her voice low: "Granny came over this morning to ask me about Baby Angel. I think he's as happy as anybody in town to have her here in Cambria."

"You're not serious! Granny Vogler?"

"I am serious. He's actually excited about her, from what I could tell."

Molly had unintentionally raised her voice as she talked. Charlie Tipsworth and Morris Layman, standing nearby, overheard. They turned to the two women.

"I wasn't listening in, since your talk's none of my business," Morris Layman said. "But if I heard you right—accidentally, mind you—it would take a miracle to make Granny look on anything going on in Cambria in a positive fashion. That's just not Granny."

Charlie Tipsworth nodded his head in support. "And I can tell you this," he said, "he might like something this morning, but by night he'll be all bent out of shape over it. Trust my word."

Molly disagreed. She said, "I'm telling you, Granny's downright happy to know about Baby Angel. He gave Johnny White a check for the baby's fund. I think he wants to get involved. Really."

Margie suddenly shushed them. She nodded across the room. Granny Vogler was headed their way.

The old man walked up and extended a hand to both Charlie and Morris and tipped his hat to Margie. "How's everybody doing this morning?" he inquired cheerfully. Charlie Tipsworth looked stunned, but returned Granny's greeting: "We're doing pretty good. Nice to see you." Morris Layman nodded politely.

Margie smiled, and said, "It's good to see you, Granny. How've you been? You ought to get around more often."

Molly soon excused herself. She had a big night to get ready for. To her great delight, she left Granny Vogler taking part in the full-throated banter common at the bait shop on a day like this. Granny, the town sorehead. And all because of Baby Angel.

As she walked home in the rain, Molly experienced a sense of exhilaration that had become rare in recent years. Like the feeling she used to get at the first signs of spring, or during those rare weeks when Roger got time off and the family could do things together. And she knew why. Lynn Swafford was coming and she couldn't wait. True, it was only a movie date, but it meant time with this man who was growing more important to her with every breath she took. She would think of nothing else the rest of the day.

Lynn picked up Molly at seven o'clock, never guessing that she had been sitting and waiting for three hours. The closest theater was in the county seat, and this meant a thirty-minute drive. Lynn half-heartedly complained about the trip—he had just made it in the opposite direction since getting off work at the sheriff's office—but Molly was happy for it. Time alone in the car with Lynn had become her favorite time.

After the small talk, Lynn turned serious. "Did you see Sheriff Higgins in Cambria today? Deputy Gidcomb was with him."

Molly said she hadn't.

"I'm sure he was coming," Lynn said. "He had another of those foolish warrants."

Molly slipped closer and took his hand. "I'm afraid he's going to find something, Lynn," she said. "I'm so scared we're going to lose Baby Angel."

"I've been wracking my brain trying to think of a way to stop him, Molly. I've tried to reason with him, I've pointed out that this could cost him the election next fall, I've done everything I can to impress on him that Baby Angel is being well cared for. Nothing works."

"I miss her so much already. And I don't know when I'll get her back again. Lynn, will you tell me the truth? Do you think we're doing the wrong thing. It seemed simple in the beginning, but it's getting way too complicated."

Lynn Swafford pulled Molly close. She leaned her head on his shoulder.

"Molly," he said, "I can't tell you what's right. All I know is that you love Baby Angel and I love you. We'll find a way to save her."

Molly told him about Granny Vogler, and the effect that merely learning about Baby Angel apparently had had on him. She talked about Granny's desire to help support the child and described the way he jumped into the conversation with other Cambrians, and how much the old man looked to enjoy the company.

120

Lynn took in every word Molly said. It was as if the simple pleasure of listening to her was all he would ask. She was still talking when they got to the movie theatre.

The theatre was nearly empty and they took seats in the middle of a row near the back. Within minutes of its beginning, they knew the movie was going to be terrible. No matter. They were there for each other's company. They would have liked to behave like teenagers, necking and petting in the dark, but they settled for the physical contact of hand-holding. This effortless intimacy carried its own thrill.

When the movie ended, they stood and stretched, blinking in the sudden bright lights. Molly was sorry that the show was over. She felt as if the warm comfort of the last two hours might never be hers again. She was taken aback momentarily by the sight of other people around them, even though it was only a handful, as if she and Lynn had been there all alone.

Although it was late—by their standards, anyway—they walked slowly back to the car, still holding hands. Molly couldn't help but be concerned that Lynn had to drive her home and then drive home himself, but her worry evaporated once she was nestled beside him again. All that mattered was his presence.

She said little as she rode through the darkness, squeezed tight against this man who made her feel alive in ways she had forgotten. Lynn talked. He told her about his sons, how they would be home for the summer soon, how he wanted her to meet them and get to know them, how he knew they would like her and he hoped she liked them. He talked about Justine and Jay, and how he had come to feel like they were his family too.

There was no mention of Baby Angel. They did not talk about Sheriff Higgins and the fight being waged by the people of Cambria. Problems of the daily world were far away.

By the time they were halfway to Cambria, Lynn also fell silent. But there was no need for talk. This night away from all others was tranquil time that belonged to them alone. They reveled in each other's presence, in the togetherness nurtured by the still, black night by which they were surrounded.

The trip was all too short. Before either of them was ready, they were in front of Molly's house. Lynn turned to her and, his hands free from driving, took her in his arms. There was a long intimate embrace and long and passionate kisses.

"I don't want to let you go, but you have a long drive home," Molly said at last. "I guess we have to call it a night."

"I don't want to leave," Lynn said.

"And I don't want you to leave."

"Then I'll stay."

"But my house is too small, Lynn. The children would hear every move."

"Miss Molly, how long has it been since you made out in the back seat?"

Molly felt herself blush, and was happy that he couldn't see it in the dark. "Truth to tell," she told him, "I never did. And I've always felt cheated, like I missed something growing up."

"Then I think it's time you catch up on what you've missed."

It was. And they did. Twice.

❧15❧

The Rider house was among the few in Cambria that couldn't easily be placed in either the Canepatch section of town or the high side. It was one of five homes perched on a narrow plateau where the gradual slope from the Ohio River to the top of the bluffs temporarily leveled out and formed a shelf barely wide enough to give these residents either a front yard or a back yard, but not both.

As Herb Rider liked to say, "We're smack in the middle, and the middle's not very big." Herb had a way with words.

Janet, unlike her husband, was somewhat reserved. Or, as Herb put it, "She doesn't talk much." Nellie, their only child, was more like her father. Nellie always had an opinion and Nellie didn't hesitate to state it. No matter what the company. Sometimes this got Nellie in trouble.

The Riders had a dog, Jasper, who counted as the fourth member of the family. Jasper was a large animal of the mutt variety. He was not pure mutt, though. You could see the lines of German shepherd, Irish setter, and maybe a couple of other breeds if you were familiar enough with them to know one if you happened into it. Herb claimed to see slight traces of Russian wolfhound and said Jasper had a true international heritage.

Janet was thrilled when Johnny White called and inquired as to whether the Riders' place on the duty roster of Baby Angel's keepers could be moved up a bit. She told the mayor she would take the little one any time, night or day, on five minutes' notice.

"That's wonderful," the mayor said, "because we need you to take her tonight."

"Like I said," Janet Rider shot back, "bring her anytime. I can't tell you how long it's been since I had a baby in this house."

The mayor promised that Birdie Wilson would be there with Baby Angel within the hour. Birdie had to pick up the baby and her things from Kelley Peterson, and he was merely waiting on word from the mayor as to where she went next. He said he would call Birdie as soon as he got off the phone with Janet, and "as you know, Birdie's thrown himself into our work to take care of that baby like Custer going after the Indians."

She didn't say anything to Johnny White, but Janet didn't appreciate his analogy. She'd read a great deal of American history and as far as General George Armstrong Custer was concerned she tended to come down on the side of the Indians. And regardless, trite analogies irritated her.

Waiting for Birdie to show up at her front door, Janet Rider tried to think of better ways the mayor could have drawn his comparison. But except for "a frog jumping on a June bug" she could not come up with anything that wouldn't offend somebody's sensibilities. And there probably were a few friends of June bugs out there somewhere. Oh, well, she decided, nobody needed her ideas on trite analogies. Nosiree, she wouldn't be their candle in the dark.

She didn't have long to wait. A soft, almost clandestine in nature, knock-knock-knocking on her front door signaled Birdie's arrival. He carried Baby Angel in a basket, covered by a blanket, and had a satchel of baby things over his arm. These had accumulated as the baby was passed from sitter to sitter, originating with Molly Hearst.

Trailing behind Birdie came Nellie, and after Nellie loped Jasper. The whole parade passed through the front door of the Rider home in a flash.

"How're you today, ma'am?" Birdie Wilson greeted her. Then, looking about, "Where should I put her?"

Janet told him to place the basket on the couch. Birdie set it down carefully, as if handling fragile merchandise. He gently pulled the blanket down from Baby Angel's face and was rewarded by a magical smile and loud gurgling noises. Nellie, standing close beside him, squealed with delight. "She's beautiful, Mom," Nellie cried. "I've never seen such a pretty baby!"

"Oh, she's a darling all right," Birdie stated proudly.

Janet Rider picked up Baby Angel and held the child close to her breast. Baby Angel's contentment was apparent to everyone in the room. "She likes you, Mom," Nellie told her mother. "Look at her, Birdie. She really likes my mom."

"This little one likes everybody," Birdie said. "Oh, excuse me, Janet, I didn't mean—"

"Nonsense, Birdie," Janet said. "I'm not that easy to offend. Except by Nellie here, who always has a way of doubting me."

"That's not true, Mom," Nellie insisted. "It's just that, well, I don't remember ever seeing you hold a baby before."

"That might be because you were the last one I ever held until now."

"Anyways, ma'am, Nellie's right," Birdie Wilson said. "Now if you'll excuse me, though, I need to get on. I'll let Johnny White know the baby's here. You'll be keeping her tonight and tomorrow, isn't that right?"

"That's my understanding," Janet responded. "And you'll pick her up about this time tomorrow?"

"Yes, ma'am, I will. You'll have all day tomorrow with her."

After Birdie was gone, Janet Rider and Nellie took turns holding Baby Angel and walking her around the house. Baby Angel surveyed her new surroundings as they went, turning her head for pictures on the walls and waving her arms as they passed bright lamps. She also kept up a running commentary, using her full vocabulary of cooing and gurgles and now and then laughing out loud.

Jasper, as soon as he had devoured the contents of his supper dish, returned to the living room. Unusual in itself, because his normal routine was to lie down in the hallway at this point in his day and promptly fall asleep. Not only did he return to the living room instead, but he fell right in behind Nellie and Baby Angel as they took their umpteenth walk around the house.

Nellie was a nimble child, even carrying a baby. Jasper was a lumbering giant. On his second jaunt around the circuit he knocked over an end table and brought a lamp crashing to the floor. Nellie screamed. Baby Angel giggled.

Jasper stood by sheepishly while Janet Rider picked up the pieces, straightened things up, and assured Nellie that no harm had been done. When Nellie went to the couch and sat, with Baby Angel on her lap, Jasper jumped up beside them. He couldn't take his eyes off the baby. Nellie started to scold, but promptly lost heart. "I know, boy, you love her too," Nellie said, stroking the old dog on the back of his massive head.

Herb Rider was late getting home that night. His boss had offered a rare chance at overtime and Herb couldn't afford to turn it down. He was surprised to see Baby Angel, and momentarily confused. He rushed to the baby and said, "There you are! I've been looking forward to you, child."

"We all love her already," Nellie said. "Even Jasper."

'No kidding! I'm surprised Jasper's not jealous."

"I thought he would be," Janet told her husband, "but he seems to have taken to her right from the start. I hope he doesn't get too attached. She'll be gone by this time tomorrow."

"Don't worry about Jasper," Nellie said. "Worry about the rest of us, Mom. I'm already hating to see her go. Daddy, this must be the sweetest baby in the world. You have to hold her for a while."

Herb Rider was a bricklayer. In recent weeks, with his masonry skill not in demand, he'd been filling his boss's need for general construction labor. He had the rough hands of a working man. Until he took Baby Angel, that is. At that point his touch became as gentle as the feather duster Janet used on her prized piano.

The whole Rider family, including the family dog, was reluctant to see bedtime come. Janet finally had to insist that the baby could not be kept up too late—although too late already had come and gone. Jasper made it clear that he would sleep beside the basket, wherever it was placed. He had become the world's most committed guard dog.

The night was wonderfully serene.

The next day, after Herb had left for work, Janet Rider went about laundering all of the baby clothes that Birdie had brought which Baby Angel wasn't wearing. She recalled the days when she'd spent much of her time washing Nellie's little things and became a bit nostalgic. How fast Nellie was growing up!

Nellie, for her part, was happy that her mother had other things to do. This meant that she and Jasper had Baby Angel pretty much to themselves. Nellie spread a blanket on the floor. The three of them lay on it and admired one another.

It was almost ten o'clock when they got the desperate phone call from Mayor Johnny White.

SHERIFF CLARENCE HIGGINS was optimistic. He still felt sure that his search for the abandoned child he knew was being hidden by the Cambrians was hampered by Judge Gilbert's refusal to grant him a broad-based warrant, but on this day he was going to be in the right place at the right time. He could feel it in his bones.

The sheriff had barely taken time to check in at the office. He signed a couple of papers, quickly downed a cup of bitter coffee, and called on Deputy Harlan Gidcomb to get moving. Lynn Swafford was scheduled to testify in court today and Deputy Gidcomb would be riding with the sheriff.

Gidcomb was a notorious suck-up. Sheriff Higgins knew it, and even though he was the recipient of his deputy's best efforts, he hated to work alongside the man. He found the pandering tedious.

It didn't take Gidcomb long to start. They were barely on the road before the deputy began to praise his boss's dedication to law enforcement and particularly his persistence in continuing the search for the abandoned child. It was Gidcomb's considered opinion that the sheriff was a model whom lawmen everywhere ought to emulate.

"I was just telling Lynn Swafford the other day how much better off the whole country would be if there were more like you," Gidcomb claimed.

Sheriff Higgins couldn't take any more. "Did I tell you I'm getting a new GMC to replace this old trap?" he said. "An Acadia, they call it. County's already signed off on it."

Gidcomb was not to be stopped. "I know you sure deserve it," he said. "An active lawman like you needs reliable transpor—"

"By the way," the sheriff interrupted, "do you know what that case is Lynn's got to testify in today? Who's the judge?"

"Yes, sir. It's the Winnowbrook case. You did some fine detective work on that one, boss. Judge Gilbert's handling it. I know he appreciates it when the prosecution's case is as air-tight as it is in this one. And that's a result of your good police work."

"Winnowbrook case? I don't recall it, Harlan."

"Winnowbrook. You know, the old lady taking her grandkids in to steal things at the Wal-Mart," Gidcomb explained. "She was a hardened criminal if there ever was one, sheriff."

"Oh, yeah. Now I remember. Pitiful old woman. And I worry a lot about those kids."

Deputy Harlan Gidcomb kept up his endless praise all the way to Cambria. At some point, the sheriff gave up. He stayed silent and let Gidcomb ramble on. By the time they turned into the dead-end street that led to the home of Herb and Janet Rider, the deputy had run out of complimentary things to say about his boss's professional ability and clumsily taken up his personal habits.

"I sure wish more in the department had your solid work ethic," Gidcomb was saying as they stopped in front of the Rider house. "Oh, are we here already?"

The warrant that Sheriff Clarence Higgins carried authorized a thorough search of the residence of Herb and Janet Rider for an abandoned child or any traces thereof. It was issued by Judge Chester Gilbert and allowed the sheriff and/or his duly appointed representative—that would be Deputy Harlan Gidcomb—to look anywhere in the house for the baby or any sign that a baby had been there. It carried no restrictions.

Deputy Gidcomb jumped out the instant they stopped. He ran around to the driver's side, hoping to get there in time to open the door for the sheriff. But even though he took time to set the parking brake, Sheriff Higgins managed to push the door open before his deputy could get a hand on the handle. Gidcomb barely missed being knocked down by the force of the swinging door. Making the best of the situation, he pretended to feel a need to hide behind the sheriff's vehicle until they had a plan of attack.

"How do you want us to approach the house," Deputy Gidcomb asked. "I don't like those big windows in front."

"Damn it, Harlan, we just walk up to the door and knock. This ain't a criminal raid or anything like that."

"Well, sure. I just thought—"

"I'll go in first," Sheriff Higgins said. "You come right behind me. Once we're inside we'll split up the rooms. You know what we're looking for."

"You can count on me, sheriff."

The sheriff headed toward the Rider house, where Baby Angel lay sleeping peacefully in her basket. Nellie Rider sat beside her, hardly able to take her eyes off the child's face. Janet Rider was in the laundry room loading baby clothes into the dryer.

Jasper was the first one in the house to sense that something was amiss. From his position beside the baby's basket, stretched full-out on his stomach, he suddenly reared into an upright position, listening intently. A car door slammed outside. Jasper raced to a picture window that offered a clear view of the street. Two men approached the house.

Moving faster than Janet Rider had ever seen him move before, the dog ran to the back entry and darted through the oversized swinging doggie door. He was on the front step before the two men got halfway there.

Jasper, given his size and appearance, could be truly fearsome if he wanted to. He wanted to. His canine senses told him these men meant to harm Baby Angel. As Baby Angel's self-appointed guardian, he would not let that happen. He barked loudly, bared his teeth, and growled viciously. The two lawmen halted in their tracks.

Deputy Gidcomb crouched behind the sheriff. "So what's our next move now?" he said in a low voice.

"We'd better split up," Sheriff Higgins said. "You work your way around the back. I'll stay here and try to distract old yeller."

Gidcomb commenced a wide circle around the end of the house and headed toward the edge of the narrow plateau that interrupted the upward slope from the river. At that point, the incline was too steep to mow. It was covered in briars and wild vines and reminded the deputy of one of his favorite blackberry patches. He looked back to make sure Jasper wasn't in pursuit.

Something moved at Gidcomb's feet. He tripped over it, which had devastating consequences. By the time he recognized the tell-tale white stripe down the back of the furry black creature it was too late. The frightened skunk emitted a malodorous spray that would mark the man from head to foot. Gidcomb bellowed in distress and Sheriff Higgins came running.

The skunk, having escaped being stepped on by Deputy Gidcomb, ran toward the open yard—right into the path of Sheriff Higgins. Gidcomb yelled, "Polecat, sheriff," but the warning came too late. Before the sheriff had time to see what was about to happen he, too, became a beneficiary of the frightened skunk's trademark defense.

The two men, drenched in skunk odor, quickly forgot about warrants and abandoned children and even self-appointed guard dogs. They hurried back to the sheriff's battered old Ford SUV and headed home. To hot showers with lots of soap. And fresh clothes, right down to belts and socks. And explanations neither of them relished having to give. And a tale that would be told by sheriff's department people for years to come.

Janet Rider had just finished loading the baby things into the clothes dryer when the phone rang. She picked up the receiver and, even before she answered, heard Johnny White's panicked voice. "The sheriff is on his way," the mayor declared. "We've got to get the baby out of there, now!"

Janet fought her own panic. "What should I do, Johnny?" she asked, trying to sound less frantic than the mayor.

"To begin with, don't answer the door."

Janet called for Nellie to run and look out front. Her daughter did her bidding, and hurriedly reported back: "Mom, the sheriff's car just left."

Out on the front step, Jasper sat and wagged his tail. For a self-appointed guard dog with no prior experience, he believed, he'd done a pretty good job.

Had the rest of the Rider family understood his role in all that had just taken place, they most likely would have agreed. They probably would have rewarded him with an extra serving of his favorite food at supper. But they didn't know.

Jasper didn't mind. He'd learned long ago that, sometimes, just doing the right thing brought all the satisfaction a good guard dog could ask for.

☙16☙

Fishing was both Birdie Wilson's passion and his livelihood. Nothing contented him more than being on the water from dawn till dusk, whether he was catching anything or not. But selling fresh fish—mostly to Tom Johnson's Fish and Fries Café—was the way Birdie supported his family. He could still count on Tom to buy all the walleye, sauger, bass, black crappie, drum, and yellow perch he caught. A fish wholesaler in Pittsburgh would take most of his flathead and channel catfish, carp, and small-mouth buffalo.

Birdie had lived his entire life in Cambria, except for one year of misspent youth in Wheeling. He had seen more floods on the Ohio River than he cared to remember. Always before, he had hated the days and weeks when the water was too high for him to be out in his boat. This time, though, he was on another mission. He was far too busy helping Mayor Johnny White protect Baby Angel from the child welfare folks to think much about the river.

Although Edna had begun to worry that he wasn't bringing any money home, Birdie wasn't concerned. He lived by the philosophy that worry was a waste of time and things always worked out in the end.

Birdie's dedication to their cause was the salvation of Johnny White, who spent way too much time running his insurance business from Town Hall to be able to fully devote himself to the struggle to save Baby Angel. The mayor was pleased to take the credit, but he relied on Birdie for most of the work. For his part, Birdie thought Johnny had created a pretty much fail-poof plan. Fail-proof, that is, as long as Birdie had his hand on the tiller.

Birdie's life revolved around Baby Angel. He expected to know where she was at all hours, where she was going next, and where she was going after that. He awoke every morning as excited as he would have been about a day on the river.

On this day, the child was safely tucked away with Jake and Carrie Garner.

Birdie was eager to talk with Johnny White, but he knew the mayor wouldn't be in Town Hall for another couple of hours. It was too early to stop by the Garner house. The only person he could think of who might be out and about at this hour was Pastor Mike. He set out for the Methodist church.

Floodwaters from the river had inundated most of the area between the Canepatch and the normal river bank. A rise of only a few more inches would bring the water dangerously close to the lowest Canepatch homes. The Wilson house was among these. Birdie considered turning back to warn Edna to watch the water closely but decided not to. Edna had lived in Cambria almost as long as he had and was just as savvy when it came to the Ohio.

The rain commenced again before he was two blocks from home. Birdie hardly noticed.

But he did notice a stranger coming toward him. She was short and round—Birdie reckoned her to be hardly more than five feet tall—wore a bright orange cape over her shoulders and a wide-brimmed black hat on her head. Trotting ahead of her was a small white poodle, protected from the downpour by a yellow slicker and rain hat.

Birdie nodded in the same neighborly fashion he would have to anyone he met on the street, friend or stranger. "Good morning, ma'am," he said.

The woman stopped squarely before him. She fixed on Birdie a gaze the intensity of which he'd never seen before. Seen? This gaze he *felt*. It was as if she could see right through his skull and take in as much of his brain as struck her fancy. Birdie was overtaken by a strong sense of helplessness.

"Might I ask for a minute of your time, sir?" the woman said. Her voice was strong and her words crisp and clear.

"Yes, ma'am. I take it you're a stranger here, since I believe I know everybody in Cambria."

"I am Madam Rowena. My assistant is Nostradamus."

At the mention of his name, the little dog sat up on his hind legs, as if about to beg for his supper.

"He sure is cute," Birdie said.

"Cute? My good man, Nostradamus is far more than cute. He is an intelligent, sensitive being. I doubt that I'd be half as successful in my profession were it not for his assistance."

"If I might ask, what is your profession, ma'am?"

"Please address me as Madam Rowena," the woman said curtly.

"Beg pardon, ma'am—Madam Rowena. What is it you said you do?"

"I am a psychic."

"Ma'am?"

"I am a psychic. Or as some might say, a seer. I am frequently sought out by those from all parts of the state to help solve crimes, or find things lost, or sometimes for the most bizarre challenges you can imagine."

"Yes, ma'am. I see." Birdie was trying to be polite.

"You do not see," Madam Rowena said. "May I inquire of your name, sir?"

"Oh, yes, ma'am, my name is Birdie Wilson."

"And you live nearby?"

"I reckon you'd know better if I said no."

"Then I take it the answer to my question is yes."

"Yes, ma'am, Madam Rowena."

Madam Rowena looked Birdie up and down, like he was a prized hog she wanted to bid on at auction and roast for dinner. Birdie squirmed under her intense gaze. He wanted to project calm. But why bother? Madam Rowena no doubt could read him like a book. A child's simple story book. A picture book, even.

Madam Rowena finally spoke again. "Mr. Birdie Wilson," she said, "what can you tell me about the abandoned child that has put this quaint little village on the map in recent weeks?"

"Well now, ma'am, we don't know she's abandoned. Maybe—"

Nostradamus growled, silencing Birdie in midsentence.

"Please, Mr. Wilson," Madam Rowena implored sarcastically. "My assistant can see through that tidy little smokescreen, and so can I. I read about the abandoned child in the *County Star*. Sheriff Higgins said the child is abandoned. The sheriff is among those who have great respect for my profession. You'd be greatly surprised at the number of times I've been called on to help the sheriff solve crimes of this nature."

Birdie slumped, intimidated by the inflexible demeanor of the woman standing before him. "Yes, ma'am," he said, "I'm sure you have."

"Then let's be honest with each other right up front. Shall we?"

"Yes, ma'am."

"Please address me as Madam Rowena."

"Yes, ma'am, Madam Rowena."

"Now, Mr. Wilson, I ask you again: What can you tell me about the abandoned child?"

Birdie's stomach began to churn. There was ringing in his ears. He felt his legs weaken. The big toe on his left foot was trying to stand up in his shoe. He was suddenly conscious of the rain. He looked about, as if seeking a way to escape. Madam Rowena's gaze never left his face.

Birdie, helplessness controlling every action now, said, "All I can tell you is, nobody around here wants her to be named Baby Jane Doe."

Madam Rowena blinked. "I beg your pardon," she said.

"They'd call her Baby Jane Doe. Nobody in Cambria wants that."

"Mr. Wilson, can you tell me where this child is?"

"No, ma'am."

"Do you mean you don't know, or can't tell?"

"Ma'am, Madam Rowena, if I told you I didn't know would you believe me?"

"Of course not," the psychic scoffed. "I knew the minute I saw you coming that you know where the abandoned child is. Right at this very minute."

Birdie fought hard not to be cowed. "Like I said," he told this

136

formidable woman, "we don't know for sure that she's abandoned. Her mama might show up any day now looking for her."

Madam Rowena made no effort to hide her skepticism. "Mr. Wilson," she declared, "if I were a policewoman instead of a psychic, I would arrest you for obstructing justice."

"Ma'am?"

"Obstructing justice. You know where the abandoned child is, and Sheriff Higgins is looking for that child. She needs to be in the hands of the child welfare department."

"They'd call her Baby Jane Doe."

Madam Rowena jiggled her dog's leash. "Come, Nostradamus," she said dourly. "Let's be on our way."

Birdie started to tip his hat and bid her farewell, but she pressed by him so quickly he hadn't a chance. Nostradamus strained at his leash and tried to look back, but Madam Rowena pulled him forward. The psychic stared straight ahead and walked on down the street at a very fast pace.

Birdie's heart was beating a mile a minute. He couldn't chance waiting until Johnny White showed up at Town Hall. He needed to talk to Johnny right now, to inform him of the presence of Madam Rowena in town. If this psychic could read his mind the way she had, she no doubt could lead the sheriff straight to Baby Angel.

He was breathless by the time he reached the mayor's house. He scrambled up the steps to the porch and banged loudly on Johnny White's front door.

"Johnny, we got an emergency," Birdie called out, even before the mayor had the door fully opened. "That psychic, she can read my mind like a phone book. She's gonna find Baby Angel. That's what she come for."

"Whoa!" Johnny White demanded. "Slow down, Birdie, slow down. Who are you talking about?"

"Madam Rowena. And Nostradamus—he's as smart as she is."

"Birdie, I don't know who Madam Rowena is, and I believe Nostradamus has been dead for a few hundred years. What, exactly, is the emergency you were yelling about? Wait, I was about to sit down for my first cup of coffee. Please, come join me."

Birdie dutifully followed the mayor inside. Johnny White pulled out a chair at the kitchen table for him and brought a cup and saucer. He poured coffee for both of them and took a seat across the table from Birdie.

"Now, then," the mayor said, "please start all over and explain to me what you're so fired up about this morning. Something about a psychic, you say?"

"Madam Rowena. And Nostradamus is her assistant. Madam Rowena is a famous psychic who knows the sheriff and she's here. Here in Cambria. And she's asking questions about Baby Angel, except she don't know her name of course. Johnny, I told her we cain't be sure she was abandoned. I said her mama could be around any day now looking for her—"

"Birdie, back up a minute. Where did you happen into this famous psychic?"

"She was out walking in the rain, just like I was. And, Johnny, she read my mind. I swear. And she's aiming to find Baby Angel. What're we gonna do, Johnny?"

Johnny White took a long drink of coffee. He put the coffee cup down and cradled it in both hands and stared at it for a long time. He said, "Birdie, I'm not sure what we're going to do. I have to think about this for a while. Where's the baby right now?"

"She's over at Jake and Carrie Garner's house. They was planning to keep her all day and again tonight."

"Where's she supposed to go next?"

"It's right on your list, Johnny. She's supposed to go to Charlie and Marylee's."

Johnny White stared at his coffee cup again. "I'll tell you what, Birdie," he said, "come around and see me at Town Hall in a couple of hours. Can you do that? I need some time to think about this."

"Yes, sir, Johnny. I'll be there."

Birdie went back out, into the rain. He pulled his hat down hard on his head. As he walked away from the mayor's house, he hardly noticed where he was going. He simply put one foot in front of the other, paying no attention to the puddles or little rivulets of water.

"They'll call that little angel Baby Jane Doe," he muttered to himself. "They will. I know it. They'll call her Baby Jane Doe."

He trudged down the slope, away from the hill section of Cambria where the mayor lived and toward the Canepatch and the river. A snow-white cat, paying no attention to the rain, ran and caught up to him from behind, then walked contentedly at his side. Birdie didn't see it. His spirits were low and he was full of doubts. Johnny White's plan for saving Baby Angel suddenly struck him as a huge failure, a scheme riddled with pitfalls even with Birdie running the show.

Madam Rowena was going to find Baby Angel. Nostradamus would lead her right to the child, Birdie had no doubt of that. And she'd give the child to the sheriff, and the sheriff would turn her over to the child welfare folks.

"They'll call her Baby Jane Doe," Birdie murmured to himself one more time. His eyes abruptly brimmed with tears.

The cat drew closer. She rubbed against Birdie's legs, as if she wanted to help lift his gloom. Birdie became aware of the animal for the first time. He stooped and stroked her silky white fur. "Pretty kitty," he said. He studied the cat closely. "Are you sure you belong here, pretty kitty? I thought I knew all the animals in Cambria, but you don't look familiar."

The cat purred and nuzzled Birdie's hand.

Birdie was struck by sudden inspiration. "Look here, pretty kitty," he said, "why don't we just say you're *my* assistant? I'll bet the two of us together can figure out a way to stop that psychic and her Nostradamus. What do you say, girl?"

The snow-white cat meowed twice and wrapped her tail around his leg. Birdie would say later that he actually had seen joy in the animal's eyes.

"Come on, then," Birdie said. "Let's go find them."

It didn't take long. Madam Rowena and Nostradamus still were on the same street where Birdie had met them earlier. This time they were walking in the opposite direction. Madam Rowena was holding her hands to the sides of her head, her elbows down on her chest. She intermittently walked a few steps, then stopped and closed her eyes, then walked ahead again. Nostradamus trotted beside her as she walked, then sat, then trotted beside her again. They repeated this ritual several times while Birdie approached from a distance.

Madam Rowena barely looked up. But she waved a hand dismissively as Birdie and the cat drew near.

"I've no time for you now, Mr. Wilson," she said brusquely. "I'm picking up vibrations from all sides. A few minutes more and Nostradamus will point me in the right direction."

Nostradamus eyed the cat menacingly. The cat arched her back. Nostradamus jerked loose from Madam Rowena and made a dash for the cat. Madam Rowena gave chase. The cat raced across the open area between the Canepatch and the river, toward the floodwaters. Madam Rowena, although she moved much faster than Birdie would have expected of a woman of her heft, couldn't keep up.

The snow-white cat stopped and waited until Nostradamus was almost upon her, then bolted ahead. Nostradamus was beside himself, having come so close. The chase was truly frantic.

At the water's edge, the cat made an abrupt right-angle turn that caught her pursuer off guard. Nostradamus could not turn fast enough and could not stop. He went into the muddy floodwaters of the Ohio River with a mighty splash. He was underwater for what seemed a dangerous length of time, then rose to the surface, paddling frantically. Still headed away from land, he swam in a circle and found a fallen log that lay with one end on solid ground and the other submerged in the water.

The little poodle pulled himself up onto the log and crouched, wet and shivering. It was clear that he wanted to come back to land but was afraid to attempt a walk on the slippery tree trunk. He began to wail mournfully. The water rushed around him in powerful swirls.

Madame Rowena arrived at the scene, flushed and panting. At the sight of Nostradamus clinging precariously to the wet log, she clapped her hands to the sides of her head and pleaded for Birdie. "Please, please help me," she beseeched him.

Birdie walked to where the psychic stood, bent over and breathless, her hands on her knees. "Ma'am, I'd be pleased to do what I can," he said.

"Can you catch my dog?"

"Why, I expect so. I sure will try if you want me to. Dogs and me get along pretty good."

Nostradamus, meanwhile, still crouched fretfully at the far end of the log, barely out of the water. Birdie approached the poodle with soothing words. He held out his hands in a way that showed friendship. The dog ceased its loud cries and grew still.

"Please be careful, sir," Madam Rowena called. "He's not easy with strangers."

"Well now, I'm not a stranger," Birdie said to the dog, still speaking quietly. "I think the two of us could be real good friends, don't you say so, boy?"

Nostradamus smiled his poodle smile. As Birdie reached the dry end of the log, the little dog moved forward ever so slightly and, gaining courage, stood and wagged his tail as if he'd never been afraid. He ran to meet Birdie and jumped straight into his extended arms and stretched up to lick his face.

Madam Rowena gasped in disbelief. Birdie turned to meet her and set the little dog down on the ground. She got down on her knees and hugged the animal tightly, cried into its fur, and called it loving names. When she finally stood, she addressed Birdie in a tone very different from that she'd used with him before.

"Mr. Wilson," the psychic said, "I'm grateful to you for saving my dog. You are a good man, sir. Is there any way I can repay your kindness?"

"Yes, ma'am, there is," Birdie said firmly, his self-confidence restored. "You can leave us be. Cambrians are doing what they think is best for that child you want to find. You can be sure we'll take good care of her. I promise you that she's better off here than she would be in the hands of the child welfare folks."

Madam Rowena smiled, for the first time since Birdie had met her in the street earlier. "I'll be on my way now," she said. "Come, Nostradamus, we've seen all of this horrid place we're ever going to see. Good day to you, Mr. Wilson."

She turned and, with Nostradamus trotting out front, walked away briskly, toward the hill side of town.

Birdie looked about for the snow-white cat, feeling that he owed her a momentous debt of gratitude. It was the cat, after all, that had saved the day.

The cat had disappeared.

❧17❧

It had become obvious to Lynn Swafford that Sheriff Higgins was growing more frustrated every day. The long drive to Cambria only to serve one warrant and look around one house took too much of his time. But Deputy Swafford also knew that the sheriff was determined to find the abandoned child. And only yesterday, Judge Gilbert had renewed his pledge to issue a blanket warrant if the sheriff could produce evidence of an unexplained child in three different Cambrian homes. So far, outside of Molly Hearst's place, there had been no such evidence.

The sheriff tended to lean on Lynn for support during the Cambria trips. Lynn knew his way around the town better than Sheriff Higgins did and, besides, the sheriff seemed to enjoy his company. That cut both ways. The sheriff had a million stories about the days when Lynn's father was his boss and always gave credit to Sheriff Swafford for teaching him all he knew about law enforcement.

The rain finally had stopped—temporarily, as they would learn later—and the sun was shining. Except for the flooding it would be an excellent day for fishing.

The sheriff was in the middle of one of his favorite fishing stories. "Your daddy was a strong man," he was saying, "but even he couldn't land that one by hisself." He laughed from deep in his belly. "That one" referred to a one-hundred-pound catfish Lynn's father had caught while fishing on the Ohio River.

"I reckon the Ohio was even more of a sewer back then than it is now," he went on. "Most people thought nothing at all about eating bottom-feeding catfish, though. We ate just about everything we caught. Except the garfish and gizzard shad. They're all bones."

Lynn nodded agreement. "Yes, they are. And Dad said a lot of people considered the carp and buffalo undesirable," he said. "We always ate them, though. Mom would bake them and they tasted fine to me."

"Depends on where you're from," Sheriff Higgins said. "You grow up on the river, you eat a lot of river fish. Simple as that."

Lynn Swafford nodded again, happy to keep the talk on fishing. He said, "You're right about the river, though. It's a lot cleaner now."

The sheriff cleared his throat loudly. Lynn steeled himself. This was a warning that the sheriff was about to change the subject, and most likely to a less pleasant one. "Lynn," the sheriff said, "would you tell me the dad-gummed truth about your take on this search we're doing? Is there any chance at all we're going to find that abandoned child the way we're going about it?"

The deputy still harbored faint hopes of dissuading the sheriff from his determined Cambrian mission. But he needed to be careful what he said. He should make it sound like what he offered simply was his best professional opinion. He was cautious in his answer.

"Well, sheriff," he said, "to tell you the truth it doesn't look too promising to me. They'll keep moving her around, and nobody's talking. Lots of dead ends, seems like."

"You got any good ideas?"

A wider opening. Lynn Swafford threw caution to the wind and gave it his best shot: "Sheriff, I have to be honest with you. I think it may be a waste of time. As far as we know, that child is being taken care of very well and we still have no real evidence of child abandonment. Are you sure there is a crime here?"

"Damn it, Lynn. You know how I feel about babies. Anybody who has one ought to be held responsible for it."

Lynn Swafford tried to back-peddle. Given the sheriff's strong feelings, he'd better not overplay his hand. "Well, I don't disagree with you on that," he said. "If somebody abandoned a child I want to get my hands on them as much as you do."

"Then how'n hell do you plan to do it? If we can't find the child, how are we going to catch whoever's responsible?"

"Sheriff, I don't have an answer for that."

"Well, anyway, we're here," the sheriff said. Lynn thought he detected a hint of relief in his boss's voice. "Do you know where the Zielinski place is at?"

Lynn knew. He gave the sheriff directions and they were at the door in no time. Margie answered the sheriff's knock and invited them inside. She said Larry was at work. She was alone in the house. Sheriff Higgins politely asked permission to look around, without even mentioning the warrant he'd left in his SUV.

"You're welcome to look anywhere you like," Margie said.

While Sheriff Higgins peered about in the two small bedrooms, Lynn opened the door to the hall closet, barely glanced inside, then went to the kitchen. Margie had set three places at the table and was pouring coffee.

"Why did you choose us?" she said quietly.

"Mrs. Zielinski, I have no idea," Lynn told her. "The sheriff goes to the judge and gets a warrant to search somebody's house. He's never told me how he chooses whose house he gets the warrant for."

"Sure seems like a silly waste of time, to say nothing of invading our privacy."

As a duly sworn deputy, Lynn said, he shouldn't comment. But he tried to show by his manner that he sympathized with her position. He thought she was getting the message, but could not be sure.

After a few minutes, Sheriff Higgins joined them in the kitchen. He promptly accepted Margie's invitation to stay for coffee and took a chair opposite her. From all appearances, the irony of accepting her hospitality after searching her house never occurred to the sheriff. Lynn sat at the end of the table.

The topic of an abandoned child never came up.

They left the Zielinski house and drove to Town Hall, where the sheriff went in to see Johnny White. Lynn had not expected this. Would the sheriff approach the mayor as if it was a friendly social call, or would he put on his "lawman's face," as he liked to say, and make this an official visit?

It didn't take long to find out.

"Johnny," the sheriff said, "I think it's time we settle something." Lawman's face.

Johnny White got up from the table where he had been working and extended his hand. "Nice to see you, Sheriff Higgins," he said. "You, too, Deputy Swafford. Now what can I do for you, sheriff?"

Sheriff Higgins: "You know damned well what you can do for me. You can tell me where you're hiding that abandoned child. We're going to find her anyway, one way or another. You sure could make it easier on yourself and everybody else if you'd just turn the child over to us without any more of this foolishness."

The mayor still wore his welcoming smile. "Now, sheriff," he said, "I think we've had this conversation before. Where on earth would I hide a child?"

"You're moving her around, that's where you're hiding her. We know what's going on and, like I said, we're going to find her. If I have to I'll bring every deputy I have in here and have the whole town staked out around the clock."

"Well, sheriff, you know that you and your men are always welcome in Cambria. It'd be a bit of a change, though, seeing that much law enforcement in town. Seems like we're usually not on your radar."

Lynn Swafford almost laughed aloud at the mayor's clever dig, but managed to hold it in. He had no desire to incur his boss's wrath. Standing behind Sheriff Higgins, though, he did manage a smile which he felt sure Johnny White saw and appreciated. He was pretty sure that Johnny already understood that the two of them were on the same side. But then he felt the familiar pang of guilt that had haunted him since he'd made his choice on this abandoned child thing because of Molly.

The sheriff and the mayor kept on with their give-and-take, neither scoring a clear advantage. But Lynn paid little attention. He was thinking about Molly.

The other two men somehow managed to remain civil. The next thing Lynn knew, they were sitting down for coffee together. He never ceased to be amazed at the sheriff's talent for accommodating those with whom he had big differences. He supposed it went with being a politician. And that gave him an idea.

At the first lull in the conversation, Lynn got in his opening shot: "By the way, Mayor White, the sheriff and I were talking the other day about the election coming up in the fall and how Cambrians are such loyal voters. You're pretty successful at winning elections. I was wondering what kind of advice you might have about campaigning in Cambria."

Johnny White looked startled for an instant, but Lynn winked slyly and Johnny caught on. "Yes, I usually manage to turn out my vote pretty well," he said. "I expect we could drum up some support for the sheriff. Maybe organize some kind of fall festival. People in Cambria go for that kind of thing. Maybe we could make the sheriff an honorary marshal."

If Sheriff Higgins had an inkling of Lynn's ploy, he did not show it. He expected a hard race for re-election. The mere mention of a fall campaign usually got him started.

"That could be a right good boost, Johnny," the sheriff said. "Lynn tells me you folks in Cambria get pretty good election turnouts. It ain't too big, but Cambria could make the difference in a county-wide race."

Johnny White showed that he was all set to play Lynn Swafford's game. With enthusiasm.

"Law enforcement's a pretty big issue around here," the mayor said. "It wouldn't take much to stir up voters about the sheriff's race. Wouldn't you agree, Lynn?"

Lynn Swafford said, "Yes, sir, from what I've seen that's certainly true."

Sheriff Clarence Higgins appeared to have forgotten the cause that brought them to City Hall to begin with. Any animosity he might have felt toward Johnny White clearly had fallen by the wayside. He was ready to join forces with the mayor. The goal was limited to the sheriff's re-election in the fall, of course, but the two politicians had just found common ground.

Deputy Lynn Swafford felt a great wave of satisfaction.

Now there was more political talk to engage in. Events to plan. Whatever else might have been on Sheriff Higgins's plate was laid aside to make room for his election to another term as the county's chief lawman.

Except for one little item. And after some half-hour of discussion, Johnny White deftly worked it into their conversation.

"I do see one potential problem, sheriff," Johnny said. "Some folks in Cambria will have to be placated a bit, some that have a grudge against you over this search you've got going on. I expect you'd need to get that wrapped up pretty soon now to have time for us to bring them around."

Sheriff Higgins stiffened. "No need to re-hash what I've already said on that," he snorted. "Come on, Lynn. We need to get back to work."

The sheriff stalked out of Town Hall and Lynn Swafford quickly followed. Outside, they found the old Ford Explorer sitting with its front bumper firmly against a small sycamore tree. The sheriff had forgotten to set the brake again. No damage done, but his failing seemed to add to the sheriff's surliness.

Lynn tried to make light of the situation but promptly saw that his joke was not appreciated. His boss was in no mood for silliness.

They drove by Molly's house on their way out of town, and Lynn Swafford's heart beat faster at the sight. He wanted to call for the sheriff to stop. He wanted to run into the house and find Molly. He wanted to taste her warm kisses. He wanted . . .

Sheriff Higgins might very well have been reading his mind. "That's Miss Molly's place if I remember right," the sheriff said. "She strikes me as a right good woman, Lynn. If I were you I'd latch onto her. Women like that are hard to find."

Lynn swallowed hard. There was nothing he'd rather talk about than Molly. But could he share his feelings about her with the sheriff and not give away his disloyalty? It was a risk he was reluctant to take. Play it down, Lynn, he said to himself. *Play it down*. He answered with an innocuous, "Yes, she does seem to be a nice woman."

Sheriff Higgins would not be dissuaded.

"Lynn," the sheriff said, "you need a woman like Miss Molly. The boys are gone now, and living alone's not much fun. Miss Molly is going to be alone too, pretty soon. Son, let me give you some fatherly advice. Show that woman your best side and let nature take its course. You might just end up making two people a lot happier in their old age."

Lynn Swafford let himself go. He put a hand on his boss's arm and said, "Sheriff, there's nobody I'd rather have fatherly advice from than you. That sounds like real good advice, too. I think I'll take it."

"If the time ever comes that I can put in a good word for you, be sure and let me know. Will you do that?"

"You bet I will. An over-the-hill guy like me needs all the help he can get."

Lynn couldn't see the sheriff's face, but he could hear the smile in the older man's voice. And what he'd just said was true. He often thought of Sheriff Clarence Higgins as a substitute for his father, who'd died of a heart attack when Lynn was a teenager. Every man, he supposed, needed a father—no matter what his age.

"You know, Lynn, giving in to Johnny White and calling off this search for the abandoned child probably would make Miss Molly happy too, wouldn't you think?"

"Yes, I expect it would."

Lynn Swafford held his breath. Could the sheriff possibly be thinking of giving up the hunt? He would love to be able to go to Molly and tell her there was nothing to fear, that Baby Angel could be hers and nobody would come and take the child away.

The sheriff was agonizingly slow to speak again. When he did, it was as if he hated to say what he had to say: "Well, son, I wish I could do it. I truly do. But it's my job to enforce the law, and it seems to me like we pretty much have to have that abandoned child before we can make much progress at finding them that abandoned her. And anyway, that child needs to be in the hands of the child welfare people. Yessir, I truly believe she does."

❧18❧

Among the dozen or so houses scattered about the Canepatch section of town, that of Pudge and Elaine Gaither and their three kids was closest to the river. A thicket of mature bamboo, with culms weathered to a golden tan, stood close to the back of the Gaither house and circled up along one side to join with a smaller patch in front. Pudge maintained a clean-cut path down to the water's edge for easy access to the shallow little rowboat he kept chained to a stout willow tree.

Pudge was clearing cane with a machete. He was intent on his work, shirtless and sweaty, his huge belly hanging over his belt and his tattooed right arm swinging the wide blade rhythmically in his vigorous attack on the tender young shoots of new growth.

The path to the water's edge was short. The swollen river had reached a stage that brought the flood to within a hundred feet or so of the Gaither house. Pudge expected to finish his task quickly.

What he did not expect was a visitor.

Birdie Wilson stopped at a safe distance. You don't startle a man with a machete in his hand. Not even a friend.

"Looks like you got a pretty big job there," Birdie said loudly.

Pudge turned slowly. When he saw that it was Birdie, a big grin spread across his face. "My favorite neighbor!" he declared. "I've not seen you around in a while."

Birdie walked nearer. "Guess I've had too much to do," he said. "Looks like you got some hard work for a man on his day off."

"I've not been working much lately."

"Looks like the water's gettin' pretty close. How you folks gettin' on, Pudge?"

151

"We're doing okay. Edna and the boys well?"

"The boys are unhappy over the high water. Cain't do any fishing. But they'll get over it."

"Don't have much choice, do they?" Pudge agreed.

"You're right about that."

"I expect you didn't come down here without a reason, Birdie. What's on your mind this morning?"

Birdie put a hand over his mouth and coughed, then spit on the ground. "Pudge," he said, "I've always admired this place of yours. You're right on the river bank, almost. And you got this big cane thicket here. You can get down to your boat real fast if you want to, without hardly anybody even seeing you."

"Well, I suppose I could if I needed to," Pudge said. "You come by just to tell me that?"

Birdie cleared his throat and spit again. He squinted into the slanting rays of the morning sun, trying to get a fix on Pudge's eyes. "You know about that baby my boys and me found on the river, don't you Pudge?" he said finally. "You know there's lots of folks in town think we ought to keep her right here in Cambria."

"I've heard talk about it."

"See, nobody wants them child welfare people to get their hands on her. They'd call her Baby Jane Doe."

"I've heard talk about that, too. So what's your point, Birdie?"

"Pudge, I've been thinking about this a lot. I talked it over with Sam Gowdy and Jake Garner and a couple of other fellows. What if the law got too close to that little tyke some day and we needed to make some kind of escape? You follow my drift?"

"You ain't makin' a lot of sense, Birdie." Pudge obviously was growing impatient.

Birdie cleared his throat one more time. Louder. And took longer. And even then hesitated a bit before speaking again: "The point is we could sneak her out right here, Pudge. Carry her down to the river, right through this canebrake here, get her in your boat there and paddle off without ever bein' seen. Wouldn't you think so?"

Pudge Gaither pulled a dirty red bandana handkerchief from his pocket and mopped at the sweat under his chin. "Well, yeah," he said. "If it ever come to that. You really think it might?"

Birdie nodded vigorously. "Sheriff's been putting in a lot of time on it," he said. "Sam and me just figured that one of these days he might get too close. Once he finds that baby, it's all over. She'd be taken to the child welfare people and they'd call her—"

"I know, Birdie. They'd call her Baby Jane Doe."

"That's it, Baby Jane Doe. And that wouldn't be right."

"So what is it you want me to do, Birdie?"

"We just need a plan, is all. So somebody can call you on short notice and you'd be ready to go."

"Call me?" Pudge expressed mild surprise. "I thought you knew, Birdy. I don't have a phone."

Now it was Birdie Wilson who pulled out a handkerchief and began to mop sweat. He looked perplexed for a moment, but regained his composure quickly. "Well, then," he told Pudge, "we'll just have to set up some kind of signal, don't you think?"

"But look here, Birdie. I don't know's I would need any advance notice. If I'm home and somebody runs up to the house with that little baby and says we need to get her out of here, why then we'll just jump in my boat and go. Ain't that all we're talking about here?"

"Yeah, that's about it. But what if you're not home?"

"Then Elaine would do it," Pudge said. "She can row as fast as I can. And she would be real happy to help save a baby."

"Still seems like some kind of signal would help, though."

"But you wouldn't have no time to send a signal in a real emergency, anyway."

Birdie wasn't completely satisfied with that, but he couldn't think of any basis for arguing Pudge's position. He thanked Pudge for his willingness to be part of the Baby Angel rescue operation, complimented him on his skill with the machete, and promised to be in touch.

Pudge Gaither stood and scratched his head as he watched Birdie walk away. Then he picked up his machete and went back to work.

⮂

BIRDIE WILSON'S concern over the lack of any way to contact Pudge if a crisis arose kept him awake that night. He vowed to himself that, come morning, he'd discuss the problem with Sam Gowdy and Jake Garner, and maybe anybody else he found standing around Sam's bait shop. All Cambrians had a stake in this, after all. Everybody's opinion ought to count.

He got to Sam's shop just after sunrise. "What'n hell got you out so early, Birdie?" Sam grumbled as he unlocked the door. "Even the buzzards ain't awake yet."

"Sam," Birdie said, "I think we got a problem."

"I wouldn't say I'm in much of a mood for discussing problems this morning, but come on in. I got to have my coffee first, whatever. You probably could use some, too."

Birdie confessed that he could use a cup of coffee, but denied that he needed it to get his head straight the way Sam implied. Sam, in turn, denied implying any such thing and accused Birdie of being too up-tight. Birdie took offense at that. Both men raised their voices.

Alma came charging from the back of the shop, disturbed by the loud back-and-forth, and demanded that they control themselves. "You sound just like two little boys on their way to school," she scolded. "What's this all about?"

Sam, somewhat embarrassed, told his wife they simply were "making plans." Birdie backed him up.

Alma's rebuke had the desired effect and Sam and Birdie sheepishly settled down over cups of coffee. "You were saying there's a problem, eh?" Sam said. "What kind a problem?"

"Pudge Gaither don't have a phone."

Sam blew across the surface of his hot coffee, then took a long swallow. "I don't know that I follow you, Birdie," he said. "I figured everybody knew Pudge didn't have a phone. Lots of them down in the Canepatch don't."

"But remember how you and me and Jake Garner was talking about a fast escape if the sheriff got too close to Baby Angel? I figured Pudge would be a real good one to make it for us. He's got that cane thicket comes right up to his back door almost, and a path cut down to the river. He can get down to his boat without hardly being seen if he wants to."

"I remember. You talk to Pudge about it?"

Birdie said yes, he had talked to Pudge. He said Pudge was willing to be part of their plan, but volunteered that he didn't have a phone and wondered how they could get in touch with him in advance. Birdie said he didn't have an answer for that, and maybe Sam had some idea how they could signal Pudge if they needed to. Or maybe they didn't need to, like Pudge seemed to think.

Sam took the easy way out. Maybe Birdie ought to talk to Jake Garner, he said. Jake was a pretty good idea man. He might come up with the answer Birdie was looking for. Sure was worth a try.

"You won't get over to Jake's house in time to catch him before he leaves for work," Sam added. "But you could probably talk to him as soon as he gets home this afternoon."

Sam's scheme worked. Birdie agreed that Jake Garner ought to have a chance to offer his opinion, especially since Jake had been strong on the quick escape plan to begin with. Birdie left the bait shop whistling a jaunty tune. The worry that had brought him to see Sam Gowdy had been replaced with a high level of confidence that Jake Garner would offer a solution.

And Jake did. Sort of.

"What we need to do," Jake said, "is to test Pudge out on this. Do a dry run, so to speak."

Since Pudge maintained that he didn't need any advance warning, Jake suggested, they ought not let him know they were coming. Just show up in the middle of the night, maybe, and bang on his door and tell him they had the baby and needed to get her away real fast. This would clue them in pretty quick whether Pudge was as good as his word.

Birdie was highly pleased—but not surprised—by Jake Garner's proposal. Like Sam said, Jake was a good idea man. And Sam liked Jake's idea, too. He wanted to test Pudge right away.

Just after midnight the following night, the three men met at Sam's bait shop. Jake insisted that they blacken their faces with soot from a barrel Sam used for burning trash, like he had seen in the movies. Sam hauled a ten-pound sack of potatoes out of the back to be wrapped in a blanket and carried with them as a surrogate for Baby Angel.

They loaded into Birdie's old pickup and raced toward the Canepatch. Birdie turned off the headlights as they got close to the Gaither house. He was going too fast for driving in the dark and crashed into the edge of the cane thicket with a loud crackling of bamboo. Sam, sitting in the back of the truck with the faux Baby Angel, jumped out and ran to Pudge's front door and began to pound with his fist. Birdie and Jake Garner took a little longer, having to pick their way through the broken bamboo, but quickly landed at Sam's side.

After what seemed to the trio much too long—given that this was an emergency—lights came on in the house and Elaine Gaither called "Who's there?" from the other side of the closed door. Then something as threatening as a rumble of thunder, which turned out to be Pudge shouting from the back of the house.

"It's us with the baby, ma'am," Sam Gowdy replied. "We need to get her in Pudge's boat to save her from the sheriff."

"Who the hell are you, and what baby? Pudge, you get in here!"

More rumbling from the back, then they heard Pudge shuffling up behind Elaine. "Damn it, Birdie is that you?" he called through the door, "You really got that little baby with you?"

Sam started to answer, but deferred to Birdie.

"That's right, Pudge," Birdie said loudly. "We need to get her in your boat, like we talked about the other day."

They could hear more rumbling from Pudge. And Elaine, questioning whether her husband had any clue what he was getting into and did he know where he was going and how long he might be gone? Which brought more rumbling.

The door burst open and Pudge, clad in only a pair of thin white shorty pajamas and his boots, stumbled out. "Sheriff anywhere close?" he whispered hoarsely.

"We don't know," Jake Garner told him. "But this is no time to take chances. Get us down to your boat, Pudge, and we'll decide what to do from there."

156

Pudge led them around the side of the house to the pathway through the bamboo thicket. The only light came from a thin slice of moon and even that was filtered through the overhead branches of trees and the bamboo. When they got into the thicket it was black as pitch.

"Who's got the little one?" Pudge inquired, still whispering.

"Sam's packing her," Birdie said. "Damn, it's dark back here! Didn't you bring a flashlight, Pudge?"

"Batteries in mine been dead for a long time. But don't worry, the boat's right here."

As Pudge spoke, his boots began to splash in the edge of the floodwaters. He found the chain and pulled the boat up to where the other three men and make-believe Baby Angel hunkered in the darkness. "Let me climb in and get to the back," he said. "Then Sam and the baby. It might be kinda crowded if you other fellows come."

"That's okay," Birdie said. "Just as long as we get the baby away and safe. Jake, me and you will wait here till they get back."

"May be a while," Pudge said. "We gotta get this baby some-where safe. Sam, you know where to go?"

Pudge pushed away from the bank with one of the oars. "One of you undo that chain," he directed.

Sam, who had just parked himself on a plank seat in the boat and sat balancing the blanket-wrapped sack of potatoes on his lap, didn't answer Pudge's question. Their scheme to test Pudge's readiness had no end point. Did they need to let him row away from the bank and take the Baby Angel stand-in up or down the river a ways? And what then?

"Did you hear me, Sam?" Pudge insisted.

"I reckon we never thought that far ahead," Sam said. "Birdie, what do you think?"

Birdie hesitated. "Well," he said, "I hadn't thought much about from here on out either, Sam. Maybe we tested Pudge enough. He got us to the boat, just like he said. He sure could get you across the river or wherever. What do you think, Jake? Maybe we done enough for tonight?"

Before Jake could answer, Pudge roared from the back of the boat: "What the hell is going on here? Is this some kind of game or something? Sam, that baby's been awful quiet. I think maybe it's time I take a look at her. Here, hand her over!"

Pudge stood and leaned toward Sam. The shallow rowboat, meanwhile, had been caught in the strong current and pulled downstream as far as the chain would allow. Fortunately, the floodwaters were not deep at this point, for Pudge's lurching swamped the boat and in an instant the two men were in the water. Pudge bellowed an oath that could have been heard across the Ohio. Sam let go of the sack of potatoes.

Still on land, Birdie and Jake Garner stood helplessly.

Sam Gowdy and Pudge splashed toward shore, Pudge still swearing and Sam coughing and spitting up muddy water. Pudge groped for the chain and began to tug. He had no intention of losing his boat.

As soon as Sam joined Jake and Birdie on shore, they turned their backs on Pudge and slogged as fast as they could up the dark path through the canebrake. Pudge's shouted epithets went unheeded. They loaded into Birdie's pickup hastily, Sam in the front seat beside Birdie and Jake in the back. Birdie backed out of the canebrake and gunned the old Dodge and they roared away.

Jake tried to put the best twist he could think of on the night's adventure. "Probably a good thing it was only a dry run, so to speak," he said. "Otherwise we would have just lost that little baby we was trying to save."

❧19❧

Molly had overslept. Not surprising, because she'd been up very late with Baby Angel. Birdie Wilson had slipped the precious little one in through the back door shortly after dark and Molly had been so incredibly happy to have her back that she couldn't bring herself to leave the child and go to bed. Baby Angel had slept through the night without a whimper.

When she did wake, Molly jumped out of bed with a sense of urgency. The mere fact that Baby Angel was once again under her roof carried far more responsibility than simply taking care of the child. Under Johnny White's revised rules, Molly was supposed to check in regularly with either the mayor or his designated contact—currently Alma Gowdy. The designated contact rotated too, no one serving more than a day at a time.

Molly wasn't sure what "regularly" meant. She assumed she ought to call either Johnny White or Alma right away, though, and report that Baby Angel was in her care and everything was okay.

Molly was concerned about more than the mayor's new system. She wanted very much to keep Baby Angel another night instead of having her moved again with the fall of darkness. Lynn Swafford was coming and she wanted to be at home with both Lynn and the baby. She spent most of her time these days thinking about Lynn. It had been only three days since she saw him, but it might have been weeks.

She called Alma at the bait shop. "I know I'm supposed to report in or something," Molly said. "Baby Angel's here and everything is fine. Do you need to know anything else?"

Alma chuckled. "Isn't this the silliest thing, Molly? I kind of think maybe Johnny White's gone off the deep end."

"So you don't know why he set up this contact thing?"

"Just some idea that it would help keep everybody on their toes, I think. If there's more to it than that, he sure didn't tell me."

Molly thanked her and cut short the call. She didn't want to mention to Alma Gowdy that she hoped to keep Baby Angel for another night. Alma was nosey. She'd ask why. And Alma loved to gossip. Better to go ahead and call Johnny White.

This wasn't the way Molly had planned to spend the summer. Jay and Justine would be gone all too soon, and she'd looked forward to making the best of this time when they were out of school. But of course she hadn't expected either Baby Angel or Lynn Swafford to come into her life.

She felt guilty that she gave too much time to Lynn and the baby—time that she could have devoted to her children. She found consolation, though, in the fact that Jay and Justine appeared to love Baby Angel almost as much as she did. And just as important, they obviously liked Lynn and enjoyed his company.

As much as she cherished Lynn Swafford, it was Baby Angel who had changed Molly's outlook on life. This child had brought her joy beyond anything she could have imagined. She'd tried to rationalize early on that it was merely the excitement of Cambria's game of cat and mouse with the sheriff which had brightened her days. But then she would see Baby Angel again, and hold her in her arms and sing her to sleep, and any doubt that it was this beautiful and innocent little girl who brought light where there had been darkness quickly vanished.

The Cambrian Project, as some townspeople had begun to call their fight to save Baby Angel, was beginning to take its toll on Molly. She lived in fear that Sheriff Higgins would find the child. Or that someone would call in higher authorities. Or . . . whatever new apprehension crossed her mind. The constant anxiety led to frequent nightmares about having the baby snatched away.

But for this day at least, Baby Angel would be hers. And again tonight, if she could pull it off.

Molly called Town Hall. When Mayor Johnny White answered

she went straight to the point: Could she please keep Baby Angel for another night? She was somewhat surprised when the mayor promptly gave permission. Shuffling the schedule a bit shouldn't inconvenience anyone, he said, and he'd let the appropriate people know.

Hearing her mother on the phone, Justine stood by to make sure that everything was all right. Her face brightened at the news. "I'm glad, Mom," Justine said. "I wish it was like in the beginning, when we had her all the time."

Molly had been thinking the same thing. "I didn't want to push my luck with Johnny, though," she told Justine.

Justine made a face at the mention of Johnny White's name. She said, "He wants to keep playing that silly game, Mom. He acts like he thinks he's a big hero."

"Well, he has done what was necessary to keep this little one in Cambria."

"Oh, sure. Poor old Birdie's done all the work."

Molly couldn't disagree with that. But she was grateful to the mayor for the support he'd given her and all the other Cambrians who were determined to keep Baby Angel out of the hands of the child welfare people. Although she did not go to Father Jacob's church, she'd heard plenty of discussion of his stories about the horrors of the child welfare system—children shuffled from foster home to foster home, never in the hands of truly caring adults.

The irony of what Cambrians were doing with Baby Angel—shuffling her from home to home—was not lost on Molly. But this was a temporary situation. She was confident that one day soon the child would be permanently committed to her loving care. Just what might bring this about, Molly hadn't stopped to consider.

Justine was occupied with the baby, pretending to check her diaper or adjust her sleeper or whatnot. It was clear to Molly that this was a ruse. Justine wanted to hold the little one and any excuse would do. And Jay, who'd just come into the room, hurried over and gave Baby Angel a kiss on the forehead, then insisted that it was his turn to hold her. Molly cautioned the two against beginning an argument.

"Mom, is Lynn coming tonight?" Jay asked.

Molly said yes, and the children exchanged knowing glances.

Justine: "Are his boys home yet?"

"I don't know," Molly said. "I guess we'll find out tonight."

"Mom, are you serious about Lynn?"

"I like Lynn very much, Justine."

"Just so you know, Mom, we like him too. Right, Jay?"

Jay said, "Sure, Mom. Lynn's a cool guy."

"I'm glad you approve," Molly said. "But let's don't get too far ahead of ourselves here. And Jay, put Baby Angel down now. She's been up long enough."

Jay did as he was told, taking his time about it. He gently placed the baby back in her basket and sat down on the floor next to it. It was as if he wanted her no farther away than arm's length. Justine sat down on the other side of the basket and the two of them fixed on Baby Angel like they were on guard.

Molly left the baby in the care of the children and set about cleaning house. She wanted to stay busy. Busy made time pass faster. Time passing faster would mean Lynn Swafford would be there sooner. Or so it would seem. And the sooner Lynn got there, the better. Molly couldn't wait.

She didn't really expect Lynn to be on time. He usually was late getting out of the sheriff's department—always more paperwork to do, he said. But this time he was early. Molly had barely started dinner. He offered to help, and after she said there was nothing much he could do he sat at the kitchen table and watched her work. At one time this would have made her nervous. Now, she was relaxed in his presence. Lynn looked very much at home sitting in her small kitchen.

"Morgan and Patrick made it home yesterday," Lynn announced. "They're looking forward to meeting you and the kids."

"Same with us. Justine was asking about them a while ago."

"Molly, is it all right if I hold the baby?"

Molly's heart skipped a beat. Nothing would please her more than to have Lynn Swafford come to adore Baby Angel the way she and the children did. She knew he liked the baby—he'd said so any number of times—but she wanted him to love the child the way she did. And if you got close to this baby you came to love her in little more than the time it took to notice the sparkle in her eyes. Of that she was certain.

Baby Angel was sound asleep in her crib. Had it been anyone other than Lynn, Molly never would have disturbed her. But she wanted to see Lynn with the baby in his arms. This child's magic would take over from there.

And it did.

Baby Angel looked into Lynn Swafford's eyes and smiled. In that single instant he knew that he wanted this child to be in his life, and he wanted to be in hers. Forever.

"Molly," Lynn said, "whatever it takes, we have to save this baby. For us."

Molly walked across the room and Kissed him. Baby Angel smiled all the more brightly. As they stood there, in the middle of the room, it was as if the three of them belonged together. Lynn and Molly felt it, although neither would have been able to put what they felt into words.

"I love you, Molly Hearst," Lynn said. "Will you marry me?"

"I love you, too, Lynn Swafford. Yes—I'll marry you in a heartbeat."

From the kitchen came a loud outburst of applause and cheering. "Way to go, Mom," shouted Justine. And Jay: "Lynn is going to be our dad! We love you, too, Lynn!"

Baby Angel cooed. And gurgled. And laughed. And waved her arms.

❧

WHEN LYNN SWAFFORD reported for work the next day, his step was quicker and his face was lit with a broad smile. Deputy Harlan Gidcomb recognized immediately that something big had happened and demanded the full story. Lynn told him. Deputy Gidcomb told Sheriff Clarence Higgins. The sheriff passed the word on to the other deputies. They told the secretary and the dispatcher. Within hardly any time at all, good feelings prevailed all through the entire sheriff's department.

Sheriff Higgins, in a celebratory mood, decided not to bother Judge Chester Gilbert for a warrant. On this day, Cambria would be spared a search for the abandoned child.

Lynn was surprised by the sheriff's decision. And happy to hear it. He had been dreading another fruitless search of some innocent Cambrian's house. But there was a greater dread—the one that had kept him awake for much of the night: Sooner or later there would come a search that was not fruitless. Sheriff Higgins would find Baby Angel. She would be taken from them. This would break Molly's heart and, now, his as well.

As the well-wishing subsided, the sheriff put a hand on Lynn's shoulder and said, "Look here, Lynn, I've been thinking. Ordinarily we'd be in Cambria this afternoon, you know, only today we won't have a warrant. So what I'd like to do is go on over there this morning and drop in on Miss Molly. I want to personally give her my best and welcome her to the family. You see any problem with that?"

"No problem. She'll be at work."

"At the Fish and Fries? We'll stop by there, then. It's been a while since I had a good fish dinner."

Lynn swallowed hard. The prospect of Sheriff Higgins dropping by to see Molly, even at the Fish and Fries Café, scared him. Too many ways innocuous plans could go wrong. He needed to let Molly know.

"Let's hit the road, Lynn," the sheriff said. And to Deputy Gidcomb: "We'll likely be gone a good part of the day. I want you to stay here and handle any emergencies, and send the other boys out with their radar guns. We've still got a problem on some of them county highways."

Deputy Gidcomb responded as if he'd just received a promotion—or pay raise. Yes, sir, he'd take care of things and the sheriff needn't worry. Make the best of Lynn's good news and visit in Cambria as long as he wanted. Give Miss Molly all the deputies' best while he was at it. Yes, sir, this was a big day in the sheriff's department and it was very considerate of Sheriff Higgins to take this little trip and welcome Miss Molly into the family—

164

The sheriff turned and walked out while Deputy Gidcomb was still talking. Lynn followed close behind.

Lynn Swafford's mind was spinning. How could he tip off Molly? Half-formed ideas tumbled and twisted. Nothing workable. No way to stall Sheriff Higgins and make a surreptitious phone call. He felt a touch of nausea in the pit of his stomach. Cold sweat breaking out on the palms of his hands.

Sheriff Higgins climbed into the old Explorer with the gaudy star and "County Sheriff" label painted on the doors. Lynn got in beside him.

"I'll be getting the new car pretty soon now," the sheriff said. "I kind of hate to see this old buggy go, in a way. You know what I mean?"

"Sure. I know what you mean."

"Our whole fleet's getting way too old, but with the county's money as tight as it is I wouldn't dare ask for any more replacements. Your car still seem to be okay?"

"My cruiser?"

"Hell yes. Your cruiser. I don't have to worry about your personal car."

"Sorry, sheriff. My head's a little fuzzy this morning."

"Having a woman say she'll marry you does that to a man, Lynn. Your life will never be the same."

The seriousness of the sheriff's tone struck Lynn as very funny. He couldn't help but laugh. "I'm glad to hear that," he said. "My life's not too great the way it is."

"So how soon you expect to change it? Get married, I mean."

"That's up to Molly. I'd do it tomorrow if it was up to me."

"Want me to try to push her on it?" the sheriff asked.

"No way! You don't push women on things like that."

Sheriff Higgins echoed Lynn's laughter. This festive mood was rare for the sheriff when he was on the job. Rare in Lynn's experience, anyway. But law enforcement isn't a particularly fun kind of work, and the sheriff was an okay guy in the right circumstances. Like fishing on the Ohio River. None of which eased Lynn's mind. They'd be in Cambria soon. Molly should be at work, but if not . . .

"Your boys are home now, I guess," Sheriff Higgins said.

"Yes."

"They grow up too soon, don't they."

"You know, one day I think that and the next day I'm glad. When they can make it on their own, I worry less about something happening to me. Know what I mean?"

"Sure. I know what you mean."

The two men grew quiet. Lynn thought about Morgan and Patrick, and yes he missed the children they once were. Missed them terribly. But they had become fine young men, sound of mind and body. And character. Maybe character was most important. If he had taught them the right things and influenced their character, then maybe his own life had been more successful than he often imagined.

Might he have another chance? If Molly came complete with Baby Angel he would be the father of a daughter. So many things he didn't know about girls. But he knew about character. He would be richly blessed if he could help Molly bring up this little girl the way she should be brought up.

Lost in thought, Lynn was barely aware that they'd entered Cambria. But here they were, and any remote possibility he might have had to alert Molly to their coming had been lost. Sheriff Higgins parked in front of the Fish and Fries Café and got out without saying anything. Lynn followed him in.

A small slate mounted on a tripod just inside the door announced today's special, printed neatly in white chalk: *Catfish Dinner with fries and coleslaw, $4.50. Includes drink.*

Max Barnes and Jake Garner sat at a table in a corner of the little café drinking coffee. Charlie and Marylee Tipsworth were eating at another table. Tom Johnson welcomed them.

"We've come especially to see Miss Molly," the sheriff said. "She working today?"

Tom shook his head. "She was here," he said. "But we've not had much business today. I sent her home to be with her kids."

"I appreciate the information. We'll just head on over to her house, then."

166

Lynn saw his chance: "Didn't you say something about a fish dinner, sheriff? Today's special looks pretty good to me."

Sheriff Higgins looked over the chalkboard menu. He turned back to Tom Johnson. "Them catfish come from the Ohio River?" he queried.

Tom chuckled. "Not these days," he said. "They come from a catfish farm in Arkansas. And I can tell you they're mighty good."

Charlie Tipsworth raised a finger and motioned toward the sheriff. "I'll sure vouch for 'em," he said. "Today's dinner is about as good as I've had in a long time. Better get one while you can, sheriff."

As soon as Sheriff Higgins sat down for lunch, Lynn excused himself and hurried to the men's room in the back. He turned on his cell phone and nervously punched in Molly's number. He let the phone ring nine, ten, eleven times. There was no answer.

❧20❧

Pastor Mike found the rainy days invigorating. Rain was God-sent, after all, and was a most important element in keeping the world alive. He loved to walk in the rain, to breathe in the freshened air and admire the lush natural beauty he found all around. Cambria had more than its fair share of magnificent oak trees and the tall cottonwoods along the river stood like sentinels marking this vital lifeline of the community.

He had grown up on the Ohio, not far above Wheeling. He could hardly imagine ever being far removed from the river.

Still, the spring floods could bring misery. The water often rose as high as the edge of the Canepatch and this year it was getting perilously close to the Methodist church. Pastor Mike had called on his followers to be vigilant. They had worked for two days filling and placing sandbags so as to build a makeshift dyke around the church on the side toward the river. Today, the water was beginning to lap against this protective barrier.

Pastor Mike believed strongly in the power of prayer. He was reluctant, though, to ask God for too much. God had a purpose in all He did. It was difficult to see how letting the church be flooded would suit that purpose, but one did not question God.

The rains to the north had stopped. Surely the river would begin to recede in a short time and the church would be spared. But Pastor Mike had less faith in his ability to forecast the perfidy of the river than he had in the infinite power of the Almighty. This was one reason he fitted well among the Cambrians, who to the last man, woman, and child were steeped in the lore of the Ohio and respected its perils immensely.

On this day, Pastor Mike did not walk in the rain for pleasure. He was on a mission. He walked fast. He found Johnny White in Town Hall, as expected. It was perfectly logical to the pastor that, with the sheriff's searches slowed to a meager single home a day, the challenge of saving Baby Angel had come to look a bit less daunting to the mayor. Pastor Mike was less certain. It really was a simple matter of odds, he suggested to Johnny White. If they had twenty homes where Baby Angel might be at a given time and Sheriff Higgins was likely to show up at one of these, there was a one in twenty chance of the sheriff succeeding in his quest. The sheriff's success would be Cambria's failure—the loss of Baby Angel. How could they improve the odds, Pastor Mike wondered, if they had no advance warning of the sheriff's next move.

Johnny White was hard pressed to reassure the young minister. "I suppose you're not a gambler, being a man of God, but twenty to one odds are pretty good," the mayor said.

But nowhere near good enough, Pastor Mike argued. Not when the payout was saving Baby Angel. They must find some way to improve those odds. And Pastor Mike had an idea: They could move Baby Angel into the Methodist church, which no judge was likely to issue a search warrant for even if the sheriff happened to suspect what they were doing.

Johnny White: "I don't see how we could make a home out of the church."

"The church basement has everything we need," Pastor Mike told him. "We could make it a fully equipped nursery. Instead of taking the baby into their homes, the women—and men too, I guess—could take turns staying there and taking care of her."

The mayor was unconvinced. The phone tree he'd set up with the firemen was working well. And Birdie Wilson was a willing runner and reliable contact man. With activity on the river at a standstill, Birdie had nothing but free time on his hands. And he took immense pride in the fact that not only had he saved Baby Angel from the river, but he also had originated the campaign to protect her from the child welfare department. He was thoroughly in tune with Mayor Johnny White's plan.

"I'll tell you what, Pastor Mike," Johnny White said, "let me talk to a few people and see what they think. Surely we could wait a day or so before we make a decision like that."

"No problem, Johnny. Check it out with anyone you like. I'll get back to you, say tomorrow?"

"Sure. Tomorrow afternoon."

Pastor Mike walked back toward the church. Off to his right, the river churned with awesome force. The current clearly was strong and Pastor Mike wondered if it possibly could still be rising. The muddy water carried a remarkable variety of debris. Brush and logs and all manner of man-made trash were being swept rapidly downstream.

He thought about Baby Angel, floating on that flimsy raft in her tiny basket. The river that day had been less menacing, but powerful as always. It gave life and it took life. How miraculous that Birdie Wilson was fishing on that particular day, at that particular time, and at that particular place.

The sheriff's Ford Explorer was parked in front of the Fish and Fries Café. The mere sight of it reinforced Pastor Mike's concern. How long would they be able to keep Baby Angel out of the hands of the child welfare people?

He whispered a quick prayer, asking God to find things to occupy Sheriff Higgins's time—things other than searching for an abandoned child. Usual law enforcement duties, peculiar responsibilities, whatever. Pastor Mike wasn't particular.

At that moment, the sheriff and Deputy Lynn Swafford left the café and walked toward the sheriff's car. And at that moment the radio began to crackle. Pastor Mike could tell from the shrill voice demanding the sheriff's attention that there was an urgent cause. He stopped within hearing distance and listened intently.

"This is Deputy Gidcomb," the shrill voice proclaimed. "Are you there, sheriff?"

Sheriff Higgins grabbed the radio microphone on the dashboard and announced his presence. "What the hell are you so excited about, Gidcomb?" he asked.

It seemed as if Deputy Harlan Gidcomb's level of excitement

rose as he spoke: "You remember them paddlefish poachers the game warden's been after? They're out there right now, just up the river a piece from Cambria."

"On that high water? They'd have to be damned crazy. You sure about this, Gidcomb?"

"The game warden got a call," the deputy assured him. "Somebody seen 'em out there snagging paddlefish and stripping the roe right out into ice chests on their boat. The warden said roe's up to pretty near two-hundred dollars a pound now and them fancy New York City restaurants can't get enough of it."

Sheriff Higgins's voice also began to rise. Not with excitement, but with anger. "What the hell's he expect us to do about it, Gidcomb? We ain't got a boat over here, and if we did have they'd see us coming and cross to the other side of the river where we don't have any authority."

"The warden thinks they'll have to come down to the Cambria pier to land, the river being so high and all. He says if you just hide out and wait the poachers will likely climb out of their boat right into your hands. They'd have the evidence right on 'em, sheriff."

"Yeah, well, got to keep the warden happy. We'll see what we can do."

Sheriff Higgins replaced the mike and turned to Lynn Swafford. "I sup'ose we can still make that visit with Miss Molly after we get done with these poachers," he said. "Maybe this won't take us too long. We got to do it, though."

Even Pastor Mike, who knew nothing of the circumstances, could hear the tension in Lynn's voice. "I understand, sheriff," Lynn said. "We've got to do our job first. If we have to we can drop in on Molly another time."

Pastor Mike stood and watched as the sheriff's old Ford roared off toward Sam Gowdy's bait shop. Then he turned and rushed into the Fish and Fries Café.

"Is Molly working today, Tom?" Pastor Mike asked loudly of Tom Johnson, who was behind the counter. Tom looked up to see who was asking. He told the pastor the same thing he had told the sheriff an hour or so earlier.

"Then we've got to call her at home and tell her the sheriff's here," Pastor Mike said. "He got some kind of emergency call on his radio, but it may not take long and he plans to go to her house when he's done. We've got to make sure she doesn't have that baby."

Tom dropped whatever he was working on and picked up the telephone. Everyone in the café held their breath as he dialed, then stood waiting. "I don't know what to make of it, but she's not there," Tom reported after a minute or so. "What do you think we ought to do?"

Jake Garner pushed back from the table where he and Max Barnes were still sitting and talking, though they'd had their fill of coffee. "We'd better go out looking for her," he said. Max nodded in agreement.

"And you should call the mayor," Pastor Mike told Tom Johnson.

Tom got on the phone at once. He called Town Hall and caught Johnny White just as he was about to leave for lunch—at the Fish and Fries. Tom urged him to hurry, but didn't tell him why. When he hung up the phone, the others were eager for a report.

"What'd he say?" Max Barnes demanded.

"He's on his way over here now," Tom answered. "He was just leaving."

"But what about Molly?"

"I don't know, I didn't ask him about Molly."

"I thought that's what you called him for."

"It was. I just didn't get to it. He was leaving for here."

Max Barnes had no response to that. He sat back down, as Jake Garner already had. Max folded his arms across his chest and leaned back in his chair, as if readying himself for a long wait. Jake had his elbows on the table with his forearms upright so that his clasped hands were right under his chin. Both watched the door anxiously.

They hadn't long to wait. Johnny White burst through the door of the Fish and Fries like he was on his way to a fire. He spotted Pastor Mike at once and headed toward him. All the others, meanwhile, surged around the mayor expectantly. Tom Johnson came out from behind the counter and pressed close.

"What's going on, Tom?" Johnny White inquired.

"Molly's missing, and the sheriff's in town."

"What do you mean, Molly's missing?"

"I tried to call her and she didn't answer. We don't know where she is."

Jake Garner: "The sheriff's heading right over to Molly's house after he takes care of something. He'll find that baby there."

"So that's what this is all about," the mayor said. "You don't have to worry. Birdie Wilson picked up Justine and Baby Angel early this morning and took the little one to another house. The sheriff can look over there all he wants."

There was a collective sigh of relief.

Pastor Mike, relishing this opportunity to push his case, told those Cambrians gathered in the Fish and Fries about his proposal to hide Baby Angel in the Methodist church. "I've talked to the mayor about it," he assured them. "I'd like to know what some of the rest of you think about the idea."

"I would be more than glad to hear what Johnny thinks," said Max Barnes. "You think it's a good idea, mayor?"

"I think it may be, but I need some time to think it through," Johnny White said. "Anybody here got an opinion on it?"

"I guess it might work okay," said Max Barnes.

"Don't see why it wouldn't," said Jake Garner.

"Probably be okay," said Tom Johnson.

Pastor Mike turned to the mayor. There was no sign of smugness, but a level of satisfaction apparent when he said, "Seems to me that what we've just been through here today speaks to the need for a different way to go on this, Johnny. I don't want to push you on it, but if you decide it makes good sense, we might ought to get to work on it."

"I'll give it serious consideration," the mayor said.

❧

SHERIFF HIGGINS parked behind Sam Gowdy's bait shop. He figured the SUV, with its obvious sheriff's department markings, would be out of sight there. Lynn Swafford followed as the sheriff made his way down toward the pier, the end of which was now submerged in the floodwaters of the Ohio. The sheriff looked about for a hiding place, pointed to a stand of young cottonwood trees and walked in that direction. "I don't imagine we need a lot of cover for this one, Lynn," he said. "Just so long as we're not sticking out like a sore thumb. Them boys won't be expecting us."

"Have you ever been in on catching poachers before," Deputy Swafford asked.

"Oh, yeah. Couple of times, maybe, but not often. The game warden's not very well set to handle this sort of thing, but usually manages without us."

"You wouldn't expect poachers to be armed and dangerous, I suppose."

"You can't ever be too sure. With paddlefish roe up to a couple of hundred dollars a pound like Gidcomb said, there's some of them boys gonna take it pretty seriously. But look here, Lynn. We're gonna need some coffee if we have to be out here in the woods very long. Would you mind chugging back to the bait shop and getting us some? I expect I can handle these poachers well enough by myself if they happen to show before you get back."

Lynn Swafford agreed, trying not to show his enthusiasm. He wanted to get far enough away from Sheriff Higgins to try calling Molly again.

He went along side the bait shop and dug his cell phone from the pouch on his belt. He dialed Molly's number nervously. To his great relief, she answered promptly. He was even more relieved to hear that she no longer had Baby Angel.

"So what are you doing?" Lynn asked.

"The kids went off somewhere and I took advantage of being here by myself to take a long, hot shower. Just got out. When are you going to get by here?"

"Honey, I'm not sure. But as soon as I can. I gotta run. I love you."

"Love you too, Sweetheart."

Lynn picked up a quart of strong coffee from Sam Gowdy, in

two paper containers, and headed back to Sheriff Higgins's hiding place among the cottonwoods. The sheriff welcomed him as if he'd been gone for hours.

"I need that coffee, boy," Sheriff Higgins exclaimed. "It's too damned wet and nasty out here. I sure wish them poachers would show up soon."

The poachers did not show up soon. After two hours with no activity, the sheriff was ready to pull the plug on the whole operation. As far as he was concerned, he informed Lynn Swafford, he did not trust the word of some civilian anyway. There was always people who thought they'd seen something crooked going on and couldn't wait to make heroes out of theirselves and call the law.

"I'm gonna call the game warden and push him a little bit on this one," the sheriff said. "We might as well get on back to the car, Lynn. Seems to me we've been wasting our time out here way too damn long."

The sheriff put in his phone call, directly to the wildlife service, and asked for Warden Ron Oliphant. The warden came on the line immediately. "What's going on, Clarence?" he said pleasantly. "Seems like I've not talked to you in a while."

"Damn it, Ron—you know what's going on. Deputy Swaf-ford and me have been sitting out here in the bushes all afternoon waiting for those poachers you were so sure about. Looks to me like you got some bad information somewhere."

"Clarence, I don't have any idea what you're talking about. What poachers? This is the first I've heard about any poachers."

"I'm talking about the guys up river snagging paddlefish. What the hell other poachers would we be looking for?"

"I think maybe you're a little bit confused about something, sheriff. Nobody'd be snagging paddlefish with the river up like it is now. Least I never heard of it. I expect it'd be a big waste of time, knowing how paddlefish work."

Sheriff Higgins's face was beginning to redden. His voice began to rise. "Then why in hell did you call Deputy Gidcomb and request our assistance, Ron? What about that civilian you said had been watching the poachers in the act? I mean—"

"Sounds to me like maybe old Gidcomb was pulling your leg, Clarence. Nobody here would have called him. Anything else I can do for you?"

The sheriff slammed down his radio-phone angrily, without responding to Ron Oliphant's final question. Lynn Swafford said nothing, careful not to bring on any further wrath from his boss.

The sheriff took a deep breath and regained control. "I've got to get back to the office and see if I can talk any sense with Gidcomb," he said. "If you want to go ahead and visit Miss Molly, feel free."

"I'd sure like to," Lynn answered, "but I don't have any transportation. I'm riding with you today, remember?"

"Well git in then, and let's hit the road. We needed to be out there looking for that abandoned child, and wasted half the day waiting for poachers that didn't exist. But Gidcomb couldn't have imagined a call like that. Where in the world did it come from?"

❧21❧

Morgan Swafford and Justine hit it off well right from the get-go. Morgan was the younger of Lynn's two sons, barely a couple of years older than Justine and still very much down-to-earth in manner despite having finished a year of college. Unlike his brother Patrick, who had made having fun his sole purpose in life, Morgan was curious about the world around him and eager to learn new things.

As soon as he heard about the Cambrian Project, Morgan threw himself into it. Wholeheartedly. He adopted the Cambrians' point of view toward Baby Angel without reservation.

Letting a child—especially a little baby—fall into the hands of the child welfare people when there were others who wanted it and would love and care for it was, in Morgan's words, "an undesirable option." He never said what information he based this opinion on and nobody asked. Justine told her mother that Morgan's views on the subject were set in stone.

Molly suspected that Morgan had been influenced by his father, but that was, of course, mere speculation. It also occurred to her that the young man may have been swayed by Justine.

Justine, as a matter of fact, had become much more forceful in her support for keeping the baby hidden from authorities. This in spite of her disdain for Johnny White. She'd taken note of Sheriff Clarence Higgins and his almost daily visits to Cambria, and she had pretty much made up her mind that whatever side the sheriff was on was the wrong side. In true Justine fashion, this was based strictly on "instinct."

Her instinct also told Justine that Morgan Swafford was a good guy. She enjoyed his company and was constantly surprised by all the things he knew.

Morgan demonstrated a knack for seeing things logically that greatly impressed her. And never more so than when, early on, he spelled out what he saw as a sizeable flaw in the way Cambrians were handling the situation with Baby Angel: "Everyone seems to be so intent on keeping her hid away that nobody's looking for a real solution. The authorities are going to find her sooner or later, and what happens then? I don't think anybody's even talked to a lawyer."

Justine allowed that he was exactly right, and she hadn't heard anybody else state this shortsightedness so clearly. In fact, she had not heard anybody else state it at all. She praised his ability to see things others didn't see.

"You're a sharp guy, Morgan," she told him. "But seeing that there's a problem is not the same as thinking up a solution. Do you know what I mean?"

"Sure I do. And a solution is obviously what I'm interested in."

Morgan had a plan.

He told Justine, "The first time I'm able to borrow Dad's car for a day, I'm going up to Wheeling and get into the library and see what I can find out about abandoned child laws." And he added, almost shyly, "You can come along if you'd like."

"Yes, I want to."

She would not tell Morgan just yet, but there was a particular reason she wanted to go. Somewhere in the library in Wheeling she hoped to find the answer to her own urgent question: Where or what was the Magnolia? If she could find the right key, she felt sure that she could unlock the mystery surrounding the origin of Baby Angel.

"Can you be ready to go on short notice?" Morgan asked. "I mean, I may not know even a day in advance when I can get the car."

"Don't worry, I'll be ready. Just let me know."

Knowing that Morgan was going to look for a way to save Baby Angel brought a level of comfort to Justine that surprised her. Why should she have that kind of confidence in this young man she barely knew? Maybe wistful thinking, but there was something about him that made you think he could do anything he set his mind to.

Justine decided not to say too much to her mother. Ask permission to go with Morgan to Wheeling when the time came, and little more. The last thing she wanted to do was give her mom or anyone else false hope. But her own hopes were sky high.

MEANWHILE, the Cambrians' daily cat-and-mouse game with the law went on without respite. Johnny White, as promised, had taken seriously Pastor Mike's suggestion that they hide Baby Angel in the Methodist church. His first call was to Father Jacob. The old priest expressed his willingness to consider the plan, but raised an obvious concern. The floodwaters of the swelling Ohio already were lapping at the sandbags that protected the Methodist church. Much more of a rise and the church would be flooded. And of course the church basement would be the first affected.

"What I'm thinking, Johnny, is that we wouldn't want to have to move that baby and her little bed and all, maybe right out in the middle of the day," Father Jacob said. "If the water goes down, well then I guess I'd be okay with Pastor Mike's idea."

The mayor called Marilee Tipsworth next. Marylee was firmly wishy-washy on the topic, to the extent that Johnny White finally ended their conversation in a state of utter frustration. He hadn't a clue as to what Marilee really thought.

Gordon and Juanita Blessing were next on his list. Juanita answered his call.

"How are you folks getting on these days, Juanita?" Johnny White asked.

She told him they were well and inquired as to his own health. They continued with such pleasantries for a time, then the mayor got down to business: "What I was calling about, is a suggestion from Pastor Mike that Baby Angel be kept at the Methodist church. Most of those I've talked with so far don't seem to have a problem with it, but nobody has been real excited about it. I was wondering what you and Gordon might think. Any thoughts?"

"Johnny, you know I don't speak for Gordon," Juanita responded. "He'd probably have something to say on it, but I won't try to guess what. As far as I'm concerned, I guess it'd be okay."

"You see any negatives in it, Juanita?"

"None that jump out at me. I expect it would be good to get the poor little thing someplace where she wouldn't have to be moved around all the time. Don't you think?"

The mayor agreed that this was likely the most positive aspect of Pastor Mike's plan. If Gordon had any strong feelings one way or the other, he told Juanita, please ask him to call. "I'm open to everybody's opinion on this," Johnny White said.

No sooner had Mayor White hung up the phone than he heard someone banging through the front door of Town Hall. He looked up, right into the face of Sheriff Clarence Higgins. The sheriff wore a look of smug satisfaction Johnny White hadn't seen before.

"Morning, sheriff," the mayor said. "Always nice to see you. Anything I can do for you?"

"Damn well betcha," Sheriff Higgins gloated. "I've got a new warrant, Mr. Mayor. Seems like Judge Gilbert got a little tired of the games you folks been playing with that abandoned child. He issued a new warrant that says we can search any home in Cambria for evidence of that little baby. I just thought you might want to know what's going on."

Johnny White was at a loss for words. He opened his mouth to speak, but nothing came forth.

"Well, then," the sheriff said, "I suppose I may as well just go on about my business. I'm going to stop in at the Fish and Fries and have a cup of coffee and wait for a couple of deputies to get over here, and we're going to work. Have a good day, Mayor."

Johnny White took a minute to catch his breath. This was an ominous development. It was one thing to keep ahead of Sheriff Higgins when he came armed with a warrant to search one house at a time, but a much bigger challenge now that the sheriff could pop in anywhere in town at any time. This was a situation the mayor hadn't anticipated.

His first instinct was to contact Birdie Wilson. If they were on schedule, as spelled out by the mayor's "duty roster," the baby should be with Molly Hearst again today—Molly badgered him for possession every time she could get it. But Johnny White wasn't as close to the action as Birdie was, and needed confirmation. Where was Baby Angel at this very minute, and did Birdie have any idea what they ought to do now? Birdie, however, didn't answer his cell phone.

The mayor called Molly.

"Molly, do you have Baby Angel right now?" he asked nervously as soon as she answered. "We got a problem."

"Yes, I've got her," Molly said. "What's the problem, Johnny? Your voice is shaking"

"We've got to hide that baby, Molly. Sheriff Higgins has a new warrant that lets him search any and every house in town. He can go wherever he pleases. He could show up at your door at any minute. I don't know what to do, Molly."

"Johnny, let me call Lynn." She'd caught the mayor's panic, as if it were a communicable disease. "I'll get right back to you."

Molly got Deputy Lynn Swafford on the line immediately. She told him about Johnny White's call, desperately hoping he'd know what to do.

Lynn tried to be reassuring. "Molly, we can still beat this," he said. "There's nothing to keep him from rushing from one house to another and I don't know how you can stay ahead of him for very long. But I'm pretty sure that the sheriff's warrant only lets him into private homes. We have to hide that baby someplace his warrant doesn't cover."

Molly called the mayor. She'd begun to repeat Lynn Swafford's advice, but the mayor interrupted: "The Methodist church, Molly. Pastor Mike already suggested that we hide Baby Angel away in the church basement. The sheriff's warrant wouldn't let him in there. You're a lifesaver, Molly."

"You can credit Lynn, Johnny. I didn't know what to do."

The mayor called Pastor Mike and brought him up to date.

"We need to get her here fast," Pastor Mike said. "And we need somebody to trail after the sheriff and let us know where he is. Someone else must get Baby Angel and get her here as fast as they can. Can you arrange that, Johnny?"

Johnny White could. And did. Less than a half-hour later, while Morris Layman sat at a corner table in the Fish and Fries Café and watched Sheriff Clarence Higgins's every move, Molly and Justine scurried into the Methodist church with Baby Angel well hidden in a roll of blankets. Pastor Mike met them with open arms.

"Bless you both," the minister said. "We can take care of this little one in the church basement for as long as we need to. Can you stay with her for now? We'll get Birdie to pick up her crib and put together a schedule of folks to take care of her so that nobody has to spend too much time here."

Molly and Justine took Baby Angel to the church basement and began to set things up to make it a home. Pastor Mike set out for Town Hall, to bring Johnny White up to date and begin scheduling Cambrians who would be available to spend a few hours at a time caring for the baby.

As he came to the Fish and Fries, the pastor noticed the sheriff's old Ford SUV parked out front. He was surprised to see a small crowd gathering in front of the café.

"What's going on?" he asked Max Barnes.

"We're here to let Sheriff Higgins know we don't like what's going on," Max retorted. "How's he come up with a right to walk into just anybody's house and look for that baby? He's in there, pastor—no, here he comes now."

Sheriff Clarence Higgins walked out of the Fish and Fries, right into the small group of Cambrian citizens bent on delivering a message of discouragement. He looked about, as if counting noses, and exclaimed loudly: "You folks go on about your business, now. I'm here to enforce the law and it's your duty not to interfere."

"We don't like it, sheriff," Max Barnes shouted. "Why don't you just go on back to the office and leave us be?" Murmurs in the crowd. Then voices rose. Others echoed Max's indictment.

Across the street, Jake Garner's old collie dog scratched herself by rubbing against a wheel of the sheriff's vehicle. It began to roll forward. It was aimed straight toward the river.

Sheriff Higgins saw what was happening. "Damn!" he roared, and raced after it. The vehicle was beginning to pick up speed, but the sheriff caught up and grabbed a door handle. He managed to open the door and fling himself into the driver's seat just as the SUV reached the edge of the water. Pastor Mike and the other onlookers stood in mute horror as the vehicle, with Sheriff Higgins inside, plunged into the flooded Ohio River. The rushing water pulled it sideways downstream. Then it disappeared beneath the surface.

"Call for help!" Pastor Mike shouted, even as he ran headlong toward the river. Without hesitation, he dived into the roiling water and began to swim toward the spot where the sheriff's Explorer had disappeared. In an instant he, too, had sunk beneath the surface of the muddy Ohio River floodwaters. The onlookers gasped in terror and disbelief.

Seconds that might have been hours went by with nothing visible in the water. Then Pastor Mike's head suddenly broke the surface. He was gasping for air, struggling mightily against the strong current. And then there was another form.

"Look!" Sam Gowdy cried. "He's got the sheriff!"

Sam and two of the other men had run to the edge of the water. Sam jumped in and swam toward Pastor Mike and the sheriff. Pastor Mike fought against the strong pull of the river's current, dragging Sheriff Higgins with one arm. Sam Gowdy met them before they were halfway to shore. Between Sam and Pastor Mike, the sheriff began to help himself, swimming weakly toward the edge of the floodwater.

A loud cheer went up from the onlookers as Sam, Pastor Mike, and the sheriff struggled onto the bank. Sam Gowdy, breathless from exertion, stooped, hands on knees, and gasped for air. Pastor Mike and Sheriff Higgins dropped onto the muddy ground, completely spent. Onlookers rushed to their aid.

After several minutes, the sheriff and Pastor Mike had recovered enough to pull themselves up from the ground. Others huddled around them and Sam Gowdy. Max Barnes, the only one wearing a jacket, took it off and put it around Pastor Mike's shoulders. Everyone else stood awkwardly. They all wanted to help, but saw nothing they could do.

Sheriff Higgins spoke, his voice choked and raspy: "You saved my life, reverend. No way I would have made it out alive. I don't know how to . . ." He began to cough.

"Pastor Mike's a hero," called someone in the crowd.

"Bravest thing I've ever seen," said another.

Pastor Mike held up his hands. "No, no," he said. "The credit goes to God. His hand was at work in this."

Sam Gowdy, finally regaining his breath, chuckled. "So maybe God was looking out for you, but you're the one that jumped in the river and pulled him out," he said. "I didn't know you were such a good swimmer."

"I'm not," the pastor said. "I've never swum five feet before. Not in my whole life."

❧22❧

Cambrians awoke the next day to a most amazing sight. Over night, the river had receded almost to its normal level. Even the oldest of the old-timers couldn't remember ever seeing floodwaters go down so fast. People gathered in small groups and expressed their amazement to one another, gazing down the slope toward the river as if to reassure themselves that it was true.

Everyone was eager to discuss events of the day before. Those who had actually witnessed Pastor Mike's heroic action and Sheriff Clarence Higgins's gratitude told their stories over and over, finding no shortage of eager listeners. Even those who hadn't been there recounted the most vivid accounts they'd heard from others. It was a near-universal opinion that the sheriff would feel beholden to Pastor Mike for the rest of his life.

"A body saves your life," Kirk Mendenhall said to any number of people, "you just naturally owe him a debt you can't hardly ever pay back."

There was lots of talk about the Ohio, as well. Granny Vogler remembered every flood of the last fifty years. He stationed himself at a point with a good river view, where a great many people came and went, and waylaid anybody who would listen with his colorful stories about floods of the past. Father Jacob apparently shared most of Granny's recollections. The two of them engaged in animated conversation for a good three hours.

At Sam Gowdy's bait shop, Birdie Wilson announced excitedly that he and his boys were prepared to get back on the water and do some fishing. Others were of like mind. Even Charlie Tipsworth, not known to be much for fishing, ventured his opinion that the

187

river looked right inviting and he might get around to casting a line himself before the day was done.

Only a couple of customers had shown up at the Fish and Fries Café by ten o'clock. Tom Johnson and Molly sat and, like everyone else, talked about the dramatic rescue of the sheriff from his sinking vehicle. Neither of them had witnessed the event, but both had heard about it in great detail from someone who had.

"Sure doesn't seem to be any doubt that Sheriff Higgins knew Pastor Mike saved his life," Tom Johnson said. "From what I've heard, it's doubtful the sheriff would have got out of his car once it was sucked under water."

"That's pretty much what everybody says," Molly agreed.

"He ought to feel pretty kindly toward Cambria this morning. You would think maybe he'd let up a little in his hunt for Baby Angel."

"We can hope. He knows how much that's irritated all of us."

"You more than anybody, right?"

"I don't know about that, Tom, but I really have come to feel like Baby Angel belongs with me."

"Yeah, well I guess the sheriff feels obligated to carry out the law like he sees it," Tom Johnson said. "And he's got that judge pushing him. Judge Gilbert. I hear he's as stubborn as a mule on Sunday."

"Lynn says it's Judge Gilbert we really have to worry about."

At the sound of someone entering, they turned toward the front of the café. It was Lynn Swafford. He was in uniform and they saw his clearly marked sheriff's department automobile parked across the street. Lynn walked briskly toward them.

Molly smiled sweetly and Tom Johnson said, "Well, looks like the law is back. Morning, Lynn."

"How you doing, Tom?" And to Molly, "Hi, sweetheart. You don't seem to be doing too much business this morning."

"Everybody's out checking on the river," Molly said. "And talking about the big happening yesterday. I guess you heard?"

"I sure did! A couple of deputies got there right after it happened and word got back to the department right away."

188

Everyone waited till the sheriff got back, and let him know how concerned they'd been, Lynn said. "You know, I warned him again about the brakes on that old Ford just a day or so ago."

Tom Johnson: "And he paid no attention, right?"

"Actually, he said they worried him, too, but he was getting a new vehicle right away anyhow so he figured they couldn't do a lot of damage."

"Well he's lucky they didn't kill him. From what I hear he'd have drowned for sure if Pastor Mike hadn't been there to pull him out."

"He knows that." An almost sheepish grin spread across Lynn Swafford's face. "And those bad brakes were a blessing in disguise. Sheriff Higgins sent me with a message: He's so grateful to Pastor Mike for saving his life that he's pulling the plug on his search for the abandoned child. He said he doesn't want to do anything more that is unpleasant for Cambrians. And I can tell you, he means it. The sheriff is a changed man today."

Molly jumped up and hugged Lynn. "Our baby's safe," she said. "Nobody else will be looking for her."

"Nobody except maybe whoever lost her. We all kind of forgot about that, didn't we?"

Tom Johnson frowned.

"You really think somebody's looking for that little baby?" he asked. "Still seems to me like she was deliberately abandoned, just like Sheriff Higgins said. Nobody's been around here asking questions, and Birdie and Sam didn't find out anything about a lost baby up in Wheeling."

"I'll admit it doesn't seem likely," Lynn said. "It's just that we have got to be open to that possibility." He looked into Molly's eyes in a way that made it clear this last remark was intended primarily for her.

"But if nobody turns up, we can keep her, Lynn," she said. "I want so bad for Baby Angel to be ours—yours and mine."

Lynn turned to Tom Johnson. "Tom," he said, "do you suppose you could do without this young lady for a little while? I mean, it doesn't look like you're going to be too busy."

"Sure. You two get out of here. And take your time. We haven't had enough business to heat up the griddle."

Lynn Swafford grabbed Molly's hand and all but dragged her out the front door. "There's something I want to do, right now," he told her.

"Whatever you say," Molly laughed. "But you don't need to jerk me off my feet!"

"Sorry. I didn't mean to be so rambunctious."

"So where are we going in such a hurry?"

"You'll see."

Lynn opened the passenger-side door of his sheriff's department cruiser. Molly slid in and squirmed across the seat until she was almost on Lynn's side of the car. When he got in, she edged against him. He put an arm around her and pulled her tight. She rested her head on his shoulder.

Neither spoke as Lynn drove straight to the Methodist church.

"I wanted us to visit her together," Lynn said as he parked close to the front entrance. "She may as well get used to seeing us side-by-side."

"Lynn, you're a darling."

"I know."

"Now don't get too smug! But thank you for coming here. I've been dying to see her. I can't get over here nearly as much as I'd like, but I have felt safer with her here."

They took a steep stairway to the church basement, where they were met by Juanita Blessing. She took them to the side of Baby Angel's crib, smiled at the baby, and left. Molly picked up Baby Angel and squeezed her tightly. The baby giggled and cooed and made noises that sounded like she had things to say and wanted to talk.

"She's beautiful, Molly," Lynn said.

"Here. You hold her."

Lynn took the baby somewhat gingerly. Baby Angel looked up into his face, her eyes dancing. Her smile grew even wider.

"She likes you, Lynn," Molly said. "You're going to make a great father. I mean, I know you're already a great father—"

190

"Shush-h-h. I know what you mean. I'm the luckiest man in the world, Molly. I've raised two wonderful sons and now I get to start over with this precious little girl. I love her already, like she was my own flesh and blood."

"We'll take good care of her."

Lynn's tone softened. Molly's intuition—or was it simply because she knew him so well—told her that he was worried about something. "I'm not such a young man anymore," he said. "I had good years to scrape and save to send Morgan and Patrick to college and still came up short. They're working part-time jobs, but they're going to owe a lot for student loans. I'm already wondering if we can manage—"

"Now you shush-h-h," Molly interrupted. "We'll do whatever we need to do."

Lynn's radio suddenly emitted a rude noise. He recognized the code, which indicated a message from headquarters. He pressed a button and said "Swafford" and Deputy Harlan Gidcomb's voice screeched from the tiny speaker.

"Hey, Lynn," Gidcomb said, "the sheriff says not to deliver that message just yet. You know what he's talking about?"

"Yeah," Lynn replied. "I know."

"Then you understand not to deliver it, right?"

"I got you. The sheriff says don't deliver the message."

Deputy Gidcomb signed off. Lynn Swafford wore an expression of dismay as he did the same.

"What does that mean, Lynn?" Molly asked, apprehension clear in her voice.

"I don't know, honey. I really don't know. But it's not good."

PASTOR MIKE was embarrassed by all the attention showered on him by his fellow Cambrians. Morris Layman came by the church the first thing in the morning to inform him that he was everybody's hero, and even Father Jacob made it a point to phone and congratulate him. The old priest lauded him for the selfless Christian spirit he'd readily demonstrated in risking his own life to save that of another.

191

"All credit goes to God," Pastor Mike told him. This was what he believed and, anyway, he couldn't think of anything else to say.

He skipped his habitual early-morning stroll, much as he would have enjoyed. If he left the sanctuary of the church, he would have to weather the glad-handing of any number of those gathered in little knots along the river front. Morris Layman also had informed him of the remarkable fall in the river level, and he'd seen it for himself through the church windows. It would be pleasant to join with the others and talk about it, if only he could avoid being the center of attention.

Pastor Mike made his home in a cramped little apartment in the church basement, put in long before he arrived in Cambria. Church members at the time had considered this an economical alternative to a parsonage and he agreed. He'd worried in the beginning that he might be spending too much time in the building and might grow weary of this modest house of God. How wrong he'd been! He never would tire of of his beautiful church home.

And now that Baby Angel had been moved into the church, he took even more pleasure in making this place his home. Yes, others would be present to care for the child, but it was as if she lived under his roof and was part of his family. It had been only one night, but he already had come to feel a strong attachment.

Saving Baby Angel now had risen to the top of Pastor Mike's agenda. He kept reminding himself that he must never fail to mention that earnest mission in his prayers.

At mid-morning, the young minister headed downstairs. Juanita Blessing was supposed to be on duty as the baby's primary care taker. He had checked earlier in the day to make sure that she arrived, spelling Margie Zielinski. Margie had been there overnight and she'd hinted that it would upset Larry if she was even a minute late getting home.

Juanita was one of Pastor Mike's favorite Cambrians. He could not recall ever seeing her without a bright smile. She always had pleasant words for those around her, and he had looked forward somewhat eagerly to her stints as Baby Angel's caretaker. When he got to the basement, to his surprise, Juanita was not there.

Molly Hearst and the man Pastor Mike understood she planned to marry stood by the crib, Molly holding Baby Angel lovingly and the man looking on with an expression of pure joy.

Pastor Mike knew love when he saw it. And this was love. True love, never-ending.

Absorbed with their fascination in Baby Angel, the couple did not hear the pastor's approach. They were obviously startled when he came close and said, softly, "She's a beautiful child."

"She's precious," Molly said. Lynn Swafford nodded accord.

"I suppose you know her better than any of us," Pastor Mike said. "You kept her from the beginning. I think everyone in Cambria thinks of her as yours, Molly."

Molly's smile was radiant. "If we can keep her, Pastor Mike, Lynn and I will be the happiest parents you'll ever see," she said.

"We want her very much," Lynn added. "And we feel like she's safer here in the church, pastor. We're very grateful to you."

Pastor Mike frowned. "I hope it's enough," he said. "I worry every minute that the law enforcement people—I beg your pardon. I know you've had to make some hard choices in this matter."

Lynn dismissed Pastor Mike's evident discomfort with the wave of a hand. "We were encouraged this morning when Sheriff Higgins said he didn't plan to keep on with his search," he said. "If we could get a break from trying to keep her hidden all the time I think we might be able to bring some closure to all this. And that would make us all very happy."

"Yes. I pray for that every day. We have to have faith."

"But whatever happens now," Molly said, "what you did yesterday, saving the sheriff like you did, certainly has helped. We're all grateful to you, Pastor Mike."

"No, no. No credit to me, Molly. God's hand was there, and the credit goes to Him."

Lynn Swafford's radio suddenly crackled. He clicked it on just in time to hear Sheriff Clarence Higgins announce himself. "Are you there, Lynn?" the sheriff called, hesitating until he got a reply.

"I'm here, sheriff."

"Where are you?"

"I'm in Cambria, sheriff. With Molly."

"Lynn, I hate to have to tell you this, especially after sending you over there this morning with my earlier message to the good folks of Cambria. And I sure hate for Miss Molly to have to hear this from me."

"You're scaring us, sheriff."

"Sorry. I didn't mean to scare you."

"What's the problem, then?"

"Lynn, right after you left this morning, I got a call from Judge Gilbert. I told him last night, you know, that I was calling off the hunt for that abandoned baby over there. But you know Judge Gilbert, Lynn. Once he gets a cat by the tail he hates to let it go."

"I know, sheriff. So what's going on?"

Sheriff Clarence Higgins sucked in his breath and hesitated. "What's going on," he said, "is Judge Gilbert says he may have to call in the state police. He says if we're not going to do our job, he has no choice but to get somebody who will. Lynn, he's determined to get his hands on that baby. I'm sorry, Miss Molly."

❧23❦

organ Swafford drove up in front of the Hearst house early. Justine came flying out, eager to get started. She crawled in beside him and pulled the door shut, slam-bang, as if there was an emergency. Morgan pulled away without waiting for her to get her seatbelt fastened.

"Good morning, Miss Hearst," he said playfully, keeping his eyes on the road and not looking at Justine.

"And a good morning to you, Mr. Swafford. Did you have any trouble getting the car?"

"Not really. I told Dad we couldn't wait any longer. If Judge Gilbert brings in the state troopers, they're going to find that baby for sure. And nobody's doing anything to save her after that. If I can get in the library and study up on the law, I'll bet my left little finger I can find a way out."

Justine squirmed down deeper into the seat. "I still don't know why nobody else has thought of that," she said. "Are you just that much smarter than the rest of them, Morgan?"

Morgan, as usual, was modest. He said, "They've all been too busy trying to keep the baby hidden. It's hard to look ahead to next week or even tomorrow when you think you hear the sheriff's foot-steps coming up to your front door right now."

"I'm proud of you, Morgan. If anybody can find the answer, you can."

"If I don't it won't be for lack of trying."

"Have I told you I'm proud of you?"

"I think you just did."

"And I meant it. Instead of waiting around to see what happens, you're trying to do something before it's too late."

"You'd do the same, Justine. In fact, you are."

"Yes. but my research won't be as important as yours. Even if I don't find out anything about the Magnolia, it probably won't make much difference."

"Maybe. But I'm betting you come up with some answers."

Justine leaned back in her seat and watched the passing scenery. She couldn't wait to get to Wheeling and get into the library. And get to work. Merely recognizing that a single faint word on the side of an old wicker basket could be a defining clue to Baby Angel's origins had given her new purpose from the time she first discovered it that day in Marlene Johnson's living room. She had become more determined than she'd ever been before and now, she might be close to an answer.

She was giddy with anticipation, but also nervous. What if she came up empty handed?

Morgan, meanwhile, was experiencing his own doubts. He had thrown himself into the Cambrian Project back in the beginning for Justine. This girl was totally dedicated to saving that baby and he wanted to help.

Early on, though, he had found an even better justification for his stand. When he and Patrick got home from college, they noticed a great change in their father. It was as if Lynn Swafford had a new lease on life, a new enthusiasm for day-to-day living. And they learned very quickly that the reason was Molly Hearst. The boys had endorsed this relationship wholeheartedly. It also had become apparent that Molly and their father loved Baby Angel very much and wanted her to be part of their family.

Morgan was hoping against hope that he could help make this happen. There might be some obscure legal mechanism available, and if there was he had to find it.

But Morgan recognized that such a law might not exist. He remembered a cautionary maxim of his grandfather's, something he had heard the old sheriff say many times: "Son, you can't flush a rabbit from a brush pile if there's no rabbit there."

Would he find that rabbit?

Traffic was light and they made good time, finding themselves in Wheeling a full half-hour earlier than they had expected. Morgan stopped and asked the way to the Ohio County Public Library and only minutes later they were in front of the modern, red-brick building on Sixteenth Street. They had to struggle to contain their excitement.

But now that they were here, their mission suddenly grew far more intimidating. Or rather, their unspoken fear of failure. The importance of what they had come here hoping to do loomed terrifyingly large.

Once inside, each wished the other luck. They clasped hands silently and looked one another straight in the eyes for a fleeting moment that was fraught with emotion. Morgan headed to the legal section, while Justine learned from a most pleasant and helpful staff member that her best bet for local history was the library's Wheeling Room.

"Check through the microfilm index," the young woman advised, "and let me know if I can help."

Justine promised that she would and went to work. It didn't take long for her to get a feeling that she very well might be seeking the proverbial needle in a haystack. She became discouraged, but no less determined.

At one o'clock, she turned off her microfilm reader and went to check on Morgan. She found him poring over an old book of state laws.

"Anything yet?" she whispered.

Morgan stretched and yawned. "Not yet," he said. "How about you?"

"No. And I'm getting tired. Could we maybe go somewhere and get some lunch?"

Morgan closed the shabby old book of laws and put it aside. "We might as well," he said, "if it doesn't take too long."

They found a coffee shop nearby and ordered sandwiches and salads. The food was good but they were too rushed to enjoy it. Less than thirty minutes later they were back at their posts.

And an hour after that, Morgan found what he was looking for.

He hurried to the Wheeling Room to tell Justine. His ecstatic expression told her all she needed to know before he'd said a word. She jumped up and hugged him, and then burst into tears.

"You did it, Morgan!" Justine said. "I knew you would."

"The answer is right there, in one of those old law books," Morgan said, words tumbling forth in his excitement like ripe apples falling from the tree on a windy day. "Any good attorney could have told the people of Cambria what they needed to do, at least after a little research. This will do it, Justine. This will save Baby Angel."

Justine hugged him again. She wanted to shout to the world how happy she was at this moment. And dance around the room. Or jump on a table.

"How about you?" Morgan asked hopefully. "Find anything?"

Justine sighed. Whatever she was looking for had proved even more elusive than she could have imagined. And what exactly was she looking for? She'd found several index references to the single word she had to work with—Magnolia—but none had led to anything useful. As a last resort, she was scrolling through rolls of microfilm on which the old newspaper files were preserved. It was a slow process, since she had to scrutinize every page. Any one of them could hold the key.

"I'll help," Morgan said. "Show me which of these film drawers you've been through."

Justine got him started. They worked at separate readers, side by side.

"You know we may not find what you're looking for," Morgan said a while later. "I've not given up, but I'm not sure how much farther back in time it makes any sense for us to go."

"I don't have a lot of hope left," Justine admitted. "I'm going to finish this reel and the two left in that drawer, then I give up. No point in wasting any more time."

Morgan was about to put a new reel of microfilm on his reader when Justine suddenly gasped. "Incredible!" she cried, alarming a librarian at a desk several yards away. "Morgan, I've found it!"

Morgan looked quickly at her screen. "Incredible is right," he said. "I never would have believed it. But right there it is, in black and white."

Morgan hugged her and the euphoric young sleuths laughed and danced up and down an aisle until a librarian shushed them. Their efforts had been productive. Very productive.

In her excitement, Justine almost forgot to take notes on the information she'd found. Not that she was likely to forget, but she needed to be prepared if someone wanted proof. Morgan had filled a page with notes and recommended that she do the same. She had to put the reel back on the microfilm reader and find the information all over again.

Once she'd finished writing, she put away the roll of microfilm and the two giggled all the way to the library exit. And exchanged high-fives and slaps on the back.

To celebrate the success of their mission, they decided to treat themselves to a good dinner before starting back to Cambria. They found a respectable restaurant, where Morgan ordered veal parmesan and Justine chose an exotic Asian dish that turned out to be mostly noodles. It didn't matter much. They still were too excited to really appreciate their food. Morgan kept smiling and Justine could not stop giggling.

Morgan finally turned serious again. "I know Dad can pull this off," he said. "Once he knows the law, he can make it work."

"How long do you think it will take?"

"A while, I suppose. But once the decision is rendered, I don't see how there could be any turning back. We have to do this, Justine, before the state cops get into it. I don't think we have a lot of time."

"Can he start on it tomorrow?" Justine pleaded.

"Probably. How about your news? You plan to broadcast what you found out right away?"

Justine hesitated. "I'm not sure," she said. "What do you think? Is Cambria ready for what I have to tell them?"

"I wish I knew the answer to that, but I don't," Morgan replied. "And I can't wait to see."

It was well after dark when they left the restaurant and drove out of Wheeling. Morgan saw a billboard for the Highway Motel. It offered cheap rates. "Want to get a room and mess around?" he teased.

"No."

"I knew you'd say that. Me neither."

"I like you very much Morgan, but I wouldn't want us to get involved like that."

Morgan put his hand on hers. "You're a sweet girl, Justine. Stay that way," he said. "Some guy is going to be very lucky to catch you a few years down the road."

WHEN IDA QUATTLEBAUM swept through the front door of Tom Johnson's Fish and Fries Café and marched smartly to the counter, the room fell eerily quiet. Tom Johnson appeared to be disconcerted momentarily by her arrival, but quickly recovered and welcomed her warmly: "Miss Quattlebaum, how nice to see you."

Miss Quattlebaum had never before set foot in the Fish and Fries. For that matter, she seldom was seen out and about anywhere in town. And even though she had spent her entire fifty-five years in Cambria—except for the hot summer months when she chose the cool breezes of upper Michigan and took refuge in her summer house on Mackinaw Island—few Cambrians knew her well and many did not know her at all. And she did not bother herself with Cambrian affairs.

She lived in the old Quattlebaum mansion, which stood well back in the woods on the high side of town, with an elderly cook and housekeeper, Mrs. Temple, and her driver, Boyd. Mrs. Temple and Boyd did her shopping. Only on rare occasion was she seen riding through town in the back seat of an ancient Oldsmobile Ninety-eight sedan with Boyd at the wheel.

On later reflection, Tom Johnson was surprised that he recognized her when she walked into the Fish and Fries. And happy that he did.

Miss Quattlebaum—no one used her first name—responded to his friendly greeting with a smile. She extended a hand and said, "You're Tom, the proprietor, I believe."

Tom actually blushed at her use of the title, having never been referred to as a proprietor before. But he still managed to keep his wits about him and acknowledged that he was, indeed, the one who ran the place.

"Yes, ma'am," he said, "I own it and it's pretty much up to me to keep it going."

Miss Quattlebaum looked about as if rating the Fish and Fries for a national restaurant guide. She appeared to be well satisfied with what she saw. "This is nice," she said firmly. "I should come here more often."

"You sure would be most welcome, Miss Quattlebaum," Tom Johnson said proudly. "We serve only fresh fish. Never anything that's been froze. Some of our best dinners are right out of the Ohio yonder." He motioned toward the river.

"Yes, Tom, I've heard as much. Now may I inquire about one of your employees? I believe you have a young woman named Molly Hearst who works here?"

"Yes, ma'am, Molly works here, but she's not here today. She's been putting in too many hours and I give her the day off. Can somebody else be of assistance?"

"No, thank you very much. I wanted to speak with her about a personal matter."

With that pronouncement, Miss Quattlebaum turned and walked out of the Fish and Fries the same way she'd walked in: like royalty appearing briefly among a handful of commoners. Only after she was well outside, beyond hearing range, did talk resume among those she left behind.

"Well, what do you make of that, Tom? Miss Quattlebaum out among us ordinary mortals," Kirk Mendenhall called from the front of the room.

"Don't be sarcastic, Kirk," Tom responded. "She seemed like a nice lady."

"Never said she wasn't."

"What the heck do you suppose she wants with Molly?" This from Jake Garner, who sat near the back, drinking coffee.

Tom Johnson raised both hands, as if offering to surrender.

"You know as much about it as I do, Jake," he said.

"Think you ought to call Molly and let her know Miss Quattle-baum's looking for her?"

"Might not be a bad idea."

Tom called Molly Hearst and told her of Miss Quattlebaum's inquiry. Molly said she couldn't imagine any reason why Miss Quattlebaum would be looking for her, that she'd never met the lady, and what did Tom think she ought to do? Tom said he didn't suppose there was anything she should do. If Miss Quattlebaum needed her real bad, she surely would be in touch.

Tom duly reported the conversation to the eagerly waiting Fish and Fries regulars. This generated a new round of speculation.

For Molly, the curiosity was overwhelming. What could Miss Quattlebaum want with her? She couldn't think of a single reason why she would be of interest to the richest woman in Cambria. Ten minutes later, when she opened her front door in answer to a firm knock, she was almost speechless.

Miss Quattlebaum extended a hand. "I'm Ida Quattlebaum," she said. "I take it you're Molly?"

Molly felt the color creep up her neck and make splotches on the sides of her face. She suddenly became very conscious of the shabbiness of her modest home. And surely she was a mess, after tossing and turning most of the night, not getting enough sleep, and presenting herself at the door without even combing her hair or washing her face!

If Miss Quattlebaum noticed any of these things, she gave no indication.

Molly replied with a simple, "Yes, I'm Molly."

"And you have a baby, I understand?"

"I beg your pardon?"

"A baby. I understand you have a baby."

"It's a long story—"

Ida Quattlebaum shifted her feet impatiently. She said, "Gran-ville told me the story, Molly."

"Granville?"

"Granville Vogler."

"Oh, of course. Granny."

"If you choose. Anyway, that's why I'm here. Granville said there is a fund to provide for the child," Miss Quattlebaum said.

"Yes, the Baby River Angel Fund. Johnny White takes care of it."

Ida Quattlebaum obviously wasn't interested in small details. "I want to go further than that, Molly," she declared. "As you may or may not know, I have plenty. I want to set up a trust fund for the little one to make sure she's well taken care of. Her whole life."

"Miss Quattlebaum . . ." Molly's voice faltered. "I, I don't know what to say."

"Please. Call me Ida. There will be legalities to take care of, of course, but I have lawyers for that. I merely wanted you to know that, from this point on, that little one—Angel, didn't Granville say?—will be provided for. Now I must rush."

On this note, the richest Cambrian turned and quickly saw herself out. Molly stood speechless as she watched her go.

❧24❧

Morgan and Justine still were giddy over their duel success in Wheeling when he dropped her off at her front door well after midnight, although Morgan tried not to let his excitement show. After he had seen Justine safely inside, he hurried home and went straight to his father's bedroom door.

Lynn Swafford was a light sleeper even under the best of circumstances. On this night he'd slept fitfully, worried about Morgan and Justine, their long drive, and what they might or might not find. He had never shared Morgan's confidence that the legal system would provide Baby Angel a safety net. When Morgan tapped on his door, he was awake and out of bed in an instant.

Morgan got straight to the point: "I found it, Dad. I know how to save the baby."

"Morgan, I'm proud of you! Let's go to the kitchen and make some coffee, and you can tell me what we need to do."

Morgan spread his notes on the kitchen table. He had careful and precise citations, solid evidence to support his case. "The law goes way, way back," he said. "But it's never been overturned—not even challenged. And one judge cited it as recently as twenty years ago. Dad, it's valid. We can do this. All we need is a friendly judge who will see things our way."

His father pored over Morgan's notes while drinking a second cup of coffee. Lynn Swafford was awake and alert now. His enthusiasm mounted as he read the text of the long-standing state law his son had discovered. By the time he'd finished his coffee his doubts had evaporated.

"Judge Winkler," he said. "Morgan, we have to get Baby Angel and Molly before Judge Harold Winkler. As soon as possible."

"Wake me up when you get up," Morgan told him. "Are you on duty tomorrow?"

"I was supposed to be, but I'll call in and tell them I have a family emergency."

"Won't they ask what it is?"

"You're right. I won't say emergency, I'll say family business that needs to be taken care of right away."

"That's accurate, Dad."

"Yes, it is. Now let's get some sleep. I'll call Judge Winkler first thing in the morning, then we'll get back to Cambria as quick as we can and pick up Molly and the baby. Morgan, you'll never know how much you've helped."

Morgan grinned and shrugged, then turned and headed for bed. His father sat up for another hour, started to go back to bed, but realized that would be useless. He was wound way too tight to get back to sleep. He got dressed and sat at the kitchen table, watching the clock. How early could you phone a judge?

Patrick joined him at seven o'clock, curious about what Morgan might have found in Wheeling. Once he had heard, he was irritated that no one had wakened him during the night.

"But that doesn't matter now," Patrick said. "More important is where do we go from here?"

"If I can get hold of Judge Winkler, I'm sure he'll help us," Lynn Swafford explained. "I'm just waiting now to call him. You think it's still too early?"

Patrick checked the time. "Ordinarily, I'd say you oughtn't to call him before nine. You might be able to get away with a little earlier time though, as critical as this is. Dad, if the state troopers get to Cambria and start knocking on doors they're bound to find the baby sooner or later. Don't you think?"

"Yes, Patrick, I do. I'm going to call the judge right now."

Judge Harold Winkler was still in bed when Lynn Swafford called, sleeping soundly. His irritation was evident when he answered the phone with a husky, "What is it?" His tone softened when he heard who was calling. Before Lynn had offered more than a few words of explanation, the judge was wide awake and engrossed in what the deputy had to say.

Patrick was beside himself, trying to guess from the one side of the conversation he could hear whether Judge Winkler was sympathetic. His father's matter-of-fact tone was of little help.

"What did he say, Dad?" Patrick demanded when his father put down the phone.

"He's cautious, Patrick, as any judge would be. That's what I expected. But he said he'll look into the law. And he implied that if he can make it work in our favor, he will. Run and wake up your brother."

While Morgan was getting dressed, Lynn called Molly. Justine was still asleep but had left her mother a note, so that Molly knew the outcome of Morgan's research in Wheeling and had eagerly awaited Lynn's call. She grabbed the phone on the first ring.

"Lynn?" Molly said breathlessly.

"Yes, Molly, it's me. You may know, Morgan found something yesterday—"

"Justine left me a note. What do we need to do, Lynn?"

"I've talked to Judge Winkler," Lynn responded, trying not to sound too optimistic. "I think he will help us, Molly. If he can. We need to get Baby Angel and appear before him as soon as possible—this morning. Can you make it?"

Molly almost laughed. "For Baby Angel?" she said. "Of course I can make it. Should I call the church and let them know we're on the way?"

"Good idea. Love you, Molly. See you real soon."

As Lynn Swafford hung up the phone, it occurred to him that he had not yet called the sheriff's department to let them know he wouldn't be showing up for work. He quickly dialed the number and, to his surprise, Sheriff Higgins himself answered. Lynn got straight to the point.

"Unless you need me real bad today," he said, "I need to take some time off to take care of something personal. I have plenty of vacation days accumulated."

"Take as much time as you need," Sheriff Higgins said. "And

Lynn, I need to tell you something: At Judge Gilbert's request, a couple of state troopers are on their way to Cambria right now. They're going to be looking for that abandoned baby."

"Will they have search warrants?"

"Don't think so. But they'll be nosing around, asking lots of questions. It would be best if they don't run into Birdie Wilson's boys like I did. You know how that turned out."

"Sheriff, I really appreciate having you on the same side—"

"Forget it, Lynn. Unless you really have something else more important to take care of, I'd get over there if I was you."

Morgan and Patrick had hurried through breakfast and were eager to go. Lynn hadn't eaten, but figured he'd had enough coffee to launch him for the day. Food seemed of little importance just now. He was worried about the state troopers. Little chance of beating them to Cambria, and who knew where they might pop up.

"I'm sorry, guys, but I think I should change into my uniform," he said. "I should have done that to start with."

Patrick: "But why, Dad, if you're not going to work?"

"Because in uniform I'm clearly an officer of the law, and this gives me authority. It might come in handy."

The boys waited, impatiently, while their father went back to his room and changed clothes. Lynn Swafford rushed. Uniform or not, he still would like to be in Cambria ahead of the state troopers. He was out and ready to go before Patrick and Morgan had much time to complain.

Driving the sheriff's department vehicle, he could ignore the speed limit on the road to Cambria. He did. The ride left Morgan and Patrick white-knuckled and queasy, but they were in front of Molly's house in less time than even Lynn might have predicted.

Molly was waiting. She ran to the car, where Morgan exited the front passenger seat and let her climb in beside Lynn. Morgan joined Patrick in back.

"I called the church," Molly announced. "Pastor Mike is expecting us. Lynn, I'm scared to death. If this doesn't work, what more can we do? I love little Angel so much . . ."

"One step at a time, honey. We're going to do everything we can to make this work. Right now it's our best hope."

When they got within sight of the Methodist church, their optimism faded. A state police patrol car was parked in front and two uniformed troopers stood behind it, talking with Kirk Mendenhall. Lynn quickly turned down a side street, hoping his sheriff's department cruiser hadn't been seen. The last thing he wanted now was to be confronted by the state troopers and have to try and explain his mission in Cambria. They and the sheriff's department, after all, were supposed to be on the same side.

Lynn worked his way to Sam Gowdy's bait shop, keeping as much distance as he could between his car and the state troopers. Sam was standing in front of the shop. He rushed to meet Lynn and Molly and the boys.

"There must be something going on," Sam said, without formal greetings.

"We've got to get Baby Angel out of the church," Molly said. "But a couple of state policemen seem to be camped out in front of the building, like they know she's there."

"I think maybe they do," Sam said. "They came into town this morning and drove straight to the church."

"But how would they have found out?" Lynn asked.

"I don't know," Sam said, shaking his head. "I understand that Pastor Mike is keeping hisself hid in the basement, so he won't have to answer any questions. He couldn't lie, you know."

Morgan and Patrick had stayed back a few steps, as if in deference to the older men and Molly. They'd been listening, though. Morgan stepped forward. "Excuse me," he said, "but if they know she's there, they're going to start pushing to get into the church and try to find her. We need to get her out. Does anybody—"

"A decoy," Sam Gowdy said. "We need a decoy."

Lynn Swafford: "That might work, Sam. Any ideas?"

"You bet. We even rehearsed it. Let me get Birdie."

While the others stood and wondered, Sam called Birdie Wilson and urged him to get to the bait shop fast. "It's real this time," Sam vowed. "We got to run that action just like we practiced it, Birdie."

Lynn Swafford was incredulous. "You mean you have actually done something like this before?" he asked. "When you mentioned a decoy, I had no idea you already had a plan."

"Me and Birdie and Jake Garner figured we might have to hightail it sometime with the baby, if the sheriff got too close. We set it up with Pudge Gaither to use his little rowboat to sneak her out. We could do it, too, if we had to."

Birdie, never one to get somewhere fast, surprised them all. He arrived at the bait shop in less than fifteen minutes, clearly excited, happy that Sam had called him, and ready to spring into action.

"What's up?" Birdie asked. He spoke directly to Sam Gowdy, acknowledging Lynn Swafford, Molly, and the boys with a nod.

"We need to do another run over to Pudge's place, just like we did before," Sam explained. "This time, we do it in front of the state police. You and me are going to decoy them, Birdie, so that Lynn and Molly can get the baby out."

"How far do we have to take it this time, Sam?" Birdie wanted to know. "I don't believe I want to get in Pudge's little boat, do you?"

Sam was reassuring. "We won't have to go that far," he promised Birdie. "Just take off and get the state cops to follow us. By the time they find out our baby is a sack of potatoes, Baby Angel will be safe on her way to wherever they're taking her. But we got to let them see us, and think we're carrying that baby."

"You got another sack of potatoes?" Birdie asked.

"Probably. If I don't I'll find something else. Don't take much to look like a baby, once you wrap it in a blanket and all."

The six conspirators got their heads together and quickly ironed out the details. Sam would slip into the church by way of the back door, carrying his sack of potatoes wrapped in a baby blanket. Birdie would drive right up to the front of the building. Sam would rush out, in plain sight of the troopers, and Birdie would drive off fast and head for Pudge's place down in the Canepatch.

"Them state boys are bound to be suspicious," Sam said. "They are gonna follow us, Lynn, and as soon as they're gone get Baby Angel and get out of there."

210

Lynn Swafford moved his sheriff's department cruiser as close to the church as he dared. Patrick and Morgan stayed with the car, while he and Molly worked their way to a position from which they could see the front of the church. The two troopers and Kirk Mendenhall were still there and the troopers showed no sign that they planned to leave any time soon.

It took Birdie and Sam only a few minutes to launch their distraction. Lynn and Molly watched as Birdie roared up to the steps of the church in his old Dodge pickup and Sam came hurrying down the steps with his sack of potatoes—or whatever he had come up with—disguised as a baby. The state troopers were talking and laughing, as if enjoying a joke, and didn't look up. Sam stopped at the bottom step and waited to be seen. The troopers did not notice.

Birdie yelled from the truck, "Come on, Sam. Let's go!" Sam didn't move. The troopers still didn't seem to notice.

Sam called loudly from the church steps: "Open the door Birdie. We've got to get this baby out of here."

Now the two troopers looked up. What was all this commotion about? Sam rushed around to the passenger side of the truck, where he was in full view of the state police officers, and shouted "Let's go, Birdie!" as he jumped in. Birdie ripped away with the maximum acceleration the old pickup could muster.

The troopers took the bait. They climbed into the patrol car—although they did not appear to hurry—and drove off after the truck. No flashing lights or siren.

Molly ran to the church while Lynn dashed back for his car and the boys. She had Baby Angel, wrapped in a blanket and looking very much like Sam's decoy, and was halfway down the church steps by the time Lynn reached that point. Kirk Mendenhall looked on with an expression of disbelief.

As Molly climbed into the back seat of the cruiser, Lynn shouted to Kirk, "How did the state cops find out the baby was here?"

"They didn't," Kirk replied. "One of them was a boyhood friend of Pastor Mike's. They were waiting around to see him."

Now it was Lynn Swafford's turn to make a speedy departure. He gunned the cruiser and headed back through Cambria. He assured a worried Molly that Judge Harold Winkler was expecting them.

"Be sure and avoid the state cops," Morgan warned.

"They'll be going the other direction," Lynn said. "Birdie planned to head straight toward the Canepatch."

"How far do you think he'll get before the troopers catch up?" Molly asked.

"Not very far. But even after they catch up and stop him, it's going to take a while for them to figure anything out. We'll be halfway to Judge Winkler's by then."

"Lynn," Molly said, "do you really think Judge Winkler will help us save Baby Angel? I'm so scared . . ."

Deputy Lynn Swafford looked in his mirror, directly into her eyes. "Sweetheart," he said, "Judge Winkler's our best hope. We have to have faith that this is going to work."

❧25❧

Birdie Wilson drove away from the Methodist church at what he considered breakneck speed. They had to get enough of a head start on the state troopers that it would take at least a few minutes for the officers to catch up. The old Dodge rocked and swayed as Birdie tried to avoid all the potholes, any one of which could have caused enough damage to break down the truck if he hit it.

"You see anything behind us yet?" Sam queried.

"Not a thing," Birdie said. "Looks like we made us a pretty good getaway, Sam."

"It can't be too good, though. They have to chase us else the decoy didn't work."

Birdie tried to keep one eye on the road ahead and the other on the mirror. His palms were sweating so that it was hard for him to keep a steady hold on the steering wheel. Sam, meanwhile, still cradled the mock Baby Angel—it was, in fact, another sack of potatoes—on his lap as if it were the real thing. He tried to turn his head so that he could see out the back window and suddenly roared with pain.

"What?" Birdie demanded.

"I pulled a muscle in my neck," Sam said. "Damn, that hurts. Birdie, why in hell don't you have a mirror on this door like there is on the other side? I thought that was the law."

"If it is, nobody ever told me. But I'm sorry about your neck, Sam. You goin' to be okay?"

"Oh, forget about me. See any cops behind us yet?"

"Something coming way back there," Birdie said, trying hard to bring an image into focus in the vibrating mirror outside his window. "Could be a cop car. I cain't tell for sure."

"Don't they have flashing lights?" Sam asked.

"None that I can see, Sam. Probably ain't a cop car."

Sam finally realized he was still holding the sack of potatoes on his lap. He heaved it onto the floor of the truck, at his feet. He said, "Maybe you ought to slow down, Birdie."

"They'll catch us real fast, Sam."

"But if they lose us, we can't be sure that Molly and Lynn will get away with the baby. Are you sure they followed us when we left the church?"

Birdie jerked the steering wheel to the left to miss a large pothole. "Man, that one would have broke an axel or something," he declared. "No, Sam, I cain't say I'm certain they followed us. We done all we could, though. If they was there looking for the abandoned child, they sure ought to have noticed us. You and that sack of potatoes, especially."

"I guess," Sam said, obviously still concerned. "I'd feel better if you'd spot 'em somewhere back there, though."

Birdie didn't answer. They were getting close to the dead-end street that led to Pudge Gaither's house and canebrake-shielded boat launch. Now that their clever decoy plan actually was being played out, Birdie was fully engaged. He thought they should carry their action as far as they could. This meant grabbing Pudge, if he was at home, and getting Sam and his sack of potatoes into Pudge's little rowboat and heading upriver. Or downriver. Nobody ever had told him which way they needed to go.

"I guess you're right about Pudge's boat," Birdie said. "We ought to get in it and try to escape up or down the river."

"That's not what I said," Sam argued. "Don't you ever listen, Birdie?"

Birdie Wilson had no chance to reply. As he slowed for the sharp turn onto Pudge's street, he spotted the state police car clearly in the mirror. Still no flashing lights, but it was coming up fast behind the truck.

"Here they come!" Birdie shouted. "They're right behind us."

Sam Gowdy forgot his strained muscle and twisted his neck to see behind. There was no police car in sight. He winced with pain. And clapped his hand on his neck like he was swatting a mosquito. "Birdie, you ought to have a mirror on this side."

"We been over that, Sam. Anyway, here we are at Pudge's."

Birdie hit the brakes, hard. Sam was slung forward, and barely caught himself before his head cracked into the windshield. The truck skidded to a stop just short of the wall of bamboo.

"Grab the baby, Sam," Birdie demanded. "We've got to find Pudge, real fast."

"But what happened to the cops? They were right behind us."

"They must have missed that last turn. But they'll figure it out soon enough. We have to get that baby into Pudge's boat."

Sam Gowdy crawled leisurely from the truck. He took his time walking around to Birdie's side of the pickup, where he plopped the sack of potatoes, still neatly wrapped in a pink baby blanket, down on the grass. He leaned back against the truck as if he intended to stay awhile and tell fish stories.

"Birdie," Sam proclaimed, "we don't have to get in the boat. We don't have to go another foot. We can stay right here and wait for the state troopers. We did our job, Birdie, and we did it well."

Birdie's shoulders slumped. He opened his mouth as if to speak but stopped himself. He started to speak again, but still said nothing. The state police patrol car reappeared, heading down the dead-end street toward them. Pudge and Elaine came rushing from the house. An old basset hound loped up from somewhere down by the river, its long ears flopping, excitedly braying its deep-throated greeting. That sent a young buck deer scurrying through the bamboo thicket. The canes rattled in its wake.

"Get down to the boat and untie it, fast, while I get the baby," Pudge yelled to Elaine.

Pudge lumbered toward Birdie and Sam, while Elaine cut back around the corner of the house and ran toward the path Pudge kept open through the bamboo thicket. She was immediately out of sight but not out of hearing range. The men heard a muffled yell followed by a watery splash.

"Lord, she must of fell in the river," Pudge roared. "Bring the baby, Birdie. I got to get down there before she drowns."

Elaine had indeed fallen into the river. The end of the path was covered in slick muck, the residue of the muddy floodwater that had covered the area. Rushing toward the boat, she slipped and went down on her backside, then slid feet-first into the Ohio. She held on to the boat chain, though, and faced no risk of drowning. By the time Pudge came stumbling down the path she was climbing back up the slippery river bank. She was thoroughly soaked, but otherwise no worse for her adventure.

Pudge grabbed her arm and tried to pull her forward. Elaine was a big woman. And her wet clothes weighted her down. Pudge grunted and heaved. His feet went out from under him. He slid into Elaine, who fell on top of him. They hit the water as one, like a plummeting granite boulder.

In the meantime, the young buck the hound had flushed from the bamboo thicket was making a dash toward higher ground. He sailed over a low fence and landed in the middle of the street at the precise moment the state police car arrived at that particular spot. The driver swerved to miss the deer. The patrol car ran off the road and came to rest in a sludge-filled ditch, leaning precariously.

Sam Gowdy turned to look. The state troopers climbed out on the high side of the car and slammed the door. They started walking in Sam's direction.

Birdie picked his way carefully down the path toward the river. He wanted to avoid whatever pitfalls had landed the Gaithers in the Ohio. His deliberate gait gave the pair time to be out of the water before he reached them. Pudge was attempting to squeegee wet pant legs with flattened hands and Elaine was twisting her hair, trying to wring out as much muddy river water as she could.

"Where's the baby at?" Pudge yelled.

"Don't have her," Birdie said.

"I can see that, Birdie. Is Sam bringing her?"

"Sam ain't got her either."

"Damn it, Birdie, I seen the baby. I seen Sam put her down on the ground while he tied his shoe."

Birdie hesitated. Did he want to be the one to reveal to Pudge the truth of their phony run from the state police? Doggone it, where was Sam Gowdy when you needed him? "Sam can explain it," he said. "Sorry you and the missus got wet."

Pudge straightened up and glared at Birdie. Elaine tugged at his arm. "Now, Pudge, be calm," she said. "We don't know what's going on yet."

Pudge was not calm.

"You . . . you," he sputtered. His face, already flushed from exertion, reddened even more in his rage. "You dumbass, Birdie, you tell me what this is all about. My wife could have drowned, and you won't say what for? Birdie . . ."

He stopped there. It was as if Pudge suddenly had run out of steam. Or out of words.

Elaine tried to soothe her husband, stroking his arm and assuring him she was okay. The two of them carefully made their way to higher ground. Elaine was barefoot, but Pudge wore heavy boots that squished in the mud. Water sloshed out around his boot tops and ran in little trickles back into the Ohio.

Birdie Wilson leaned forward and reached out to help Elaine. "No reason to call names, Pudge," he said.

"I'm sorry, Birdie," Pudge answered. "I didn't mean nothing by it. I was just so flusterated, worrying about that baby and all."

"Well, the thing is, we don't have the baby. This was all bait to fool the state police."

"Bait?"

"You know, bait to mislead 'em, get 'em to follow us."

Pudge made no effort to hide his confusion. "You want to cause more trouble by misleading the state police?" he asked.

"It was so Molly and them could get away with Baby Angel. No way they could have took her with that state police car setting there in front of the church. Sam and me decided to use that plan we'd worked out, us and Jake Garner you remember, and they'd figure we was running out with the real baby. And it worked, too. Sam's setting up there now with that sack of potatoes and the state cops likely are up there talking to him, mad as hell."

Birdie Wilson's prophecy was correct. He and Pudge and Elaine sloshed their way back up the path through the bamboo thicket, rounded the end of the house, and found Sam trying valiantly to explain to two disgruntled state troopers exactly what he was doing with a sack of potatoes wrapped in a baby blanket. Sam was not doing very well.

At their approach, one of the troopers held up a hand in a signal for them to stop. "Now who are you?" he demanded.

Elaine took the lead, smiling and using her most pleasant tone of voice. She introduced herself, then Pudge and Birdie Wilson. "We live here, Pudge and me," she explained. "Mr. Wilson and Mr. Gowdy just came by for a visit—and to look at Pudge's boat. We river folk depend a lot on our boats, you know."

The trooper softened. "I'm Sergeant Wiley, ma'am, and this is Patrolman Wolowiec. We're from the district state police office."

"And what brings you to Cambria today?" Elaine said sweetly.

"You've got a judge over in the county seat who seems to think there's an abandoned child here somewhere," Sergeant Wiley said. "Our commander sent us over to ask around a bit."

"You don't say! Have you found out anything?"

Patrolman Wolowiec stepped forward. "Nothing yet, ma'am," he said. "But we could be onto something here. Do you have any notion why Mr. Wilson and Mr. Gowdy would come flying up to your front door carrying a sack of potatoes wrapped in a baby blanket? And how'd you and Mr. Gaither end up all wet, anyhow?"

"Oh, that," Elaine said with a laugh. "I slipped on the muddy bank of the river and fell in and my husband gallantly jumped in to pull me out. Wasn't that heroic!"

"Yes, very gallant," Patrolman Wolowiec said, his tone less edgy. "Why were you down by the river in the first place?"

"Why, to show Birdie—Mr. Wilson—Pudge's boat," Elaine said.

Patrolman Wolowiec looked at Sergeant Wiley somewhat helplessly. The sergeant took over the questioning: "What was Mr. Gowdy doing while you all were down at the river?" he asked.

"I don't really know, sir," Elaine said. "You can't see up here from the river. But I suppose he was just waiting for Mr. Wilson."

Sergeant Wiley excused himself and led his fellow officer off to the side. After a brief, low-voiced conference, they returned to the group. "Mr. and Mrs. Gaither," Sergeant Wiley said, "would you excuse us now, please. We appreciate your cooperation. We need to speak with these two gentlemen now. It was a pleasure to meet you, ma'am, sir."

He tipped his hat as Pudge and Elaine turned and walked to the house. He whirled to face Sam Gowdy: "Sir, either you tell me right now what this is all about, or things get hairy. Your choice."

Sam, who'd been leaning on Birdie's truck, stood up and looked the state trooper straight in the eye. "Birdie and I came out to look at Pudge's boat, just like the lady said," he declared.

"Explain that sack of potatoes."

"Just a sack of potatoes. Don't quite know what there is to explain, officer."

"You know damn well what there is to explain. Why do you have a sack of potatoes wrapped in a baby blanket?"

"Sir?" Sam Gowdy replied. "Oh, that. Well, it's not really a baby blanket. Or leastwise it's not a baby blanket anymore. I suppose it used to be. Now it's just something we use around the bait shop to cover things, like open tackle boxes and such."

"Then explain why it's wrapped around that sack of potatoes lying there at your feet."

"Well, as you most likely know, potatoes are dirty—come right out of the ground," Sam responded, drawing his words out deliberately. "I didn't want to mess up Birdie's truck there so I wrapped that sack of potatoes in the blanket, if you want to call it that, to keep from getting dirt in the seat."

It clearly had become a struggle for the sergeant not to let his exasperation show. He looked to Patrolman Wolowiec, almost pleadingly. His fellow officer shrugged and said nothing.

"Mr. Gowdy, that does not explain a couple of things that we need to know," Sergeant Wiley said. "Where were you taking that sack of potatoes? And why were there potatoes in the church?"

Sam Gowdy brightened. "Simple," he said. "We was bringing the potatoes here to Pudge and Eilene."

"Any particular reason why you were doing that?"

"Kind of like payment for taking time to show us their boat. We figured anybody could use a sack of potatoes, wouldn't you think?"

"Yes, of course. But why were there potatoes in the church?"

"Well, there's lots of good Christians in the church, and they share what they have."

Patrolman Wolowiec stepped forward and interrupted. "We're wasting our time here, Larry," he told Sergeant Wiley. "We might as well get back over to the car and call a tow truck. You're not going to drive out of that ditch without one."

Birdie Wilson: "I'd be glad to give you a pull if you've got a chain in the trunk. This old Dodge's stout as a Caterpillar tractor."

Sergeant Wiley said they didn't carry a chain. He appreciated the offer. He'd get on the radio and call for a tow.

"It'll take a while," Birdie told him. "There ain't no towing ser- vice in Cambria. 'Spect it'll be at least a couple of hours."

"We've got nothing but time," Patrolman Wolowiec said. "Our morning's pretty well shot, thanks to you guys."

"Tell you what," Birdie suggested, "whyn't we give you a ride back into town. Drop you off at the Fish and Fries. That'd sure be a better place to wait. Wouldn't you say, Sam?"

"Sure would. It's getting to be about lunch time, too, and Tom serves up some mighty good fish plates, with all the coffee or iced tea you can drink. I believe I'd think about it if I was you two."

Sergeant Wiley spoke for the state troopers. Birdie Wilson's offer made good sense, and they'd take him up on it. And thanks very much. Patrolman Wolowiec nodded agreement. They walked back to their immobile patrol car and arranged for a tow truck driver to meet them at the Fish and Fries. The towing company dispatcher confirmed Birdie's prediction. It would be at least two hours before they could get there.

Sam Gowdy, after he carried the sack of potatoes over to Pudge's front door and deposited it on the step, climbed into the back of Birdie's truck and pulled the pink baby blanket over his knees. Birdie turned around started back to town.

When he stopped to pick up the two state troopers, Sergeant Wiley joined him in the cab. Patrolman Wolowiec took a seat in the bed of the pickup beside Sam. If he noticed the pink baby blanket, he kept it to himself.

They were at the Fish and Fries in a matter of minutes.

Birdie stopped directly in front of Tom Johnson's café, got out quickly and led the troopers to the front door. Sam followed. Birdie opened the door, held it wide, and made a sweeping gesture of welcome with his free arm.

As the four men walked in, Pastor Mike got up from a table near the door and rushed to meet them.

"Ed Wolowiec!" the young preacher almost shouted. "Heavens, man, it's been a long time."

Patrolman Wolowiec dropped his reserve and greeted Pastor Mike with a warm handshake and then a strong embrace. The two stood back and looked at each other, as if studying faces to make sure of their respective identities.

"Folks," Pastor Mike announced loudly, "I want you all to meet the best friend I ever had. Ed Wolowiec and I were the most feared twosome on the Pittsburgh YMCA youth hockey team. When this man took the ice, opposing players ran for cover. Ed, it's sure good to see you!"

"Same here," the patrolman said. "It's been a long time, Mike."

Tom Johnson hurried from behind the counter. He introduced himself to the two state police officers and pulled out chairs so that they could be seated at one of his best tables. Pastor Mike joined them.

"It's not often we get a visit from the state's finest, as they say, here in Cambria," Tom announced. "Gentlemen, lunch is on the house. Anything you want."

Sergeant Wiley started to protest, but saw there was no use. The two troopers leaned back in their chairs and smiled.

❧26❧

lthough Deputy Lynn Swafford's speeding sheriff's department cruiser had put a safe distance between them and the state troopers, Molly still was nervous. She sat hunched in the back seat, Baby Angel asleep in her arms, and worried about what lay ahead. Uncertainty kept crowding out all the optimistic possibilities that raced through her mind.

Lynn studied her face in his rear-view mirror. He could see the apprehension in her eyes. "We made it," he said. "You can loosen up now, Molly."

Molly wasn't easily soothed. "That's just one little step," she said. "What's going to happen now?"

Lynn tried to be reassuring. "It's all in the hands of Judge Winkler," he told her. "And he's a good man, Molly. If there's a way that he can save Baby Angel, he will. Trust me on that."

"I trust you, Lynn. But it's hard to feel like we're home safe yet."

Morgan, who was riding in the back next to Molly, put a hand on her arm. "We're almost there," he said. "Dad's right. The law is on our side in this and Judge Winkler knows how to use the law."

Molly managed a weak smile. She said, "If it weren't for you, we might never have had this chance. We're all more grateful than you can imagine."

"It was my pleasure," Morgan said. "And by the way, did Justine tell you what she found out in Wheeling?"

"I didn't have a chance to talk to her. She left me a note, but she didn't mention that. Do you know?"

"I know, but it's complicated. I'd rather have Justine explain it to you, herself."

Molly was about to ask more when Lynn Swafford suddenly burst forth with a stream of mild profanity. This was so unlike him that it grabbed the attention of his three passengers.

"What, Dad?" demanded Patrick, riding in the front seat beside his father.

"I can't believe this," Lynn said. "Look behind us."

They didn't have to look. Sheriff Clarence Higgins, driving his new GMC Acadia, pulled up beside them with lights flashing. He signaled for Lynn to pull over. The deputy slowed almost to a stop, then crept along the narrow highway until he came to a place where the shoulder was wider. He parked on the edge of the road and Sheriff Higgins stopped behind them.

"What the hell could he want?" Lynn protested. "This is the last thing I expected."

Sheriff Higgins got out and walked to the side of Lynn's car. Lynn already had lowered the driver's window. He looked into the face of the sheriff but said nothing, waiting for his boss to speak first.

"Good morning, Lynn," the sheriff said politely. Then, tipping his hat, "Good morning, Miss Molly, boys."

Lynn Swafford's tone betrayed his irritation: "You got a problem, sheriff?"

Sheriff Higgins's smile disappeared. "No, sir," he said, "I don't have a problem, son. You do."

"Then I guess you better tell me what it is."

"You'll be glad I did," the sheriff said. "When Judge Gilbert called in the state boys, he asked them to do two things. First, get over to Cambria and start asking questions and, second, watch this road this morning and try to intercept you if they happen to catch you headed this way. My guess is there's a state trooper settin' somewhere down there watching and waiting."

Deputy Lynn Swafford wiped his forehead with his hand.

"That sneaky SOB," he said. "But what would they stop me for? They wouldn't charge me with speeding in this marked department car, would they?"

"They wouldn't have to." The sheriff looked at Molly and Baby

224

Angel in the back seat. "Judge Gilbert would have you charged with some crime, Lynn. Like obstructing justice. Unless that child on Miss Molly's lap is your cousin's granddaughter or somebody like that, it would be easy enough to prove that you're carrying the very abandoned child we've been looking for. And since you were one of the lawmen supposed to be doing the searching, you would not have a leg to stand on."

"What should I do, boss?"

"That depends on exactly where you're headed, son."

"You might as well know," Lynn said. "We're on our way to see Judge Winkler. We think there may be a way he can save Baby Angel."

Sheriff Higgins laughed. "Save her from us nasty lawmen? I sure hope you know what you're talking about," he said.

Lynn: "I guess we're still most worried about saving her from the child welfare system."

Sheriff Higgins was serious again. He mapped out a route to Judge Winkler's house, using back roads. Not only that, but he promised to drive ahead, with lights flashing, as if escorting Lynn after he'd been stopped by the sheriff for a traffic violation. Like he already was in custody, so to speak. Just in case.

They formed a two-car caravan, led by the sheriff in his sparkling new SUV with its full array of emergency lights flaring, and left the highway at the next side road. Sheriff Higgins was true to his word. He drove a roundabout route that led them, eventually, to the front door of Judge Harold Winkler's well-kept but modest country home.

Sheriff Higgins went ahead of the others.

Judge Winkler answered the door promptly. Molly knew that he was expecting her and Lynn Swafford and the baby, but she noted with surprise that he seemed to be expecting the sheriff as well. This left her a bit confused. The immediate exchange between the judge and Sheriff Higgins did nothing to clear things up.

"Good morning, Clarence," the judge said pleasantly. "You here on official business, or is this a friendly visit over a cup of Mrs. Winkler's wonderful coffee?"

The sheriff extended his hand and replied, "Something of both, I'd say. Good to see you again, judge."

Judge Winkler escorted the party into his living room, got them comfortably seated, and went straight to the point. "I know why Deputy Swafford and Mrs. Hearst are here," he said. "I've done some homework and I'm prepared to act on something that's gone on far too long. Now, Clarence, I need to know right up front what your interest is in all this."

Sheriff Higgins stood. He walked over to where Molly sat, hold- ing Baby Angel.

"Judge Winkler," the sheriff pronounced, "I have every reason to believe that this is the abandoned child our county law enforce-ment—and now the state police—have been looking for."

"I see. And you have evidence of this, sheriff?"

"My best evidence is that neither Deputy Swafford nor Miss Molly can tell you who this baby is or who she belongs to. Ain't—isn't that right, Lynn?"

Deputy Lynn Swafford flushed with anger. He turned to Molly and shook his head. He said, "Sheriff, I never expected this of you. What a lousy—"

"Now hold on, Lynn," Sheriff Higgins demanded. "Let this play out, will you? Judge Winker here will need to make some hard de-cisions this morning, and I want him to have all the facts. Okay?"

Lynn said nothing more.

Judge Winkler stood in the middle of the room. He faced the sheriff directly, yet took great pains to address himself to all those present. "This is indeed a difficult situation," he pronounced. "Let me be very careful here, and in the words of men far wiser than I, proceed with deliberate speed to get everything resolved fairly and humanely. And most important, I suppose, legally."

"That's what we all want," Sheriff Higgins said.

"So, then. Sheriff, do I understand correctly that you are charg-ing Deputy Lynn Swafford with—what, kidnapping, concealing a fugitive from justice, what, exactly?"

Sheriff Higgins: "I'm charging him with obstruction of justice, your honor."

Molly gasped. She started to speak, but Lynn Swafford motioned her not to.

Judge Winkler frowned. "That is a very serious charge," he said. "Deputy Swafford, you're entitled to a fair hearing. And a trial, if it should come to that. And an attorney, of course—"

Lynn Swafford stood and looked the judge in the eye. "I waive all those rights," he said.

Molly could contain herself no longer. "This is outrageous!" she protested. "Judge Winkler, you can't do this. The sheriff led us here under false pretenses."

Lynn put a hand on her shoulder. "Molly, I think I see what's happening," he said. "Give it time, okay?"

Judge Harold Winkler ignored the interruption. He proceeded: "In that case, I can move straight to a preliminary hearing. Deputy Swafford, how do you plead to the charge of obstructing justice just levied against you by Sheriff Higgins?"

"Not guilty, your honor."

"I thought so. I'm ready to issue my ruling. Sheriff Higgins, in light of the fact that you have no specific evidence to back your charge, I find Deputy Lynn Swafford not guilty. Now we can get on to other things."

Sheriff Clarence Higgins smiled broadly. He clapped Lynn on the shoulder and leaned down and kissed Molly on the cheek. Then he shook hands with Judge Winkler.

The sheriff said, rather loudly and in somewhat formal tone of voice, "I suppose that being the highest-ranking police officer in the room I need to present the next case, your honor." He turned to Molly. "May I hold the little one?" he asked.

Molly loosened her grip on Baby Angel. Sheriff Higgins took the child, and held her gently in his big arms as he turned again to the judge.

"Judge Winkler," the sheriff said, "we have every reason to believe that this little baby was abandoned by someone on purpose. They left her floating down the Ohio River on a flimsy little raft that was almost sure to have sunk and left her to drown. The good people of Cambria, and especially Miss Molly here, have taken care of the little one and made sure she got everything she needed."

Judge Winkler reached out and took Baby Angel, who smiled happily and remained totally quiet.

"Now tell me this, sheriff," he said. "In all the time since the baby was found, has anyone come looking for her? Has there been any inquiry that you're aware of, either through the sheriff's department or other law enforcement agencies?"

"No, sir, there hasn't."

"Not a single one?"

"No, sir. Not a single one."

Judge Winkler crossed the room and returned Baby Angel to Molly. "She's a little darling," he whispered. Then he reassumed his judicial attitude. "Thanks in great part to the research of my legal assistant, Mr. Morgan Swafford here, I've found that there are laws—or at least one law—that gives us direction here," he said. "It's been on the books for a good many years, and few people are even aware of it."

The judge paused dramatically as if to give his words effect. He smiled at Morgan.

"Now," he continued, "under the provisions of this law—chapter and verse will be recorded in the proper paperwork—by authority of this law I hereby declare that this baby was deliberately orphaned, that no known family exists, and that she is free to be placed in adoption. Does any soul present have reason to object?"

Total quiet.

"Okay, then," Judge Winkler went on. "Having so ruled, I stand open to a formal adoption hearing."

Tears streamed down Molly's face. "Judge Winkler," she whispered hoarsely, "does this mean—"

"Yes," the judge said softly, "it means that I'm open to a request that I give this baby a home. Appropriate paper work will be filed in good time."

Lynn Swafford took Molly by the arm. The two stood before the judge, as if they awaited his pronouncement of marriage. Baby Angel cooed softly. Morgan and Patrick, and then Sheriff Clarence

Higgins, stepped forward and stood beside them.

"Your honor," Molly said hoarsely, "I want this child so much. I've come to love her like my own, and Lynn—Deputy Swafford and I—we can take care of her and devote our lives to her."

The judge took Molly's arm and placed a hand on Baby Angel's head, as if conducting a kind of religious ceremony.

"It is my decision, and I so declare," Judge Winkler said, "that this child be given in legal and permanent adoption to Mrs. Molly Hearst and Mr. Lynn Swafford. I further rule that her name be recorded as Angel—would you want that to be Hearst or Swafford?"

Molly and Lynn, at once: "Swafford."

"It's done," Judge Harold Winkler pronounced. "This court now stands adjourned."

Molly could not find words to express her happiness. Everything had happened so fast. Could she be sure that Baby Angel was really theirs—hers and Lynn's—and that the danger of losing this beautiful, special child really was past? She looked plaintively at Lynn Swafford, and then at Judge Winkler. The judge might have been reading her mind.

"Mrs. Hearst—Molly," Judge Winkler said, "you have nothing to worry about. I've ruled, all the legal paperwork will be filed, and no one in this county will challenge me. Outside of this county, there's nobody who will know or care. And even if they did, the law is on our side. What happened here this morning is perfectly legal. It would stand up in any higher court in the land. And you can thank young Morgan here for discovering the obscure law that made it possible."

The judge put an arm across Morgan's shoulders. Morgan blushed, but his pride was evident.

"I'm more grateful than I could ever tell you," Molly said. "And you, too, Morgan."

Sheriff Higgins shook Judge Winkler's hand, then turned to Molly. "Miss Molly," he said, "I apologize for the tom-foolery. The good judge called me this morning and said we needed to get Lynn in here and charge him, so that he could be cleared. Double jeopardy and all that. Nobody will try to pull anything on him now that he's been formally charged and found not guilty."

Molly wiped a tear from her cheek. "I'm sorry I doubted you, sheriff," she said. "But I didn't know what was going on."

"Of course you didn't. No way you could have."

The sheriff kissed Molly on the cheek and shook hands with Lynn Swafford.

"I really don't know what to say, sheriff," Lynn said modestly. "Except thank you."

"Son, I couldn't be happier with the way this all worked out. You know, the more time I spent over there in Cambria pushing Judge Gilbert's warrants, the more sheepish I felt. Then, when Pastor Mike saved my life, I couldn't help but think there was a message there. A message that I was doing wrong."

"But you were just doing your job," Lynn said. "I'm afraid I didn't live up to my oath of office very well."

Sheriff Higgins laughed heartily. "Depends on what part of the oath you're talking about," he said. "Ain't there something in there about serving the public good? You helped save this little one and make sure she has a home. I'd say that's pretty much in the public good."

"And you, young man." The sheriff turned to Morgan. "You did a good thing, going up there to Wheeling and finding that old law. Judge Gilbert is a real stickler for the law, you know, and I expect he'd be hard put to argue with what went on here this morning."

Judge Winkler had disappeared, but returned momentarily with his wife on his arm. Mrs. Winkler greeted each of them individually. She took Baby Angel from Molly and walked about the room, expressing her delight over the child's new parentage. There must be a celebration, she insisted, and asked the judge to bring coffee and cookies from the kitchen. He did.

As soon as everyone was served, Patrick clinked on his coffee cup with a spoon to gain attention. When the others quieted, he stood.

"I'd like to make a toast," Patrick announced. "To our father and to Molly. In case anyone here doesn't know, they're going to be married. So here's to the greatest dad any son could ever ask for and our new mom that we already love."

He lifted his coffee, and others chimed in, "Toast" and "To Lynn and Molly."

Patrick clinked again with his spoon. "I forgot to mention the most important member of the family," he said. "Here's to Baby Angel, our new little sister."

Another round of murmurs. "Toast" and "To Baby Angel."

Judge Winkler: "By the way, Lynn and Molly, if you two would take that step right away it would simplify my paperwork. No point in waiting, right Lynn?"

"I'm ready," Lynn Swafford said. "It's all up to Molly now."

Molly beamed. Her joy permeated the room like the pleasant aroma of a bouquet of fresh-cut flowers.

❧27❧

Molly planned her wedding in the car on the way home. Lynn was agreeable to everything she proposed, and Patrick and Morgan sat behind them and played the role of cheerleaders. By the time they got back to Cambria, wedding plans were almost complete. The ceremony would be right away. Molly and Lynn would go to the courthouse and pick up the license in the afternoon, and details would be put together hurriedly. It would not be a lavish event.

Justine met Molly and Baby Angel at the door, nervous as a cat. "Mom," she said, "I've been dying to know what happened. This has been the longest morning!"

"Baby Angel is ours now, honey," Molly told her, almost choking up. "Judge Winkler approved her adoption and we—Lynn and I—are her new legal parents. And Justine, Lynn and I are getting married Saturday, can you believe it? I want you to be my maid of honor. Jay and Morgan and Patrick will be Lynn's groomsmen."

Justine squealed with delight. "I'm so, so happy for you, Mom!" she said. "And now I have a little sister. Baby Angel—"

"Her legal name now is Angel Swafford."

Justine tried to hug Molly and the baby at the same time. Although Baby Angel was being squeezed between them, she made no protest. Justine chattered excitedly. "Do we have a lot to do now?" she asked. "I mean with the wedding coming up so soon and all. Where do we start?"

"It's not really that big a deal, honey," Molly said. "It isn't like we're having a big wedding, or sending out invitations or having a reception or anything like that. But I do need to call Johnny White right now and see if he can marry us. And use Town Hall for the wedding ceremony."

☙

JOHNNY WHITE sat down at his computer and began to write. He finished a dozen lines, then went back and started over. After some twenty minutes of writing and rewriting he had a page-long document that was close to what he wanted. He made a couple of quick final revisions and printed ten copies to be posted in the most conspicuous places in town. This is what his poster said:

PROCLAMATION

Be it known to all interested parties that:

Whereas the child known as Baby Angel has been a blessing to the Town of Cambria, bringing the town's residents together in a spirit of cooperation virtually unknown before, and

Whereas Molly Hearst, resident of Cambria, and Lynn Swafford, county sheriff's deputy, were highly instrumental in saving said Baby Angel from the child welfare department in what came to be known unofficially as the Cambrian Project, and

Whereas said Baby Angel was in no small measure responsible for bringing Molly and Lynn together, and

Whereas Molly and Lynn are to be joined in holy matrimony Saturday at 10 a.m. in the Town Hall, and

Whereas, all Cambrians are invited to the wedding,

Now be it declared by the Mayor of Cambria that Saturday, the day of the wedding, be recognized as Molly and Lynn and Baby Angel Day and, further, that said Saturday shall be celebrated by all Cambrians as an official town holiday.

(signed) Johnny White, Mayor, Town of Cambria

☙

SATURDAY DAWNED bright and clear. There was a gentle breeze that made ripples on the surface of the placid Ohio and rustled the leaves of Cambria's plentiful oak and maple trees. Birds sang and squirrels frolicked in the streets. No dogs barked and not a loud voice could be heard.

At half-past-nine o'clock, exactly thirty minutes before the ceremony was to begin, a parade of county sheriff's department vehicles rolled into Cambria and made its way to Town Hall. Leading the convoy was Sheriff Clarence Higgins in his shiny new Buick. His passengers were Deputy Lynn Swafford and Patrick and Morgan. All were dressed in their nicest suits.

The second vehicle was Deputy Harlan Gidcomb's patrol car. The deputy had personally washed and polished the vehicle the night before. He chauffeured Judge and Mrs. Harold Winkler, who by Sheriff Higgins's direct orders were to be treated as honored guests.

The sheriff's department automobiles lined up along the street and the deputies filed into Town Hall and quietly took seats. Already, townspeople had begun to arrive. Birdie and Edna Wilson were among the first, with Kyle and Ross in tow. Birdie was clean-shaven and wore his favorite yellow tie. With a nod from his father, Ross stepped beneath the bell tower, took the rope in both hands and clanged the Town Hall bell twenty-five times. The initial clang sent a small flock of pigeons flying.

The first civilian vehicle to arrive was Ida Quattlebaum's ancient Oldsmobile. Boyd, wearing a new black chauffeur's uniform complete with highly polished boots, stopped directly in front of the building, got out and opened the rear door and, to the utter surprise of onlookers, Granny Vogler alighted. Miss Quattlebaum was right behind. She took Granny's arm and the two paraded into Town Hall as if they expected all eyes to be on them.

In a surprising display of cooperation, Pastor Mike and Father Jacob, rather than compete for the best seats down front, took chairs near the back of the large meeting chamber. They promptly began a friendly though vigorously animated conversation.

Margie Zielinski wore a new dress she'd been saving for a special occasion. Larry shuffled along at her side, smiling and nodding. Tom Johnson closed the Fish and Fries Café, unheard of on a Saturday morning, and he and Marlene also were among the early comers. Right behind them were Gordon and Juanita Blessing. Gordon wore a poorly fitting suit he'd bought Friday afternoon at a thrift store just for this event.

Morris and Ethel Layman, Charlie and Marylee Tipsworth, Jake and Carrie Garner—all of the most prominent Cambrians arrived at Town Hall well before ten o'clock. Max Barnes looked taller than usual, and other townspeople quickly noted that he wore new shoes with very thick heels. Sam and Alma Gowdy entered with Pudge and Elaine Gaither and found seats near the front.

Kelley Peterson and Janet Rider, whose husbands had to work on Saturday, came together. They took the first empty seats they saw, near the back.

The assembled guests kept up a harmonious babble of chatter and laughter indicative of the festive mood. Until Johnny White walked in. Everyone fell quiet as the mayor strode to the front of the room. He turned to face them and welcomed them all on behalf of the town of Cambria. At a signal from Johnny, Karen Barnes stepped forward. In a truly astonishing a cappella performance, she brought many in the audience to tears with a beautiful rendering of "Because."

Karen took her seat and all eyes turned to the side doors. Sheriff Higgins stepped in with Lynn Swafford at his side and the two walked proudly to where Mayor Johnny White waited. Next came Jay, Morgan, and Patrick. There was a hush and then loud murmuring as Molly entered from the other side, accompanied by Justine. Both wore knee-length pink dresses and both carried white orchids.

The ceremony was brief. And precise. Johnny White had pared his wedding formalities down to the bare bones and practiced these well. He came to the vows in short order. Molly's "I do" almost was drowned out by loud cooing from Baby Angel, who up to this point had slept quietly in the care of Juanita Blessing.

The mayor pronounced the couple man and wife, and the guests cheered. Lynn accepted with enthusiasm the mayor's invitation to kiss the bride. The new Mr. and Mrs. Lynn Swafford embraced and the guests cheered again. Cambria would celebrate this event for the rest of the weekend.

Patrick and Morgan congratulated each other first and then the newlyweds. Jay stood by, looking embarrassed, until Justine took him by the hand and led him to his mother and new step-father.

Molly circled her arms around Jay, then pulled Justine into the hug as well. Lynn Swafford gently patted them all on their backs.

As the crowd began to surge forward, Molly ran to Juanita Blessing and took Baby Angel. "You've been a good girl, sweetheart," Molly said. "We're all one happy family now."

Justine joined them. "It's been a long road for my little sister," she said.

"You know what?" Molly said. "We've been so busy I forgot to ask what you found out in Wheeling. Morgan said it was too complicated for him to start on, then—"

"Not really complicated, Mom. I found exactly what I was looking for in the Wheeling library. The Magnolia was a packet boat that carried mail and passengers up and down the river. One day it hit a submerged log and sank. All twenty people on board were lost, including women and children—one of them a baby girl."

"But that's not possible," Molly exclaimed. "We would have heard about a terrible thing like that."

"But, Mom—it happened a hundred years ago."

Molly paled. "Justine, if what you say is true, it means Baby Angel is . . ."

"You can say it, Mom. It means she's a real angel."

Baby Angel smiled shyly, as if she knew a secret. Her eyes were as bright as the nearest stars on a cold, clear winter's night.

Other Books by Robert Hays

FICTION
A Shallow River of Mercy
Blood on the Roses
Circles in the Water
The Life and Death of Lizzie Morris
Early Stories from the Land
(editor)

NON-FICTION
Patton's Oracle
Editorializing 'the Indian Problem'
A Race at Bay
State Science in Illinois
G-2: Intelligence for Patton
(with Gen. Oscar Koch)
Country Editor

About the Author

Robert Hays has been a newspaper reporter, public relations writer, magazine editor, political campaign manger, and university professor and administrator. A native of Illinois, he taught in Texas and Missouri and retired in 2008 from a long journalism teaching career at the University of Illinois. He also has spent a great deal of time in South Carolina, the home state of his wife, Mary, and was an active member of the South Carolina Writers Workshop. He served in the U.S. Army and holds three degrees, including an inter-disciplinary Ph.d., from Southern Illinois University. His publications include academic journal and popular periodical articles and twelve books, including his collaborative work with General Oscar Koch, *G-2: Intelligence for Patton.* His most recent non-fiction work is a biographical memoir about General Koch, his close friend and collaborator, who was World War II intelligence chief for General George S. Patton Jr. Three of his five novels have been honored with Pushcart Prize nominations. Robert and Mary live in Champaign, Illinois. They have two sons and a grandson.